Friend (With Benefits) Zone

Also by Laura Brown

Signs of Attraction

Friend (With Benefits) Zone

LAURA BROWN

AVONIMPULSE
An Imprint of HarperCollins*Publishers*

Digital Edition JUNE 2017 ISBN: 978-0-06-249559-4

Print Edition ISBN: 978-0-06-249561-7

FIRST EDITION

17 18 19 20 21 HDC 10 9 8 7 6 5 4 3 2 1

To my wonderful husband.
You've been my support and
my rock throughout this writing process.
You've listened to me babble plots and helped
(sometimes against your will) figure out solutions.
I would not be where I am without you—
certainly not as inspired to write about love.

Acknowledgments

SOMETIMES WRITING A book goes smoothly. Other times it does not. This novel did not. I won't bore you with the details. Just know that a lot of blood, sweat, and tears went into FRIEND (WITH BENEFITS) ZONE. And not all of them mine!

This novel went through a few major changes, and thanks to that I've had a lot of help along the way, including help on areas that had a date with the cutting room floor. It's been quite the journey, and I couldn't have done it without all my readers, from beta to critique, and those willing to handhold me through the process.

In no particular order, I'd like to thank Karen Mahara, Heather DiAngelis, Robin Lovett, Adrienne Proctor, Emma Wicker, Ann Marjory K, Laura Heffernan, and two sensitivity readers who gave me fantastic feedback on a character I later opted to revise to be a mirror to myself.

I'd also like to thank the writer community in general. I can't imagine taking this journey without the incredible support, sounding board, and comic relief that the community provides.

A special shout-out to my husband, who decided to break his wrist right as I was faced with a huge deadline. And another shout-out to my son, for keeping Daddy entertained while I chained myself to my laptop.

I am blessed with the best agent and editor. They helped me over the hurdles I faced, giving me the tools to create the end result I needed.

And thank you to my readers. I received some encouraging words from those eagerly awaiting my next novel. I do hope you enjoy.

Friend (With Benefits) Zone

Chapter One

Jasmine

CHILLY MIDNIGHT WIND blew my trench coat up as I stared at the fluttering note taped to my basement apartment door. I needed to get out of the freaking cold air, but I stood rooted to the spot by a sloppy handwritten letter that didn't even mention my name.

To Whom It May Concern,

Your residency is terminated. Please collect your belongings and move out ASAP.

I'd seen one too many letters like this in my twenty-one years. Some taped to doors, others shoved underneath them, and still more sent certified mail. All back when I lived with my mother. This was the first I had managed to collect on my own.

I shouldered the door open, then used my hip to force it closed. The letter—now crumpled in my hand—landed on my wobbly kitchen table. I still hadn't found the right combination of books to keep it level. Not that I had many books to begin with.

The wind outside stopped, but my postage-stamp-sized studio didn't exactly come with heat. I flicked on the tiny portable heater and sat on my bed, waiting to thaw out.

I never wanted to be in this situation. Not again. Served me right for accepting a cheap Craigslist apartment. I paid my rent on time, in cash. I kept to myself. If I'd somehow created too much noise, then they needed to tell me. Deaf ears couldn't tell.

I took in a deep breath of questionable moldy air. Thirty days. That was standard for evictions. I could work out something in thirty days.

I had to.

With a bit of warmth finally reaching my skin, I changed out of my clothes and into a baggy tee shirt, then added sweats and a sweatshirt. I had to tighten the drawstring to keep the pants up, but the extra fabric helped keep me warm. Clothes stolen from Dev, my BFF. Perks to having a guy friend. I had no clue if he knew I'd stolen his clothes or not. I didn't care. He'd give me the shirt off his back if I asked; nothing wrong with skipping a step.

From my bed, the entire studio apartment stretched before me. Okay, so *cramped* was a better word than *stretched*. A half kitchen that consisted of a mini fridge, a sink, and a microwave, a small table, one lousy tiny window, and the bathroom that held a stall shower and just as much water pressure as heat: almost nonexistent. The only positive thing about this place was the rent, cheap enough that I could save as much money as possible. My phone vibrated, and I picked it up, welcoming the distraction.

Dev: How did the date go?

Considering I sat on my bed wearing his clothes instead of being warmed up without any clothes on at all? I sent back a thumbs-down image.

Dev: That bad?

Me: Greg was disappointed I wasn't in my bar clothes.

Served me right for picking up a guy at the bar I worked at. He had seemed nice and far more of a gentleman than most of my customers. He even knew a few signs. I had hoped for a little fun, a departure from my daily life. In the end, we had nothing in common. He wanted the shot-girl image, not a real person.

Dev: That asshole. Want me to beat him up?

Me: I know you have a love affair with your punching bag, but this one requires no fists. Sorry.

Dev: You OK?

I stared up at my ceiling. The man always managed to read between the lines.

Me: I'm fine.
Dev: Liar.

I scrunched my nose and tapped at my phone until his image appeared on-screen, too-long hair included. "I just had a bad date. Are you done picking on me?" I signed.

He tried to keep a straight face, but his eyes laughed at me. "I wanted to make sure you were OK."

I held the phone farther back and let him see I was ready for bed. How much more fine could I get?

"So that's what happened to my college sweatshirt."

I angled the phone to the emblem on my leg. "Pants too."

Dev laughed and shook his head. "Come over. You don't have to stay at your crappy apartment tonight."

"I happen to like my crappy apartment." Okay, that was a lie. I hated this place. But I liked my privacy. And even if I stayed at Dev's a few times a month, that didn't mean I needed to right this second. Not when I'd be losing this place soon.

I didn't sign that. My problem. I'd handle it. I'd learned a long time ago to never let a wannabe social worker get involved unless I wanted to give up control. Dev had no boundaries when it came to helping others.

"Please?"

"Are you seriously begging me to come over at midnight?"

Dev had the decency to shrug.

"Tomorrow. Come to the bar. For now, I have a date with my pillow." Sure, the pillow was flat as a pancake, but I wanted alone time.

"Fine. If you change your mind, come on over."

I nodded and ended the call. I had his spare key, but we both knew I wouldn't use it.

My eyes traveled over the room once again. The cracks in the walls, the cracks in the cement floor. I had snagged the place for one reason and one reason only: to save money and buy my own bar.

Like my father had. I wondered if he'd recommend it or if he'd try to convince me to choose a different career. Maybe we would have worked side by side, handling customers and drinks. In truth, I'd never know what might have been.

I pulled out my notebook, the one with the pale blue cover on which I had penned *Jas's Bar.* Here I planned out everything I could for owning my own bar. From rules and regulations, to which brands I wanted, to recipes and other ideas. I mapped out my finances, what I'd need to make this a reality.

I wasn't there yet. Hence the cheap apartment and meager living.

Maybe I should have crashed at Dev's. A little comfort went a long way when life spiraled out of control. I knew I was young and I had time. But I wanted my happy. I'd paid my dues; I deserved my dream.

I was still staring at my notebook when a light flashed by my tiny window. Outside someone stood with a flashlight, shining it into my apartment. I didn't need to adjust to the light to know who that someone was with the one, two, three blinking pattern.

It took five steps to stomp over to the door. Dev came in once I wedged it open. He pushed the door closed.

"You can't have your clothes back," I signed, even as I was grateful to see him. When Dev was around, even this place sorta felt like a home.

"I don't want my clothes back. Not now, at least. I wanted to make sure you were OK."

I held out my hands, showing that I was fine. Even if I did scan my coffee table and breathe in relief that the eviction letter was facedown in a crumpled mess.

He studied me, searching for all my little tics that spelled I was in trouble, tics only he knew. I blanked my face; otherwise he would latch onto there being a problem. A big one. Dev shoved a hand through his hair, those wavy locks rioting into one massive sexy-as-hell bedhead. I missed the days when he was a spindly little thing, before he grew into this hunk I could never unfriendzone. He meant too much to rock the boat, and I didn't dare risk losing him. He scratched at a day's worth of scruff, the black stubble contrasting with his pale skin. Then he kicked off his shoes, tossed his coat on the back of a chair, and plopped down on my bed in a way that had to have a spring or two digging into his back.

He didn't budge.

I wanted to laugh. Forget me time—neither one of us had given the other the right to be alone since we first met. Still, I couldn't let go of our usual bickering match. "Go home."

He folded his hands behind his head, not moving. I crossed my arms. A few seconds later he sat up, grabbed my laptop off the floor, and flipped it open. "We'll watch a movie."

"My laptop can't handle Netflix. You know that."

He closed the laptop. "Right. Forgot." He unlocked his phone and placed it on the bed.

"Tiny viewing tonight?"

"You refused to come to my place." Underlining meaning: we could have watched on a large flat-screen TV.

Since there was no budging him now that he had settled in, I climbed onto the bed with him. He picked up the phone so we could watch, and I settled my head on his chest.

I didn't pay much attention to the action flick he put on. Most days I loved the intensity of those movies. Tonight, those explosions felt too close for comfort. Instead I made a mental list of my options. Had to before Dev found out. He'd want me to stay with him. And being cuddled up with him, I had to admit, had potential. More so when I placed my hand on his firm stomach and took in a deep breath of the ocean scent of his soap. Problem was, I needed to be on my own two feet. The last person to take care of me—my mother—had failed. I couldn't trust anyone else.

Not even Dev.

Chapter Two

Devon

My task—to reach over a sleeping Jas and pluck my hearing aids off her bedside table. Challenge level—low. This early in the morning, she'd be in a deep enough sleep that I'd have to resort to a bucket of cold water to wake her up.

I leaned across her, gathered up my hearing aids, then sat back to put them on. The silent room squeaked into sound, adding a mechanical humming noise to my ears. Could have been something from the pipes, could have been background from the aids. I didn't know. Didn't care, really. In her tiny-ass apartment, there wasn't much to hear.

She shouldn't be in a place like this. Life had a penchant for handing Jas the bad end of a stick. She'd weathered so many bad storms, and yet her spirit remained intact. A little bruised, a little weary, but still a fighter.

There were days I'd swear she was stronger than me.

Maybe it was odd to have shared a bed with my best friend, but certain things had become normal before we hit puberty. Before my awareness of her shifted and I had to stuff it into a box. Back then, Jas had needed comfort and a safe place to stay. Now...it was habit.

I shoved my feet into my shoes with too much force, throwing my balance off. My hip bumped into her kitchen table before I could regain my footing. Papers fell to the floor, and I bent to pick them up, freezing at one crumpled paper and the words *residency is terminated.* My hands tightened around the edges, all but tearing the page that appeared torn from a notebook. My jaw ticked as I swallowed that strange combination of emotion Jas created so well: anger and fear.

"Liar," I signed to Jas, even though she remained fast asleep. "You're not OK." The paper looked illegal as hell, but then again, so did Jas's apartment. I took a picture of the letter with my phone before putting her mail back on her table.

I wanted to write her a note, tell her to come with me to Support Services, where they could help her fight this. But Jas did things on her own. If I wanted to help her, I'd have to be sneaky about it.

With one last look at Jas and a prayer I'd manage to help her for a change, I left. I needed to go to my classes but figured I had just enough time to make one more important stop first—I headed closer to Boston, to Support Services, the Deaf social work agency I volunteered at.

I arrived five minutes before opening. The doors were already open and a crowd hung out in the waiting area. People sat in chairs or stood, all signing back and forth. Most of it ASL, some more gestural or reminiscent of signs from a different country, a few speaking along with their hand movements.

The place was home.

I waved to the receptionist and headed to see Katherine, the social worker I had interned under last semester. I was strictly a volunteer now, but she hadn't stopped being my mentor.

Something I was grateful for this morning.

I found her at her desk and flicked the light switch to gain her attention. "Got a few minutes?" I signed once she looked up.

She studied my face and didn't miss a beat. "What's wrong?"

I loaded the picture of Jas's letter and slid it under Katherine's nose.

"Yours?"

I shook my head. "No. A friend's."

"Rent issue?"

Jas might be careful with her money, but not at the expense of others. "No."

"Anything you know might have been a problem? Is this the first notice?"

"She keeps to herself. No problems." But I had no clue if this was her first notice or not.

Katherine leaned back, nodding slightly as she thought. "Your friend should have thirty days before the landlord goes to the next level. Then the courts become involved."

"But she did nothing wrong."

"Doesn't matter. A landlord can evict for any number of reasons."

I shoved my hand into my hair and tugged at the long strands.

Katherine studied me. "You care about her."

"She's my best friend." I cared more than I should.

"Sometimes staying with a friend during a transition period is the best thing." Her expression shifted to one of contemplation, and I knew we were about to shift topics. "You're graduating soon, right?"

"Two months." And if I could stop time, I would, because after graduation things would be different. For starters, I wouldn't be here, and that grated.

"And you'll have a degree in social work?" Her pointer finger stretched out that question a bit much. I smelled a trap.

"A minor in social work. My major is accounting." Not my choice. My father was an accountant. My brother had recently become one. I was expected to follow suit and had learned long ago that my wants didn't matter.

Katherine nodded, a deep pensive nod that could make a grown man squirm. Not that I squirmed visibly. I tapped my foot on the floor. "We need a new social worker. Full-time. I think you should apply."

I stopped tapping. A job. A job I actually wanted.

"I'm supposed to join my dad's accounting firm."

Katherine smiled. "We all like your father; it's wonderful to have a Deaf accountant. But we need you. Here. And we know you want it."

I ran my hand across my scruff. I'd been torn between the two careers since freshman year—before that, if I was honest. Now the clock was ticking, and I had to make up my mind, fast, and stick to whatever path I chose.

"Think about it. You decide what's best for you." She glanced behind me, and I turned, finding a client waiting. "I expect to see your application in May."

I nodded and left. Off to a class I didn't care about, to worry about a friend who wouldn't easily accept my help.

Chapter Three

Jasmine

AFTER A BUSY night at the bar, my feet protested all movement as I exited my car and headed to my basement apartment door. All I wanted to do was change into Dev's sweats, curl up in bed, and sleep. I pulled out my keys and jiggled the small metal piece into the lock. The key wouldn't fit. The same slot that used to accept me with open arms. It refused to budge, insisting we no longer matched. Yesterday they left the note, and today my key didn't work.

Fuck.

I shivered, the wind brutal against the low insulation of my trench coat, seeping inside to all the skin exposed by my miniscule cocktail-waitress getup. I checked my keychain, but I had the right set of keys. Why the hell didn't my door work? I tried it again before pounding on it with both my fists. This couldn't be happening. Not today, not now. Not when I was dead on my feet after a ten-hour shift.

The single-family house in front of me remained dark and quiet while I struggled with a busted lock. Or a changed one. I moved to the window. Too narrow, I'd never fit.

Inside, my studio was dark. Panic gripped me at being separated from my belongings. Yet I didn't care about most of them. Only one item couldn't be replaced: my memory box. Clothes, toothbrush, memories, all gone.

I looked at the dark sky and the moon hiding behind a shadow of clouds. A moment of peace and tranquility, even when life didn't go as intended. At least I had my fallback plan, the same one I'd had in place since I was ten years old. As I headed to my car, I pulled out my phone and sent a text to Dev.

Me:	Need a place to stay. Do NOT type: I told you so.
Dev:	What if I type it backward?
Me:	I can read backward, same thing.
Dev:	Damn. What happened?
Me:	Don't know. Key not fit.
Dev:	Assholes. Come here, we'll figure it out.

I shoved my phone back in my bag, a little warmth thawing out this messed-up cold night.

On my drive, I passed a car or two, but otherwise the night slept. Dark skies, dark road, my headlights lighting the way. I liked this time of night, when the world left me to my own devices. There was peace in the early hours of the morning. I imagined my father liked this time, could all but see him walking home, taking slow steps to enjoy the night sky.

And now my box containing the only articles I had left from him, mainly random small items, a few pictures and recipes, was trapped in a place I no longer had access to. Yet another landlord held my belongings hostage.

Anger bubbled up inside, and I had no one to blame but myself. I banged on my wheel, signing profanities into the air. I should have listened to Dev. If I had showed him the letter, we could have packed up all my belongings and brought them back to his place. Then my box would be safe.

The light ahead turned red, and I braked, resisting the urge to put my head on the steering wheel. Once before, I'd set the horn off by doing that, having no clue I'd disturbed an entire apartment complex. Another day in the life of Jasmine Helmsman.

By the time I made it to Dev's place, rage had taken over. Every time, every damn time I managed to get one foot in front of the other, life pushed me back.

I stomped up the stairs in Dev's building, wishing he was hearing and I could bang the shit out of his door. I could, if his brother was home or if Dev had his hearing aids on. Neither were a sure bet. I settled for pressing my thumb into the doorbell and holding it down, imagining the strobe flash and flash and flash.

The door flung open. "What the hell?" Dev signed before grabbing my arm and drawing me in. "Are you

OK?" He looked me up and down, as if my physical appearance would change simply because my lock did.

"I'm fine," I signed with more force than necessary.

Without missing a beat, Dev pulled me into a tight hug.

My anger vanished. His arms wrapped around me—my own personal blanket—while his head tilted until it rested on top of mine. Like I belonged there. No one hugged like Devon Walker. I buried my head in his shoulder, not caring that my curls were caught in his whiskers. Only his comfort reminded me of all my troubles, hitting me like a brick. Here I was, held by a guy who had more stability than I ever had. He'd always have a place to call home. I was homeless.

I pulled back before his warmth caused me to shed a tear. I didn't cry, hadn't for over ten years.

"You need anything?"

I dropped my purse on the floor. "Everything."

He eyed my trench. "Bar clothes?"

When would I have changed? I popped the top button on my father's old trench, not hard to do since it was barely holding on, and glanced down.

"I'll get you some clothes." He turned and headed for his room.

I ran after him and tapped his shoulder. "Do you have anything smaller than normal?"

I made it to his nose now, but I'd be below his chin once I took off my boots.

"Hasn't stopped you before." I laughed, and he put a finger to his lips. "Quiet, Blake's got an early morning tomorrow."

Dev had the type of family who annoyed each other but stayed close. I had the family who died or faded away.

I followed him into his room. He pulled out a tee shirt and tossed it my way, and I threw my trench over his chair.

"Any more letters?" He leaned against his dresser.

I froze with the shirt halfway to my head. He stared back at me with those cool blue eyes, completely unfazed. I pulled the shirt over my head—it covered me down to my knees, concealing my clothes. "How did you know about the letter?" I wiggled out of my tube top and skirt, tossing them on the chair with my trench.

"I found it this morning."

Something didn't add up. "And you didn't say anything?" Dev was the type to find a problem and jump right into problem-solving mode. "Unless..."

"They shouldn't have changed the locks. They aren't following appropriate protocols. You should be able to fight this—"

I raised a hand to cut him off. "I'm not going to fight for a crappy apartment."

Dev's jaw clenched. "The only other suggestion is staying with a friend."

"Which is why I'm here." I climbed into Dev's bed and put my head on his pillow. This had to be temporary, like each time before when I needed a break from life or had been dealt crap like this. It did comfort me to know I had a place to go. He had my back, always. I never had to ask, the offer was open for me to stay when I needed, though I did my best not to abuse the option.

He sat on the edge. "You can still fight."

"Not now, please." I had no energy left for Dev's desire to help others. And less energy to fight. If an apartment didn't work, I left. End of story.

His shoulders tightened, but then he let go, and they relaxed. Small win for me. "What are you going to do?"

I stared up at his ceiling. "No clue. Put everything on hold and find another apartment." I'd never find another with rent that cheap; my next one would cost an arm and a leg. I probably needed to consider getting a roommate, but I did best on my own.

The bed vibrated, bringing my attention back to Dev. "No. You can stay here."

I sat up. "Where? You share a two-bedroom with your brother."

His lips quirked. "You're here a lot of the time, anyways."

"Once in a while. Or has your love life grown sad?" I pouted, my bottom lip sticking out.

"Shut up."

"What happened with Natalie? She lasted a full two and a half weeks. I think that's a new record for you." Dev had commitment phobia down to an art. I could never figure him out. He had a stable life and should be looking forward to settling down. Instead, he played harder to get than I did.

Dev shook his head, and I knew he wasn't going to give me any answers. For a guy who helped everyone whether they wanted it or not, his own life was locked down tight.

"I'm serious, you can always stay here. Blake seems happy with his boyfriend. I would guess they might move in together soon, anyways."

Living with Dev had always been an idea, but he'd moved in with his brother when he started college, and I'd had my own path to take. I couldn't explain the weird feeling in my gut at the thought of staying here. One that had nothing to do with my desire to support myself.

I shook it off and got out of his bed, heading to the bathroom to wash my makeup off before I transferred it to Dev's clean sheets.

His room was dark by the time I returned. Didn't matter, I knew the layout, same way I knew his covers would be flipped back for me. The streetlight sent slats of light across the room, enough to make sure I didn't trip over anything. And then, there was Dev, face lit up from his cell phone, smiling at something.

He put his phone down as I slid into his bed. No matter how I climbed in, I always ended up at his side, curled up with him. It was habit.

I rested my head on his shoulder and tangled my cold toes with his for warmth. He fixed the blanket, then wrapped an arm around me. We didn't sign good night, too heavy into our routine. My eyes closed as soon as my cheek made contact with him, the heat of his body warming me through his shirt.

Relaxation took over. Snuggled into him, I drifted, the comfort and warmth and caring lulling me into some of the best sleep I ever had. Only with him. Always.

Chapter Four

Devon

My backpack hung over one shoulder, weighing me down with textbook after textbook on accounting. I had a class in twenty minutes. And then two more after that. I needed to open the door and get into my car.

I stood still. Back in my room, Jas slept, curled up under my covers with her blond curls splayed out over my pillow. She had no home, no belongings, and here I was heading off to classes I didn't give two shits about.

Screw it. I dropped my bag and pulled out my phone. I sent a text to my interpreters, letting them know I would be a no-show at class today. Call it some fucked-up signal crossing in my brain, but if a person needed my help, nothing else mattered.

And if that person was Jas, then all bets were off.

Keys in hand, I finally made it out of my apartment and into my car. I had purpose now, and that purpose involved hunting down Jas's landlord.

I had my fingers crossed the guy would be home in the middle of the day as I pounded on his door. I strained my limited hearing for any sounds of life, but all I got were cars traveling on the street behind me and the frigid wind rustling against my microphones. I raised my fist to knock again when the door shifted open.

A little old lady stood on the other side.

I couldn't hear little old ladies—something to do with pitch and my ears—but had been told my "accent" was pretty obvious. "Hi, my name's Devon Walker. Jasmine Helmsman used to live here; I want to know what happened," I spoke.

She looked me up and down with her little-old-lady eyes, nothing like the sugary-sweet grandma the media insisted all women grew into. She opened her mouth, and I caught the word *game*. That couldn't be right.

"I'm deaf. Can you write it down?"

Instead of grabbing a pen and paper, she opened her mouth again and yelled at me. I plastered a smile on my face that I didn't feel at all. I wanted to yell back at her for being an idiot, but I caught a few words, namely that she didn't trust me.

"Why were her locks changed?"

She yelled some more, and I caught something about family needing a place. I ground my teeth. They could have told Jas, given her a chance to move, instead of this shit. But I bit back my anger. I pulled out my phone and wrote a message about how they couldn't kick her out, not like this. It was illegal, regardless of whatever Jas thought about not signing any papers.

The lady pushed my phone away without reading and moved to close the door in my face. I shoved my shoulder into the jamb, holding it open. My window of opportunity was closing.

"I want Jasmine's belongings. I'll be in and out in fifteen."

She crossed her arms across her housecoat. "Fifteen…cops in twenty." Then she grabbed a cane, not waiting to see if I comprehended her or not, and hobbled around the building to the little basement apartment. She let me in, said something I could barely hear, and left me alone.

What a bitch. I thanked my lucky stars that Jas didn't have much in the way of belongings. She lived simple and light, because shit like this happened.

If this apartment was legal, I'd have her fight them. But as it was, the place didn't even have a full kitchen.

I found her duffel bag and unzipped it on her unmade bed. Her closet had no door, and her limited clothes hung in the open space—mostly small black outfits she wore at the bar, the rest jeans and tee shirts with a few sweaters. I collected them all in one fell swoop and shoved them in her bag. She'd complain about the wrinkles, but wrinkled clothes were better than no clothes. A canvas hanging shelf held more of her shit, including bras and panties. I unlatched the top of the shelves and collapsed them into the bag, hiding temptation from view. The duffel still had room, so I collected the rest of what I could find until the zipper struggled to close.

I brought the full duffel to my car, then grabbed the box I had hanging around in my trunk. Cranky landlady sat in a chair by the front door, watching me. She looked like the type to have a shotgun too.

Back in the apartment, I grabbed everything I could uncover, but still the box wasn't full. I made sure to find the old shoe box—reinforced with pink camouflage tape. The one item she went back to get each time she was evicted.

That was who she was. She'd leave the laptop and clothes but take a few trinkets from her dad. It was part of the reason why I went for her necessities first.

I rounded the building and saluted the old lady, not bothering speaking. She nodded and headed back into her house as I climbed into my car. I drove away, knowing I'd done something more meaningful with my day than if I had attended my accounting class.

After dropping off her stuff in my room, I headed to Support Services for my volunteer day. I went back to the computer I used to update their website. It was mindless work, for me at least, but it helped out and made sure all the outdated information shifted to current.

I focused all my attention on the website until a little girl with hair in poufy pigtails ran over to me.

"Guess what?" She bounced as she signed. "They found an apartment for Mom. We're moving! I'm going to have my own bedroom." She grinned from ear to ear.

I turned away from my computer. "That's wonderful. I'm happy for you." Ana lived at a women's shelter with her brother and mother. I wasn't aware of the full story but thought domestic abuse might have been involved.

"Me too! I have to pack. And paint the walls. I want pink." She jumped and ran back to the waiting area, no doubt sharing her good news with others.

I got up and went to Katherine's office, finding her there with Bea, Ana's mother. "Ana told me the news. Congratulations."

Bea smiled even wider than her daughter had. "Finally, a home for my kids."

"Now they can fight out of view."

Bea laughed. "I have already explained they can't be loud and bother the neighbors." Her kids were both hearing, and I had a good guess the noises I heard from the hall were related to them. "I think I need to find my old baby cry light, catch them yelling."

I thought of the items I collected from Jas. They fit in my car, as she had next to nothing. A family of three would have a lot more. "Need help with the move?"

Bea reached out and wrapped a hand around my bicep. "Yes, he's strong; he can help."

Katherine stifled a smile. "The move is on Wednesday. If you're available, it'll have to be outside of your volunteer duties."

"I'll be there."

Katherine faced Bea. "I guess you've found yourself some manpower." She leveled me with the same look she used to get a client to agree to something important. "I want that application from you."

If only it didn't come with a lot of family baggage.

Chapter Five

Jasmine

Society informed me that mothers were supposed to be warm and caring. Mine was a user. I should stay with her—after all, I sent her a check every month to help out—but I didn't think my mental health could handle being under the same roof as her again.

Still, it was an option, and I was in no position to discount options. I stole another pair of sweats from Dev and headed to the next town over.

Mom lived in a subsidized apartment, on account of her miniscule income. The buzzer system was all sounds, not deaf friendly at all, so I had an illegal copy of her keys. Better than yanking on the door like an unwanted guest while waiting for the mysterious sound to alert me to it being unlocked. I let myself into the building and took the stairs up to the fourth floor.

I could knock, but Mom rarely got up, and I wouldn't hear her tell me to come in. I found her where I expected, in her lounge chair in front of the television. Takeout from multiple restaurants covered the kitchen table. My heart went out to her, just a little. She'd been a shit mother after Dad's death had thrown her into a deep depression, one no one could pull her out of. But she was still my mother.

I stomped and waved until she looked my way. "Hi, how you doing?"

Her eyes narrowed, her hair dull and lifeless against her pale skin, blanched by the harsh fluorescent lighting. "Why here?" Mom's ASL wasn't the best, lots of choppy movements and messed-up words, but she could communicate when she wanted to.

Okay, so it was going to be one of those days. I could tell her I came to visit, which I did at least once a month, but instead I cut to the chase. "My landlord changed the locks."

She turned back to the television. "Not my problem."

I tightened my fists at my side and signed to her back, "Dad would've helped." Granted, our financial troubles were partly due to the debt Dad had. But he did his best. Always.

"He can't help. He's dead."

Shit, she must have caught my reflection in the television.

"Where are you going to live?"

Should have known that would be her response. Yeah, she had a studio, but I could crash on her couch as long as her neighbors didn't report me to the association. Not like she'd ever offered.

"Don't know. But I won't be able to help you until I'm on my feet."

She clicked off the television. "You owe me."

I shook my head. "I don't owe you anything." I didn't know why I continued to see her. I guess out of some long-buried family connection, in a perverse hope that one day, she'd wake up and I'd have a parent back. Said hope dwindled by the day, and now only a few threads remained.

I didn't look at her, so I didn't know her response. A box of black trash bags sat on her counter; the cardboard hadn't even been cracked since I bought it. I filled one with all her takeout and other shit, eyes away from her.

Story of my life.

My eyes traveled to the menorah Mom had set up on a low shelf and never taken down after the holiday ended. She never lit it. Never celebrated the miracle of lights. And yet the menorah remained, a lingering connection to our religion. As if she still wanted a miracle herself, but didn't know how to get one.

I shook those thoughts aside and collected the trash. I glanced back at her once, from the door. Not sure why. I didn't really expect any response. She had resumed watching her show and didn't turn my way. I didn't stomp, or wave, or flash a light. I simply took her trash with me.

One option crossed off the list. One left.

I tossed her trash in the large container outside, then pulled my coat tighter around myself for warmth. Dev's tee shirt and my trench did nothing to shield me from the crisp spring air.

I wiggled my phone out of my back pocket after I climbed into my car.

Me: I've got work tonight.

The words were right there, *I'll come back after*, but I couldn't type them. The offer was there for me, but acknowledging it? That took balls.

Dev: Come here first. You are staying, right?

And there it was, ready for the taking. No choice but to accept.

Me: I can help with the rent, or food, or something.

Dev: Stop. You stay. End of story. Please.

Please. Did Dev really type that?

Me: Are you begging?

Dev: You'll know if I'm down on my knees. Cut the shit. You've got a place. And I've got a surprise for you.

Me: If it's a puppy you need your head checked.

Dev: Where are you?
Me: On my way to work where it's at least warm.
Dev: Come here.
Me: What did you do?
Dev: Come here and find out.

I wanted to be stubborn, but curiosity got the best of me. I started my beat-up old Civic and headed back to Dev's place. The heat didn't exactly work, but at least the sun warmed up my car a few degrees.

My phone lit up from its spot in my cup holder.

Dev: You coming?
Me: Can't text and drive.
Dev: Then stop checking your phone!

I braked at a red light.

Me: Stop texting me and I will.

At his apartment, I hurried through the wind and up the stairs, found his front door open a crack, and let myself in. I felt him standing nearby, but my eyes were trained on the coffee table, where my box sat in all its loud pink camouflage glory.

My heart stuttered. His baby blues shone with a good dosage of pride, but I had no desire to pick on him. "You got my box?"

A grin lit up his face. "I got everything I could find, but I knew this was the most important item."

A weight lifted off my shoulders, and I flung myself at him.

Dev's arms came around me, holding me tight. I buried my face in his shoulder, taking from him whatever he gave. He was my family, more so than those I shared blood with.

I pulled back before I did something foolish, like cry, and collected the box. One peek inside the lid, and I knew it held everything it needed to.

"Thank you," I signed small, impossible to express the full gratitude I felt.

"Don't thank me yet. I had to touch all your underwear."

It should have been a joke. I know he meant it that way, but his expression shifted. Instead of a teasing glint to his eyes, something darker simmered just below the surface—a darkness part of me really wanted to explore.

Why was this any different from sleeping beside him in his bed? I tried to come up with a joke, to right the weirdness now between us. But I liked the heat in his gaze, the way he looked at me. I wanted to pretend it could be more than our usual friendship for just one moment before I went back to believing it could never be.

I STOOD UNDER the shower stream at Dev's place, hair completely soaked and cleaned and conditioned for the first time in months. By the time I finished, my fingers were pruney, but I felt clean and refreshed.

I wiped steam from the mirror, detangled and gelled my hair. In Dev's room, I changed into fresh clothes, even if they did have a few wrinkles. A section of Dev's closet had been cleared for me, and two drawers were empty and open. I didn't have much, and he knew it, considering he'd packed for me. What did he think I was going to fill the space with? At least if this didn't work out, I could easily pack up.

One room I did take up space in was the bathroom. The Walker brothers had this long counter they kept empty, but now it held my crap. It took work to transform into a bar girl, but it was a part of my day I looked forward to. A chance to put on the flirty-girl persona.

I leaned over the bathroom counter, applying a thick coating of eyeliner—a technique Mom had taught me, side by side in front of the mirror, me copying her movements, before depression latched its cold, hard teeth on her. The image of her, hair blonder, skin less pale, came to mind as if a ghost in the mirror. Along with that long-forgotten emotion of familial acceptance. One of my few happy memories with her after Dad died—applying makeup. I shook the image clear; moments like that had been fleeting, but powerful.

Just as I held the mascara wand to my lashes, the light flashed and I nearly stabbed myself in the eye. I turned to the open door, where Dev propped his shoulder against the jamb. "What the hell? I nearly took my eye out!"

He studied my face. "You're fine." Then his gaze traveled down my black tank top and biker shorts to the pink nail polish on my bare toes. "Really fine."

This was our banter. A line like that deserved a shoulder punch from me or a turn back to the mirror. He hung out at the bar all the time; there was nothing new about the situation.

I went back to applying mascara. Dev didn't move.

Nothing had changed. I tossed my mascara on the counter and reached for my lipstick.

Something had changed.

My hands shook, and it took twice as long as usual for me to paint my lips. Staying with Dev was a bad idea. I'd figure out something else. I replaced the lipstick and faced him, ready to tell him thanks but no thanks. Only his eyes held a glint I wasn't used to seeing.

"I'll sleep on the couch." It would be too weird to sleep next to him. Not when I wasn't thinking of him as a platonic friend. Not when I was far too aware of the muscles I knew were under his shirt.

Dev straightened, and I tilted my head up to keep him in view. He hesitated. He felt it too. "Or I can, no big deal."

Very big deal. The first time I stayed over was the night Dad died and Mom was stuck at the hospital in a hysterical dehydrated fit. The Walkers had set me up in their spare room, but I sneaked into Dev's bed. Even at ten years old, there was no one who held me quite like he did.

"Right, no big deal."

He stood there another minute before shaking his head and leaving me alone. Tomorrow I needed to come up with a new life plan, one that got me out of murky waters with my best friend.

Chapter Six

Devon

The need to help Jas consumed me. The undeniable urge to do something, anything more for her. To wave a damn fairy wand and fix all her problems, bring her father back, prevent her mother's depression, and keep money from ever being an issue.

I had to think, find some unturned rock that held all the magical answers to fixing her life. The itch was there, telling me an answer existed inches from my grasp, waiting for me to shift just enough to find it.

While I searched for the rock, another idea sprang to mind. It was small, but the smallest of gestures had been known to create the biggest results. I pulled out my phone and sent a group text to our mutual friends, Pete and Nikki.

Me: Bar. Tonight. Jas evicted.
Pete: What the hell?
Nikki: How's Jas?
Me: What do you think?
Nikki: She need a place, or do you "have her"?
Me: What does that mean?
Pete: Let them live together, maybe they'll figure it out.

I placed my head on the back of the couch. No one was going there. Especially not Pete. If he revealed my secret, I'd reveal his.

Me: Drop it.

Nikki texted a winking emoji. Helpful.

I didn't leave to join Jas at the bar, not right away, and I hadn't the foggiest idea why. I'd never hesitated before. Never needed to.

I did now. Maybe I'd been in love with her for so long I'd forgotten how to mask it. I had to do better—that line was not to be crossed. Ever. Jas was my family, not someone I screwed around with. I needed her in my life, and she needed me. Being friends kept us as we were meant to be.

The dive bar where she worked consisted of a run-down building next to other run-down buildings. I parked in the lot abutted by a tree, its roots creating some interesting parking spaces. The wind tunneled between the buildings, blowing against my aids and creating loud microphone noises. I hurried into the warm yet dreary bar and searched for Jasmine. She stood at a table where a bunch of college guys sat. Jas handled communication via a whiteboard she kept attached to her hip, and one guy wrote on her. Part of her appeal, I thought—the up-close kind of contact.

It made my blood boil as usual and eradicated any chill from outside.

The guy had his head too close to her breasts, his hand nearly on her ass as he wrote, and there was nothing I wanted to do more than punch the hell out of him. Especially when his hand snaked around to grab her ass. Before I could move, Jas backed out of his reach, collected her board, and wagged a finger in front of his face like a schoolteacher reprimanding a student. It got his hands off her, but I knew he'd be jerking off to her image later.

Jas shifted, catching me at the door. A smile brightened her face as she nodded toward the bar. I'd hung out here since before I could legally drink. This bar was the *don't make us ask for your ID* kind of place, the reason why Jas had worked here since she was seventeen.

A few older guys sat at one side of the bar, and I settled at the other end, sitting on a round stool with a cracked red leather cover. Jas came over and handed her board to her bartender/boss, Len, then grabbed a beer for me without asking. She popped the cap and placed it in front of me. "Don't trust me to come back to your place?" she signed.

I brought the beer to my lips. "You've had a shit day. I thought you could use some friends."

Her eyes narrowed, then darted over my shoulder. I didn't have to turn. I knew reinforcements had arrived.

Nikki sidled up next to me, with Pete on the other side of her. "That apartment was crap, and you know it," she signed.

Jas let out a breath. "It was cheap."

Pete leaned forward, the tattoos on his tanned arms flexing as he moved. "So's Devon."

I reached behind Nikki and whacked Pete on the back of his head.

"True." Jas's brown eyes held a tease but lingered on mine for too long. The air between us grew thick with a new kind of tension, the kind of tension that made breathing an option and my pants too tight. I wasn't mistaking this shift. I held her gaze, searching for answers, refusing to check her slender neck for signs her pulse was as crazy as mine was.

Jas broke eye contact and collected Nikki and Pete's drink order. She avoided looking at me as she checked on Len, who had finished her orders. She gathered her full tray and swayed away from us, balancing all those drinks on slender arms that were a hell of a lot stronger than they appeared.

Nikki crossed her arms and leaned back, dark eyes flitting back and forth between Jas and me before staring me down. "See?" she signed, before recrossing her arms.

"See what?" I all but dared her. If any talk about us existed behind our backs, no one dared mention it to Jas and me. We had shot down any romantic notions for years, our standard responses accepted far and wide. There was no reason to change things now. None at all, even if I'd been better at hiding my feelings back in school.

Nikki turned to Pete. "We should tell them."

Pete shook his head. "No. Their problem, not ours."

"You want them to keep playing this game?"

"Sure, it's fun."

Someone bumped my shoulder, and I turned to Jas leaning against me, her empty tray dangling at her side. "They picking on us again?"

"Of course."

Our usual banter. Same conversation, different night. Except for the way her shoulder continued to touch mine. I tried to remember if this was normal or not. All I knew was that it didn't feel normal. Not anymore.

Nikki spun around to face us. "You two are yin and yang."

I arched an eyebrow.

Pete popped a nut in his mouth. "Truth. You should get it tattooed."

Jas shook her head beside me, her blond curls swishing into my periphery.

"That's an idea," Nikki signed. "You two together are complete, you balance each other the way no one else will. Why not show it off with a little ink?"

Jas shifted next to me. "Your point?"

Nikki fought an upturn to her lips. "Nothing. Nothing at all."

Jas took off, returning a minute later and banging Nikki and Pete's drinks on the counter, liquid splashing. "Play nice, or go home."

I didn't catch Nikki's response but I did see the flush to Jas's cheeks before she moved away.

"Be nice," I signed to Nikki.

She held her hands up. "I'm nice. I swear." She pushed my shoulder. "Open your eyes."

"No." I turned away from her. It was the most confirmation I'd ever given. And I didn't dare give more.

THE MINUTE NIKKI and Pete left, Jas picked up a rag and started wiping down tables. Tables that didn't need to be cleaned. Not at this hour, with only a few stragglers remaining. Her message was clear: she didn't want to talk.

I waved her down and had to include a few foot stomps before she looked my way. "I'll see you at home?"

Her shoulders stiffened, and I braced myself, but she nodded before turning back to the spotless tables.

I headed home, all the while wondering if she needed a little space. I could sleep on the couch, give her my room. Or would she interpret it as me treating her with kid gloves? Didn't matter, being too close to her was bound to get my signals crossed. I couldn't keep her in the same box she'd been in for over a decade. Not when the thought of her made me hard.

I needed to get my head on straight, and some time with the punching bag in the basement usually did the trick. Didn't explain why I stood staring at the couch as if it was a goddamn crystal ball or some shit. I hadn't moved when the door behind me opened. Blake entered, goofy smile on his face, razor burn on his neck, and—

"You skipped a button."

He looked down at his shirt, one side higher than the other. "You don't care."

I shook my head. I didn't. Blake worked hard; he deserved to play hard. "How's Shawn?"

At the mention of his boyfriend's name, his smile widened. My days with Blake as a roommate were definitely numbered.

Blake looked around. "Where's Jasmine?"

"Work. She'll be home soon."

Blake's smile fell. "And you were waiting for me?"

I scratched the back of my neck. "Debating if I should stay on the couch."

"You haven't stayed there before."

I hadn't had my bottled-up desire this close to the surface. "I can't do that to her."

Blake's eyebrows scrunched together. "Do what? Sleep with her?"

I shifted my stance. Those words no longer had a platonic connotation.

Blake laughed, the sound connecting with my hearing aids until I flicked one off. "Want some advice?"

"No." Only I still didn't move.

"Stop fighting yourself. Allow whatever needs to happen, to happen."

"And when it fails?"

Blake ran a hand through his hair. "And when it doesn't fail?"

"Neither one of us are good at commitment."

"Except that you've been friends since elementary school. Maybe you both are really good at it."

With that, he turned and headed down the hall.

I left the living area and entered my room, determined to make things a nonissue. Any more acknowledgment of this shit would just mess things up further.

I got ready for bed and busied myself by playing on my phone when Jas showed up. And all I could think about was the way the light hit her cheek and how I wanted to trace the path with my hand.

She waved and grabbed the tee shirt I had given her yesterday before slipping off to the bathroom. I tried to convince myself everything was fine; if Jas didn't want to acknowledge the couch offer, then I wouldn't either. Except the thought of my clothes against her bare skin sent all my blood rushing south.

Well, at least that was still the same. Not quite to this extreme, but yeah. The downside of having a smoking-hot best friend.

Jas returned and dumped her bar clothes in a corner. My tee shirt grazed her knees. I couldn't help but wonder which of her underwear she wore underneath, if any at all. "So, are you the yin or am I?" Her lips curved as she signed.

I had to blink a few times to get my head back on track and off what she looked like under the shirt. "Your skin is darker than mine." I nearly punched myself. Way to let go of thoughts of her bare skin, Dev.

She kneeled on the bed. "I'm, like, two shades darker."

I took in the warm olive tones of her face, arms, and legs, then turned to my arm, the pale shit that didn't tan. "Fine, you can be the light one. It matches your hair."

She narrowed her eyes, staring at me with tiny little slits threatening to shoot dangers. Then she laughed, and I didn't bother quieting her. Truth be told, I lived to make her laugh, loved the way it tugged at my heart when her whole face lit up. "You've had the lighter life."

I didn't argue. Both my parents were alive and financially stable. Add in the fact that with them being Deaf, I never lived in a place where I couldn't communicate or wasn't understood.

Jas climbed into bed with me. Even though I had a queen, she curled right up like she had when I still had the twin. Her head on my chest, legs tangled. My arm went around her, an automatic response to the light floral scent attacking my nose.

She raised one hand. "Light off," she signed in my view, before settling back in.

Stubborn. I had to shift us both to reach the damn light, but soon we were curled up in the dark, only a few streaks of light peeking through the wood blinds.

Jas's breathing slowed as she drifted off to slumberland. Meanwhile I stared at the slats of light on my ceiling, doing my best not to think of how close her knee was to my crotch, or how her breast pressed into my chest, or even how far up her leg rubbed against my thigh.

Sleep would be a long time coming. Always was when she shared my bed. I might need to reconsider the couch for my own sanity. Until then, I held her closer and tried my damnedest not to think of what could be if things were different.

Chapter Seven

Jasmine

I WOKE UP to a hand on my ass. In those rare moments between asleep and awake, I had no clue about my surroundings, only that the warmth penetrating through me sent tingles up my spine. Thanks to my thong, the hand was flesh against flesh in the best possible way. I wanted the hand to tighten. To claim and make good use of the desire spreading through my veins.

Then it all came crashing back. My eyelids flew open. Dev slept next to me—well, under me, as I was sprawled out across him. Not that unusual. Except for the hand.

Dev remained fast asleep. Instead of moving and breaking our awkward connection, I shifted, my breasts rubbing against his chest, hips digging into his, body tightening at the sheer pleasure of it all. My shirt was somewhere around my waist, and the heat of him seeped through my clothes.

His hand squeezed my ass, shifting my thong, and my breath backed up in my throat. Holy shit. He wasn't doing anything, and yet my core clenched, and it took everything in me not to push into his hand.

Get out, Jasmine. Get out now. Stop getting off on your sleeping BFF.

I slipped out of bed, moving slow enough not to jar him awake. He rolled over, and I pulled down my shirt to once again cover myself. My pulse raced, and I tried to take deep breaths and slow it down, but all I saw was Dev. The bed hair, the stubble accentuating his pink lips. His hand that had been keeping my ass warm now above the covers.

I turned before a cold shower was in order.

I pulled on jeans and made my way into the living area, where Blake sat at the kitchen table, coffee in one hand, book in another. The studious Walker brother, complete with neatly combed short dark hair.

I stomped on the floor, and Blake looked up, sending me a smile. The man needed a pair of reading glasses to take off and complete the image.

"Good morning. I finally see my newest roommate."

"Haha." I joined him at the table.

"You doing OK?"

I nodded. "I'm fine."

He leaned both elbows on the table, shifting it toward him. "I smell shit."

"That's your coffee; you didn't add any sugar."

He leaned back. "Do you need your own room? I could possibly give you mine."

My jaw dropped. "Moving in with someone?"

He dipped his head, but his cheeks pinked. Busted. I prepared to tease, until I caught the telltale Walker uncomfortable sign: a neck scratch. "What's the problem? I thought you and Shawn were in love." I prolonged the sign for *love* in a light tease. I liked Shawn. He didn't need to learn ASL to date hearing Blake, but he had done so, knowing Blake's entire family was Deaf.

He scratched his neck again. "Living with someone is a big step, don't you think?"

I raised my eyebrows and signed nothing. I had just come from his brother's room, after all. "I have no idea what you mean."

A smile cracked his face. "I mean what other people think."

"I stopped caring about that years ago. You should try..." My hands stilled as I figured out the real problem. "I thought your father supported you?"

Hand. Neck. Scratch.

"Wimp. If the building ever caught on fire, you and Devon would be afraid to tell your father."

Blake shook his head, but a relaxed smile crossed his face. "I suspect he's waiting for this phase to end."

"A phase? I don't remember you ever being straight."

He picked up his coffee mug, only to put it back down without drinking. "Shawn isn't some random boyfriend."

I squirmed. "Now the truth comes out. It's not just living together, it's 'meet my future husband.' "

Scratch, scratch. Cheeks pink. And the final piece slipped into place.

"They haven't met Shawn, have they?"

Blake shook his head.

"What are you waiting for?"

Something switched in Blake's face. "What are *you* waiting for?"

"What do you mean?" I had a sneaking suspicion we were no longer talking about his parents.

He stood, taking his mug with him. "You're not that clueless." He glanced behind me, toward Dev's room, and my blood ran cold.

He turned, letting me off the hook. I needed to get back at him, make light of the situation and throw him off the scent, the problem being that I really wasn't that clueless. He was right. Truth was, I was too damn scared to find out what could happen.

NIKKI BEGGED ME to join her at the mall after her classes finished for the day. I wasn't much into shopping—browsing and not buying grew old very quickly—but I enjoyed friend time. I followed her around the store as she picked up shirt after shirt, holding them up, putting some back. I only ever bought what I needed. Started doing so a year after my dad died, when the reality of the debt he left hit. I told myself we'd bounce back and I'd buy fun stuff again.

We didn't bounce back. Things grew worse. Since I was on my own now, I saved as much as I could. I refused to be without food again. And until I had my own bar like Dad used to have, I'd continue saving.

So even though she held up the cutest little dress, I didn't grab one in my size. I had enough, no need for more.

Until she showed me the tag, with the ridiculously cheap clearance price. Then I was powerless to resist. My find for the day in hand, I couldn't get my head out of my present predicament.

"Am I crazy to think about living with Devon?"

Nikki paused mid rack search and put her armload of clothes down. "What?"

I had the sudden urge to rub my neck. "Me. Devon. Living together. Crazy, right?"

Nikki shook her head, black curls brushing against mahogany cheeks. "Crazy would be not living with him."

"I should find my own apartment."

Nikki's hand shot out. "No. You keep searching for these cheap places and end up with no heat. It's not safe."

"No different from when I lived with Mom."

Nikki wiped an imaginary board. "No. Not going there. Stay with Devon. Save money. Buy your bar. Maybe add a few other good things to your life."

I didn't care that we were in the middle of a store, I sat down on the floor. "I'm tired." Always thinking, having to stay two steps ahead of finances and evictions, never having stability—it all wore thin. If it wasn't for my friends, I had no idea where I'd be.

Nikki sat across from me. "So let someone else take care of you for a change."

I smiled, thinking about my dad making me soup when I was sick. And then twelve-year-old Dev bringing me home with him after school to do the same. "I let others take care of me."

"Once in a while. And it's all pretend; you still control everything."

"Can you blame me?"

Nikki's face softened. "No." She rose and re-draped her items over one arm. "But I still think you can trust Devon," she signed one-handed.

The answer bubbled up, but I kept my hands still. What I couldn't trust was my attraction to him. I'd done my best to ignore it, strangle it, diminish it. It lived when it shouldn't.

Which didn't explain why his little half smile, the barely there curve that lit up his entire face, always got to me. It started off as this warm place, this special acceptance I got from him, and grew into me wondering how it would feel to have that smile against my lips.

After Nikki and I split up, I drove around, a bit aimless since I had the night off. I ended up parked outside my father's old bar.

It'd been empty for a few years. Dad hadn't been gone six months before Mom was forced to sell the place. Not that owning a bar was something she dreamed of doing, but if Dad hadn't died with the place mortgaged up to his eyeballs and behind on almost all the bills, maybe we could have kept it afloat.

Maybe.

It changed hands two more times before collecting cobwebs. The lease sign hung in the window, loud and proud. And a stab to my heart. If I was older, if I had more money, I'd snatch it up in a heartbeat. But even if I had enough for the rent, I didn't have enough for any supplies, never mind the cosmetic work the place surely needed.

I pulled out my notebook and set it on my crossed legs. I thumbed through the pages, thinking of all the things I remembered from my father, from being at this very location, in hopes I could add an idea or two. Once upon a time, his tall frame stood behind the bar, hands on the top, ruling his world with a smile on his face.

One day. I had my notebook. I had my dream. Another delay sucked, but I'd do this. I had to.

I got out of my car and walked over to the window, cupping my hands to see in through the glare. The tables were laid out like Dad had them, chairs turned upside down on top. Everything was achingly familiar, down to the silly singing fish hanging above the bar. For whatever reason, the subsequent owners had done little to change the appearance.

Which made it easy to travel down memory lane, to the days when I got off the school bus and came straight here. I washed counters, dried cups, and chatted with my dad.

He always signed when I was around, something that confused new customers. The regulars soon learned some basic ASL so they could communicate with me. I never felt out of place or unwanted here. This bar was home.

Or maybe my father made it that way. I rubbed at the ache in my chest and returned to my car. One day, I'd have my own place, and it would be home.

If I continued to save. One point in favor of staying with Dev.

Chapter Eight

Devon

Blue light leaked through the side of the copy machine. When the machine finished, I took the paper out and placed another in. Over and over again, the same job I'd done since high school.

Once I graduated, I wouldn't be doing this. One small relief in the grand scheme of things. But the question remained: Where would I be? Where I wanted, or here?

Blake came out from his office in his dress shirt and tie, a full-on professional appearance. I had on a dress shirt, the collar unbuttoned, and with the exception of special occasions, this was about as professional as I wanted to get. He bypassed me and headed over to the receptionist. Arms resting on the high divider, he leaned forward, hands out of view as he spoke to her, no signing. Their voices crisscrossed, nothing more than a light murmur to me. She'd been with us for a while and knew enough ASL to communicate with Deaf clients—the standard *hi, how are you, please wait*—and yet I couldn't have this type of casual conversation with her.

I could at Support Services though. Everyone there knew a decent amount of ASL—they wouldn't work in a Deaf environment if they didn't. They had interpreters on staff to help with any outside meetings with hearing people or phone calls.

Here Dad had an interpreter on staff to help with his hearing clients. And he already planned to hire another one when I joined.

I collected my papers and headed to the back room to file them. I was proud of my father; he hadn't let his hearing loss get in the way of his dream. Because of him, I had grown up knowing that my ears didn't have to stop me.

No, my only obstacle was what my parents wanted.

I grew up in a Deaf home, in the Deaf World, and that's where I wanted to work. More like Mom, who worked in a Deaf school, than Dad. I wanted to help others like me who had hearing loss—maybe even ones who didn't have the opportunities I had. One thing was for sure, I didn't want to do their taxes.

The never-ending trap between what I wanted and what was expected of me became clear when I was still a kid. Dad only paid attention when it suited him. Anything Blake or I desired otherwise didn't matter. If we weren't signing what he was looking for, it was as though the words didn't exist. I could tell Dad what video game to get me for my birthday until my hands were numb, and he'd get me something else. The worst part was always the ending, where he never even acknowledged I had told him anything differently. Eventually Blake and I stopped telling Dad anything except what he wanted to see. It was the only way to be heard.

Dad entered the back room, shifting through the papers until he found the one he was looking for. "We'll have to hire another assistant next year. Know anyone in your classes who might be interested?"

I was the only Deaf person in my classes; he'd need an interpreter to communicate with them. "I'll see if I can find someone."

Dad nodded. "Good."

My window of opportunity would close the moment he turned and walked away. "I want to help people." Good lord, what was I? Five?

Dad put his papers down. "I have a client who can't leave the house. Why don't you visit and find out what he needs?"

Not what I meant. "I meant using my social work training."

"That's why I'm sending you and not Blake."

Oh good, I'd get a few small opportunities to do what I wanted while being suffocated. I raised my hands to sign more, but the interpreter showed up at the door. Dad quickly rattled off the client's name in a blur of finger movements and left me alone.

I collapsed into a chair. It wasn't that he was being an asshole or inconsiderate. He had dreamed for twenty years of his two sons joining the business. A kind of power duo. We could take care of anything and anyone.

It worked for Blake, but Dad never once asked if my minor should have been my major. And odds were, he never would.

A HALF HOUR later, I pulled up to a quaint little house in the suburbs. Grass freshly mowed, flowers and shrubs carefully attended to. Either this guy had a major green thumb or money to spare.

When I rang his doorbell, no lights flashed, and for the first time since Dad sent me here, I wondered what this dude's communication style was. Dad wouldn't send me to a hearing person's house. Would he?

The door opened, and an older guy with a nearly bald head stared back at me. He said nothing. Signed nothing. So I tossed both forms of communication at him. "Hi, I'm Devon Walker, here from Walker and Associates. I'm looking for Charlie."

The man's eyes narrowed. "Mick's son?" he signed, mouth closed, face stoic.

I nodded.

"Which one?"

Since I already told him my name, I figured out which direction he headed. "Deaf."

Charlie cracked a smile. "Come in."

I followed him through a house as put together as the outside to a kitchen table covered in papers. Once we settled in, I pulled out my papers. "My dad said you needed help?" Because, shit, he'd given me nothing else to go on.

Charlie nodded and shuffled through the massive collection of papers on his table before pulling one up. "The IRS sent me this."

I took it from him—a clean open slit at the top, clearly from a knife or envelope opener and not a thumb in the flap—and opened it up. The papers had been folded back up, not a wrinkle on them. I unfolded and read, some shit about incorrect taxes being paid. I had part of his information with me, but it would take time to research where the problem originated from, and I might not have the piece I needed.

"I'll bring this back to the office with me, if that's OK with you, and we'll figure it out. No worries."

Charlie smiled, but there was a sadness behind it. "Thank you. So you're leaving now?"

"You want me to leave?"

Charlie didn't respond. He launched into a discussion about the Red Sox, which I gladly participated in. Chit-chat wasn't for accounting, but no one was here to rush me along. It was a strong part of Deaf Culture. As a social worker, I'd be able to have these types of conversations, especially if my clients were Deaf. So I accepted a coffee and hung out for an hour.

I asked questions. It was my nature, ask and problem solve. Which was how I ended up adjusting the captions on his television and fixing a leak in the kitchen sink.

As I drove away from the house, all I could think of was that he was a nice guy and this was the type of work I wanted to do. I hadn't felt this good after a day of work since…ever.

I needed to sit Dad down and have this discussion already. But when I got back, he was busy with appointments, and I had an IRS issue to investigate.

Next chance I got, I had to do it. No excuses.

Chapter Nine

Jasmine

My phone flashed, forcing me to tear my eyes away from Dad's bar.

Dev: You off tonight, right? We should do something.

Dev: Movies? Bowling?

I wanted to wallow, pointless and ridiculous behavior.

Dev: Please, something, anything but taxes.

Warmth spread through me as a smile crossed my face.

Me: Want to help my mom? I'm sure she hasn't done any in a few years.

Dev: No. Hell no. She can use a hearing accountant, one that's not still in school.

Me: Party pooper.

Dev: Fine, I'll check with Pete. I thought you might want to watch hot guys blowing up stuff.

Me: Did you really type hot guys?

Dev: Blake claims so.

I laughed. No matter what shit life threw at me, Dev always managed to make me laugh.

Me: I could go for some hot guys.

It took him some time to respond. I imagined him typing a word, then deleting it, then typing it again.

Dev: I'm hot.

Yes, he was, but where the hell did that come from?

Me: Blake can't claim this one, he's your brother and biased.

Dev sent me a frowning emoji.

Me: Besides, I was promised guys, plural, blowing up stuff.

Dev: I could blow up stuff.

I closed my eyes, as my head went in a very dirty direction. My hands trembled when I picked up my phone, and it took me a few tries to get the right letters out.

Me: Movie.
Dev: Fine. Meet me at home. I'll check the times.

I tossed my phone on the passenger seat and started the car. Home. He didn't call it *his* home; he said *home*, like he was including me. He always had. Made me wonder what made a place *home*. Mine were always just a place to sleep. But Dev's childhood home held a warmth foreign to me. Even his apartment had that special comfort. And I knew that comfort went beyond heat and safety. It was that special feeling he extended to me.

I feared I craved that kind of a home more than I should.

As promised, the movie involved explosions and hot guys, even if one sat next to me and hogged the popcorn. Our captions were on little devices connected to our cup holders, preventing me from leaning into him like I did when we were at his place.

The forced barrier was a welcome addition to the mounting tension in my veins when I was around him. It all but simmered between us, across the armrest and through our jeans where our thighs touched. I could easily place my hand on his thigh or brush our arms together. Dev was the one who moved. A small shift and his pinkie wrapped around mine. Such a simple movement, but my heart beat faster.

I forgot to worry about his presence, the vibrations of the movie taking me over. I liked explosions in theaters. They shook the seats, lending to an air of reality. And for however long the movie lasted, my own world didn't matter.

When the movie ended and the lights turned up, I leaned over the armrest between us and snatched the popcorn. The empty popcorn.

"You ate it all," I signed.

"An hour ago." Dev laughed and popped his caption device from the cup holder. "You want more?"

My stomach grumbled, but I shook my head. The popcorn was way too expensive. And I'd already had enough. "I think you're going to lose a roommate soon."

Dev paused. "You leaving already?" Something in his eyes cut me more than normal.

"No, not me. I mean your brother."

He nodded. "That's been coming for a while now. I don't know what's holding him back."

"Seriously?"

"What am I missing?"

I had the sudden urge to point to myself. After all, we were at the movies. He'd paid for the tickets and popcorn; it was the type of night that under different circumstances would be considered a date. "He's worried about your father. Sound familiar?"

Dev's hand went to his neck. "He's got nothing to worry about."

And yet, the hand told a different story. "Neither do you. Why can't you just tell him you don't want to work for him?"

Dev paced in a circle. "Confessing things isn't easy." He stood two feet away and locked eyes with mine. My pulse picked up, and the world around us faded away.

This was bad, very bad. Very, very, bad.

"Dad's wanted this since I was born. I can't break his heart."

I closed my eyes and took a breath. We were having two conversations at once, and we both knew it. I forced myself to look into his baby blues. "You won't." I needed to get this second conversation buried again. Because what he needed to do with his father was different from what could happen between us. And I still wasn't sure there could be an *us*. "Your dad might be upset, but he'll be proud of you. I know he will."

"We'll see."

I had a sneaking suspicion I hadn't squashed the second conversation. I needed an out, an escape. "Ice cream?"

Okay, so I had a nervous tic too.

"I'm surprised you haven't wanted it yet."

I broke eye contact and nearly stumbled over my feet as I tried to quench the thoughts threatening to destroy our friendship.

Shit.

We left the theater and took a short drive over to the frozen yogurt place. It might be cold outside, but it was never too cold for ice cream.

We studied our options, waving away the overeager employee who tried to speak to us. Dev leaned into me, his arm touching my shoulder. "You get the strawberry, and I'll get the chocolate?"

"Of course."

We filled our bowls, then added toppings before paying and taking a seat by the window. Before I even touched mine, I took a large spoonful of his in order to exploit the amount of chocolate in his overloaded toppings. And as always, Dev did the same with mine.

At least, I assumed he did. The chocolatey mess was too good. I had to close my eyes as it invaded my system. I began to wonder why I let him get the chocolate until I took a bite of my own and the sweet fruit intermixed with the hot fudge.

Heaven.

The table vibrated beneath my arm. "Don't enjoy it too much." Yet the twinkle in his eyes said go right ahead.

I stole more of his ice cream. "Too late."

He smiled and tried to bat my spoon away from his ice cream. "I will beat you."

"Nope, my turn."

He dueled with my spoon, plastic against plastic, until mine loosened in my grip and went flying to the floor. I propped my hands on my hips, but the bastard laughed at me. So I stole his spoon.

I had ice cream in my mouth when I realized we had company. Some leggy blonde I had never seen before hovered over us. Or, rather, hovered over Dev.

He rubbed his neck. Interesting. Which of Dev's exes would this be? I hoped it was Natalie. I hadn't gotten the chance to check her out yet. I grabbed his ice cream and leaned back with it, fighting at the uneasy churning in my gut.

Blondie shoved two hands on her hips and began speaking to Dev, red lips flapping. I hoped Dev had his hearing aids on, because that was the only way he stood a chance in hell of hearing her.

Dev angled forward, half signing as he spoke but not enough so I could understand him. Blondie was not impressed and jabbed a finger in my direction. I flashed a smile and shoved another bite of ice cream in my mouth.

Shaking his head, Dev pulled out his phone and tapped at it, thumbs flying, before holding it up to Blondie. She took the phone and read, a scowl crossing her otherwise not-too-bad features.

While she read, Dev stole his ice cream back. "Natalie?" I asked.

He stared at the ice cream. "Yeah."

"What's the problem?"

He shifted and turned to Natalie, not able to meet my eyes. I returned to my own ice cream, only now I had lost my spoon and my distraction. I'd met plenty of Dev's dates before, but this one had my jealous inner beast ready to crawl out. I'd kept her tame for so long that I was tempted to act on impulse. I wanted to drag Natalie away and ask her what really happened between them. Deep down, I was afraid of the answer.

Chapter Ten

Devon

NATALIE REFUSED TO get the hint. She stood there, heels planted, ruining my night with Jas. She let out a huff and began tapping on my phone with one long manicured nail. While she pecked, I reached across the small table. Jas had just scooped up a hefty part of her ice cream, and I angled her wrist and claimed it myself, ignoring her narrowed eyes.

My phone landed in front of me.

She's the one. Right? The reason why you can't commit to anyone. Because you've clearly committed to her.

I made sure Jas couldn't see the words and quickly typed back.

Jas is a friend.

I held it up to Natalie, and she shook her head. She held up finger quotes, and I lip-read *friend.*

I think it's time to admit she's more than just a friend.

Natalie didn't wait for me to read; she stalked off before I could respond.

When I looked up, Jas was gone as well. I had a moment of panic, worried what Natalie would say to her. Jas appeared a few second later with a fresh spoon for me. "What was the problem with that one?"

I dug into my ice cream. "We didn't match." No one did. No one would. Not while I had feelings for Jas.

Jas leaned forward. "I didn't realize clueless blondes were your type." Her words were light, but something lurked deep in her eyes. I'd call it possessiveness if I didn't know better.

I tugged at one of her curls. "And this color is what?"

Jas leaned back and brushed her curls out of my reach. "Dyed."

I shook my head and returned to my ice cream. I'd known her since kindergarten; she had always been a blonde. And yet I had stumbled into an unknown area with her. I had no idea if she was jealous. But there was a part of me that hoped she was.

"I ATE TOO much," Jas signed, hands going to her belly as I let her into the apartment.

"Good." I hung up my coat, trying not to think about how I wanted my hands to be on her body and how maybe she was cold and I could warm her up.

I turned back around to find Jas on the edge of the love seat, chatting with Blake and his boyfriend. Shawn was the type who always smiled. He had shining brown eyes against tawny skin and that slicked-back hair thing that apparently drove my brother crazy. Jas slowed down her signing, but Shawn and Blake had this subtle communication system going—Shawn would tap Blake when he missed something, and Blake would voice.

Instead of paying attention to the conversation, I had been lost in my own thoughts, studying Shawn's face to gauge his comprehension level. Jas's hands were a blur in my peripheral vision, and when I finally focused, I realized I needed to have paid attention when she started. "I think he's dating the wrong kind of women," Jas finished.

Blake and Shawn both darted their eyes to me. "I agree," Shawn signed.

I sat down on the love seat next to Jas. "What does that mean?"

"You seem to be afraid to go after the type you really want," Blake signed, glancing back and forth between Jas and me.

"The great Devon Walker is scared? Maybe he needs someone strong enough to put up with his shit." Jas seemed to hold in a laugh and got up, heading toward the bathroom.

How about you? But I kept my hands clutched by my sides. I waited until the bathroom light disappeared behind the closed door before leaning forward. "You finished?" The guys stole a loaded glance. Christ, my brother talked about me with his boyfriend. I didn't want to see any shit they decided to unload, so I veered the conversation way off track. "Did your mom figure out the health insurance connector?" I asked Shawn, voicing with my signs.

Shawn leaned forward, an unconscious act; he did it to be louder for me without yelling. "Yeah, she needed some help, but my brother got through it. Thanks for the tip. We had no idea there were so many options out there."

Another good part of Shawn leaning forward: Blake leaned back and interpreted. Shawn threw a few signs in, but without Blake I would have been lost.

Shawn held out a fist, and I bumped it. "That's wonderful." I had learned of the resource at my volunteer job and had to share when I learned Shawn's mom had lost her health insurance. The least I could do for a guy Blake was serious about. Family helped family.

I signed good night to the guys and headed into my bedroom. Only I had missed Jas leaving from the bathroom.

She stood by my bed, back toward me, and was changing into her nightclothes. She wore nothing but her panties, and I couldn't stop my gaze from sliding down her naked back, over the round exposed butt cheeks from her thong, to her long, toned legs. My blood rushed south, and my fingers itched to touch her and make her come alive in my hands.

She pulled on a tee shirt—my tee shirt—and I stumbled back. I shouldn't have been there; I shouldn't have seen that. And yet, I wanted to. I wanted that shirt off so I could spin her around, press her against me, and kiss the hell out of her.

I closed the door and hit my head against the wood. I couldn't stay in the living room, not with Blake on a date.

But I needed a moment to collect myself and get my head in gear. So I did the only sure trick: I spouted accounting facts guaranteed to kill any boner.

Only it wasn't working. My signals were getting mixed up. Because no amount of accounting hell would change how much I wanted her or shrink the wood in my pants.

I had to decide if risking our friendship could ever be worth it. If not, then I had to man up and move on.

The only thing I knew? I could never hurt Jas.

Chapter Eleven

Jasmine

My father's box sat on my lap. I brushed my fingers over the top. It wasn't anything fancy, just an old shoe box from a pair of shoes I outgrew years ago, the size and brand freezing his belongings in time. Over the years, the cardboard bent and tore, so I covered parts in pink camouflage tape to protect the valuable contents inside.

The tape made the lid snug, and I had to wiggle it in order to pop it open. The first thing I pulled out was always the hardest to find, his wedding band. Mom didn't want it, but I did. I didn't know why; it was a simple gold band, no different from any I could find in the stores.

It fit him.

On me, it barely clung to my thumb. Made me feel like I was still his little girl, even if he was the one wrapped around my finger—or thumb—now.

I kept the ring on as I sifted through. A tie, a Queen CD that he used to play loud enough for me to feel, and a grouping of recipes.

Once upon a time, they'd been organized in separate cases. I'd snatched them out when Mom had gone on her purging spree. Now food recipes and drink recipes were stuck together, intermixed, like his life. Bar. Home. They were one and the same. My father had lived for his family and his bar.

And the stress of it killed him.

Stress, chronic heart problems in the family—who knew what really did him in? But he'd been too damn young to die. I'd been too damn young to lose my father.

I flipped through the recipes, pulling out a drink combination that had to be a joke, but it sounded so bad I had to try it. It had been years since I'd seen this one. Certainly not since I had gone to bartending school. Little good it did me; my boss didn't need me behind the bar, and no one else wanted to take a chance on a deaf bartender, assuming my ears meant I couldn't do my job.

I wondered if Dad would have let me work for him, with him. Maybe he would have taught me the ropes, helped me figure out effective communication.

Didn't matter. He was dead and couldn't help me.

Still, the cards held ideas I wanted to put to use in my own bar. I shimmied off the bed and grabbed my notebook, jotting down his joke recipe. Either it would turn out to be legit and I could put it on the menu, or I'd have a gag drink ready to go.

The next card gave me pause. Matzo ball soup. I hadn't had any since Grandma got sick, a few years after Dad died. Hadn't had a Passover Seder since then. And yet, the smell of the soup filtered to my nose. Back before I lost my father, before finances sucked, before my faith faded to the occasional lighting of a menorah on Chanukah.

I pulled out my phone, looked up when Passover started this year. Tomorrow night. I looked up at the ceiling. "You planned this, didn't you? I don't know how to make soup!"

As always, the ceiling didn't answer.

I flipped the card over in my hand. Dev had enjoyed the Passover food when Dad was still alive. I could barely remember what was needed for the first night's Seder meal, so that was out. But soup, soup I could do. A small thank-you to Dev for always having my back.

I should have remembered that finding Passover supplies so close to the holiday would be a bitch, especially in a non-Jewish area. I traveled up and down the food-store aisles, searching for matzo meal, before stumbling across a small table covered with macaroons, matzo, marshmallows, and jelly fruit slices. But no matzo meal.

Screw it. I had time; I'd have better luck in Brookline. I headed into the city. I was sure there were real Jewish stores I could go to, but that was never my family's style. We were the very reformed type who only celebrated the main holidays. Dad was trying to get me into Hebrew school when he died. He was the religious one in the family, and he wasn't even that religious.

At the second store, I found half an aisle filled with Passover stuff: cereal boxes, coffee, cake mixes, cookies, as well as everyday stuff made special for the holiday.

I stood there, somehow feeling connected to those who had gone before me. It was a weird experience that a part of me felt at home standing in the middle of a grocery store.

A lot of the food looked good, tempting. And expensive. I'd come here for soup. I picked up my matzo meal—and chocolate chip macaroons since I couldn't help myself. Then I got the other soup ingredients: broth, chicken, celery, carrots, and an onion. The rest of it would be odds and ends Dev and Blake had in their cabinets.

Back at the apartment, I set to work. It had been so long since I'd had a kitchen to work in—most of my apartments had barely any space, if they even had a stove. I chopped and minced, and soon the smells of chicken and onions floated in the air.

The smell was home. It was my father and tradition. Anger bubbled forth. If Mom had been willing to try, I could have continued to learn about my faith. Instead I'd been left with broken pieces and half-formed concepts. Tradition would have made each of our random apartments feel more like home.

Or it wouldn't have changed anything. Maybe once my life settled down, I'd do my own research. There were occasional interpreted services at a local temple. The next time I heard of one, I'd go.

Until then, I had soup. Sure, a day early, and I'd still eat bread and all the crap I wasn't supposed to for a week. But soup was good.

The ground vibrated, and I turned to find Dev at the edge of the kitchen, nose sticking in the air. "You cooking?" His eyebrows scrunched low on his face.

"I can cook."

"I know you can. Haven't seen it in years." He walked over to the pot and looked in. "Soup?"

"Matzo ball soup. Dad's recipe."

His face softened. "Glad I saved that box for you." His smile tried to melt me. "Funny, I got something to go with the soup. I noticed Passover started soon and wanted to get you something." He reached around and set his backpack on the table, pulling out a bag and then a box of matzo.

I laughed and shook my head, spreading my arms around the kitchen. "Do you see any matzo?" I'd made a conscious choice not to buy any when I was at the store. Of all the things tempting me, matzo was near the bottom of the list.

Confusion crossed his face. "No."

"I dare you to eat only that for bread for a week; it's heavy as hell. It's been years, and I remember that."

"Deal."

I laughed; he was going to hate me in a few days. I tried to remember what else we couldn't eat, but the rules were fuzzy. One day, I'd figure it out. One day.

I WIPED DOWN the worn wooden bar top as I looked around. All my customers were happy with full drinks, so I took a moment to alternate my weight, taking pressure off my feet. These boots looked kick-ass, but after several hours, they hurt like hell.

Another thing I should consider replacing, perhaps with something a little more suitable for long hours standing. But every time I spent money, my dreams slipped further and further away. Vicious cycle of life.

At least my belly was full of good soup. I'd even crumbled some matzo and sprinkled it on top. A day early and without any of the tradition I once had, but it warmed me even hours later. Made me a little sleepy, but no worse than when I worked on an empty stomach.

A new group of guys arrived, snagging one of the round tables. I collected my whiteboard and attached it to my hip, crossing the room to where they sat. Smile firmly planted, I waved, signed "deaf," and pointed to my board. In permanent marker, the top read: *Hi, I'm Jasmine, I'm Deaf, write down your order.*

The guys smirked, and I resisted an eye roll. Yes, I wore a short black skirt and a black tank top, but only because I wanted to. This was my image of my job, and if it helped boost my tips, then all the better. My reflexes didn't need any help. If they got too handsy, they didn't get a drink. Simple as that.

I jutted my hip out to the first customer. Sure, I could detach the board, but I found this method to be easier and flirtier in most cases. It also reduced grumblings over having to write their order.

They chatted over me as they wrote, nothing new. I became part of the furniture since I couldn't communicate. On rare occasions, customers gestured or wrote back or showed off the two signs they picked up in elementary school. Not this group. I backed away from the last one when his hand snaked around to my ass. Didn't stop him from grabbing me, but I prevented my skirt from being raised. I checked my board and saw that he'd written down enough. I knew what he wanted. I flashed a smile and waved before turning around and rolling my eyes. With my orders, I rounded tables on my way to the bar and handed my board over to Len so he could prep the drinks.

I brushed my hair back, tempted to pull it into a ponytail and get it out of my face. But since it covered some of my skin, it lent an air of mystery. Even if I was hot and sleepy and starting to regret the soup.

I needed a distraction and scanned the bar area, not surprised to find Dev at one end. My aching feet and tiredness vanished. Time for a little fun. Since he'd agreed to our deal about the matzo, I was going to torture him. Step one, he had to follow the rules, and the main one involved yeast. I bumped shoulders with him. "You think you're getting a drink?"

"Why not?"

I tried to hold back the smile but failed. "You're eating the matzo, right?"

He narrowed his eyes. "Yes." His hand movements were slow and elongated.

"Beer has wheat and yeast in it. You can't have it if you accept the matzo challenge."

"That wasn't part of the original plan."

Len nodded my way and pointed to my full tray. "It is now," I signed. I picked up my orders and headed off, leaving Dev without a drink of his own, doing my best not to laugh.

I delivered the beers, careful of any more ass grabbers, but they seemed too distracted staring at my breasts. Some days the customers were gentlemen, other days they were grabbers.

"You don't play fair," Dev signed from across the bar, after my drinks were served.

"You're just figuring this out now?"

His jaw clenched. "Twenty-two years old, and she's refusing to give me alcohol." He didn't sign it to me, but he didn't hide his hands either.

Len was MIA, probably out back smoking, so I slipped behind the bar. "You want a drink? I'll give you a drink." I pulled out my phone and the picture I had snapped of Dad's crazy concoction. An old-fashioned with basil simple syrup instead of a sugar cube.

Even if Dev gagged, it'd be worth it. And, bonus, I'd know whether it stayed on my bar plans or not.

I busied myself fixing up the drink. Without looking up, I knew he watched me; something about his gaze always touched my skin. I'd know where he was in a dark room.

With the drink finished, I sniffed it. It seemed to be okay. Alcohol wasn't for me, sans a few sips here and there, part of avoiding addictive behavior and all that shit, but I would take a sip of this.

After Dev.

I slid the glass on the bar top until it rested under his nose. "What's this?" He pointed to the drink with an air of distrust.

"Something my father left me." His jaw worked, and I swallowed a laugh. I knew he wouldn't be able to refuse me. "His soup was good, right?"

Dev shot daggers with his eyes, but I held firm. I knew he was seconds away from caving. Sure enough, before I reached the count of ten, he picked it up and took a sniff. Eyes on me, clearly suspecting foul play, he brought the drink up to his lips.

My humor died as his mouth parted and pressed against the glass. The liquid floated toward his face, wetting his top lip. How easy it would be to lean across the counter and take a taste against him.

I took a step back instead and forced the smile back on my face. "So?"

"It's not beer." Yet he took another sip.

"Good? Bad?" The man was killing me.

He gripped the top of the cup and slid it across the bar top to me. His eyes held mine in a challenge, and I couldn't look away even if I wanted to. I picked up the glass and brought it to my own lips. For the first time ever, I saw heat come into his eyes as the liquid touched my tongue. I welcomed the sweet tang, anything to diffuse the building tension between us.

I gave him back his drink. "Not bad. Point for Dad."

Dev nodded, turning the glass around so his lips touched the pink spot where my lipstick had rubbed off.

My knees threatened to give out. We were playing with fire now.

But the tables needed my attention. I grabbed my board and scurried off. Like it or not, I couldn't stop thinking about kissing my best friend.

Chapter Twelve

Devon

I PULLED MY shirt over my head, tossing it in the corner to my hamper. Jas was at work, so for the moment I had the room to myself.

The apartment still smelled of the chicken soup she made earlier. My room held a light floral scent that I associated with her. She was up my nose, in my head, and driving me insane.

I wanted her. In many ways I always had—couldn't quite pinpoint when friendship merged into something more. Didn't matter, since I couldn't stop thinking about her now. Each touch, each look burned with need. And moments like tonight, when she looked at me like I tried not to look at her, only wound me up further. I couldn't think of being with anyone else. I wanted to kiss her plump lips, run my hands into her tight curls, feel her curves underneath me, and...

Get a grip. These thoughts headed into no-man's-land. I couldn't change things. Could I?

I pulled out my phone, sent a text to my brother.

Me: You awake?
Blake: Yeah, what's up?
Me: You alone?

I had no problem if Shawn stayed over, but I had my limits.

Blake: I'm alone.
Me: I'm coming in.

I left my shirt off and crossed the hall to his room. He sat up in bed, also shirtless, and I hoped his lap stayed covered by the sheet, just in case.

"What's up?" Blake signed.

I perched on the end of his bed, not quite sure how to sign what I wanted to sign, if I even wanted to. I picked at the small hole in the knee of my jeans and tossed out the first words I could. "You think I should be dating someone specific, right?"

Blake sat up straighter. This whole thing with Jas required kid gloves, a topic danced around for years now. I never threw it out for discussion, and no one ever out-and-out challenged my real feelings.

He rubbed the back of his neck. "Of course you do this now, when she's living with you."

No mistaking what his answer would have been if he didn't have other things on his mind. "We see each other all the time. It's no different." No pretending on my end either.

Blake's eyebrows shot up. "No different? She's sleeping in your bed," he signed, his hands making large movements for emphasis.

"Same as she's done since we were kids."

"You two are crazy, you know that? It's not normal."

It was for us. "I can sleep on the couch."

"And what happens when you're not there? What happens when you fight and she feels she can't stay?"

"Nothing's happened, and you expect us to fight?"

"Yes."

Then that was my answer. I couldn't do this. "I can't date her." The words felt wrong on my hands, and it had nothing to do with the admission.

"You can't *not* date her. You'll never find someone else unless you let each other go."

"Not happening."

Blake laughed. "You signed that awfully quick."

I raised my hands, but nothing came out.

"Find out what her plans are, long term. She can stay, but you two need a foundation."

We had fifteen years of foundation. "What about you?"

"What do you mean?"

"Why haven't you introduced Shawn to Mom and Dad? Isn't that part of a foundation?"

Blake broke eye contact. "Dad doesn't like change."

"No, he doesn't." I tried to think of the last boyfriend Blake introduced to them and had to go back to high school.

"You talk to him yet?" Blake asked, turning the tables back on me.

Proof we were related; neither one of us shared important things that Dad might not like. "Tried, but not really."

"He's got that disappointed-puppy face that cuts right through."

That wasn't my concern. "He paid for a degree I don't want to use."

Blake rubbed his neck. "I guess we're both wimps."

I laughed. Yeah, we were. But there was one place I didn't want to be a wimp anymore, and that had nothing to do with Dad.

The bed vibrated under my hand. "You're really going to go for it with Jasmine?"

Multiple answers flitted around my mind, but only one mattered. "I love her."

"That's old news."

I laughed, years of hidden tension breaking free. "So that's my answer." Jas wasn't some random fling or a quick fuck. She'd always been a person I wanted by my side, forever. I got on my feet. "Nothing fast, she's too important to me for that."

"See you on the couch in the morning."

Yeah, the couch. Like that'd be comfortable. I tried to escape, but Blake waving caught my attention. "I heard the door close. She's home. What's your move?"

I stared at him. I had no clue. How did I forever alter things with my best friend?

I turned, catching the blur of blond curls as she passed by, then popped back out, checking on me. I waved and closed Blake's door behind me. "How was work?"

Her eyes skipped my face, zoning in on my chest, all but tracing me. I'd been shirtless around her countless times, and she'd never reacted like this. I wanted more, wanted to know what thoughts plagued her and how I could act on them. She shook her head and checked her wrist for her nonexistent watch. "You left maybe ten minutes before I did."

She collected the shirt she'd been sleeping in and vanished into the bathroom. I headed into my room and grabbed one of my pillows and a spare blanket. Then I stared at my bed, imagined Jas in it, alone. What it would be like to lay her down, strip off her clothes, and…

I took in a breath. I couldn't share a bed with her. Not anymore. Nothing had happened, and yet whatever bubbled between us had boiled over.

Somehow, I needed to explain this to her.

Lost in my head, I didn't notice her coming back. Not until she touched my arm, and I jumped like a scared little kid. Her face makeup-free, all she wore was the tee shirt. No amount of makeup or bar clothes could compete with her natural beauty. Her eyes were wide with amusement until they narrowed in on the pillow and blanket. "What the fuck?"

I rubbed the back of my neck. "I thought it would be best if I slept on the couch."

She didn't move. Her facial expression didn't change. Yet I knew thoughts ping-ponged in her head. One of us needed to leave or make a joke. Or we'd finally call attention to what had grown between us.

I took a step toward her, testing the water. She took a step back. But the irises in her eyes darkened, and dammit, there lay an invitation.

We both breathed heavily, neither moving. We knew each other like the back of our hands, but from here on out, everything was new.

"You're too tall for the couch." Her hands moved small, soft. I wanted them on me.

"I don't sleep flat."

She cocked her head.

"When I'm alone." Maybe that was why I didn't sleep much when she joined me.

"What are we doing?"

The feet between us could've been miles, and yet the pull grew stronger than ever. No more denying, no more pretending. In a few short words, we'd both acknowledged that something was there.

Had been there.

I shifted my feet. "I can leave." An offer. I leave, we bury this shit again. No questions asked.

Jas tipped her head up, curls tumbling down her back. She breathed in, and I couldn't ignore the rise and fall of her chest, not when I could make out the shape of her nipples through the cotton. Then she pierced me with her brown eyes. "That's not an answer."

Offer shredded. I took another step to her. She didn't move. My breaths came in fast spurts. She was there, right there. Everything I had dreamed of potentially minutes away from my grasp.

I reached out and caressed her jaw, her skin smooth and soft. My thumb traveled over her bottom lip, and she opened for me on a little gasp. A taste, I needed one more than my next breath, and I leaned in, eyes locked with hers. She tilted her head up to mine, letting my fingers brush down her neck. But even as her body said yes, there lived a hesitance in her. I didn't know if it was the newness of this, the change, or what. I only knew I had to take my hand back.

Slow, or we'd combust. "I'm sleeping on the couch. Because it's too damn hard sleeping next to you and not touching you."

I held my breath, those words flying in the air from my hands. She bit her lip, her gaze not on my eyes. "Why now?"

"Too long."

She nodded, the tension threatening to bend the walls. I wanted that lip out from her teeth and in between mine. But I also noticed she hadn't confirmed anything, even though we both knew the truth now.

It cooled me down. Here I had just revealed a part of my feelings, and she kept her hands still.

I backed up. She let her lip free. Instead of reaching for her, I kept the distance we now required. "Good night."

"Wait." She stepped forward, answers written across her face. The need to share shone in her. I held her eyes, begging her to join me in this shift of our relationship. "Good night."

She didn't reciprocate. I stood there a moment longer, hoping for a change that wasn't coming. Then I left the room and settled down on the couch. Sleep would be a long time coming. Blake was right, I shouldn't have done that, not now. Instead of moving things forward, I might have fucked up everything with my best friend.

She deserved better than this. What the hell had I been thinking? Laying it out like that. I should have asked her out. Made my intentions clear, rather than pussyfoot around the issue.

It was out there now, nothing stopping me from bringing it up. From asking her out. See if she took the bait. Maybe I'd get a different reaction out of her.

I'd give her some time, then make one more attempt. If she shot me down…well, that's what I got for trying to change things, for trying to acknowledge what we both damn well knew was there.

Chapter Thirteen

Jasmine

I ALMOST KISSED Devon. His lips had been right there; one step into him, and I wouldn't be in his bed alone. His scent surrounded me, and I rolled over, buried my head in it, and breathed him in.

I should have kissed him. I wanted to. He wanted to. He wanted to change us, who we were, who we'd become. Change, such a simple concept for him. It meant good things and potential. Change, for me, had almost always meant bad.

I couldn't risk losing him.

And I would lose him. If we did this, we had three weeks, tops, before he did whatever Dev did to sabotage a relationship. Three weeks, and I'd lose more than him as my friend.

That thought should have been enough to kill the desire. Had been for years. Not this time. Risk had no effect on the thoughts plaguing me. Thoughts of Dev's lips and hands and how damn close we were to crossing that line. A line my body wanted to cross. Excitement ran rampant through me, convincing me change could be a very good thing.

I twisted in his bed, unable to stop the shifting of my body against the soft sheets. Everything needed to go back as it was, as it had been.

My body stilled, and I stared up at the ceiling. Too bad we'd crossed the line. Or Dev had. I'd toed it and hurt him by not crossing it. He put on a good front, but I knew I'd hurt him. And now he wasn't here. Not to talk to, not to curl up with.

My head swam in circles. Over and over. Yes, kiss Devon. No, keep him as a friend. Yes. No. Sleep. I needed to sleep, clear my head, and figure out the best way to move forward.

I tossed and turned in Dev's bed. Several times I contemplated joining him in the living room, if for no other reason than to get some rest. But there was a reason he was there and not with me. He probably wouldn't even want me there. So I stayed.

Morning found me groggy. I stretched my limbs, adjusting to the light. Dev and Blake would be gone by now. I had the entire apartment to myself.

Which also meant Dev had been in the room. I sat up and looked around. He'd worn only his jeans when he'd gone to bed; poor guy hadn't even been able to change into his pajamas.

I went to the bathroom to get myself ready for the day, only to end up staring at my reflection. Crazy half-curly, half-limp hair, with a good three inches of roots showing. My natural shade was somewhere between blond and brown. Why couldn't it stay the vibrant color of my youth instead of fading to this lackluster crap? And this was what Dev had seen when he'd gotten ready for classes.

Never before had I cared what I looked like when around him. He'd seen me when I played in mud, when I had the flu, after my wisdom teeth had been extracted. He'd seen me with bloodshot eyes and falling apart after Dad died. And yet now I worried about bedhead and a few inches of roots, when the man knew damn well the color of my hair.

I closed my eyes and hung my head. I needed my friend.

I finished getting ready and picked up my phone, tapping until I uncovered my text thread with Nikki.

Me: You got time to dye my hair today?

What was wrong with me?

Nikki: I'm free after this boring lecture ends. Please tell me you want to go purple this time?

Would Dev like me with purple hair? I shook those thoughts free. *I* didn't want purple hair, screw Dev.

Me: No purple. You can go purple.

Nikki: It has potential. Wait for me to shop.

I made my way into the living area. The matzo box sat on the counter, and from habit or genetic memory or whatnot, I headed for it. Enough pieces were missing to indicate that even with everything going on between us, Dev kept to the challenge.

I pulled out the jam and smothered the large square cracker. It was crumbly and bland without the sweet strawberry flavor, a flat piece of bread that didn't have time to rise. It was also tradition, and even though I knew the taste grew old after a few days, I enjoyed the missing connection to my religion and ancestors. I hadn't minded too much when Dad was alive. As the family chef, he made all this yummy Passover food. When he was gone, it became the matzo show for a week unless one of my grandmothers gave us something.

I'd have to search for more of his recipes, if there were any I had salvaged.

I SCANNED THE aisle, searching for the tags indicating sale prices. I wasn't brand loyal—all I needed was something cheap and in the right color.

Nikki browsed next to me, her own black curly hair held back by an elastic band. She picked up the blond kit I had just put back on the shelf and held it up to her face. "What do you think?"

I took in the color, pictured it against her dark skin instead of the model's pale one. "Nice! You need bleach first." I looked around the shelves and pulled the bleach before shoving it at her. Then I grabbed the "close enough" shade for myself.

When I faced her, she stood gawking at me.

"What?" I signed, even as I forced my feet not to fidget.

She studied my hairline. "You normally go another two months first."

I worked at a dive bar—no one cared about my roots. If I even tried to hide my real reason, she'd beat me down in ten minutes. "I almost kissed…someone." I couldn't use his sign name, it felt too real.

Nikki propped a hand on her hip. "Almost. Someone. And you're blushing. You never blush unless…" Her eyes bulged as her hands trailed off. "Devon! You kissed Devon!" Then she jumped up and down, like she was eight and I just offered to get her an American Girl doll.

"Almost. I didn't kiss him." Yet. I tossed my hair dye into her basket. This was weird. We usually talked about whom I had kissed or Dev had kissed, not the possibility of us kissing each other.

"Details. Tell me what happened." Nikki continued bouncing on her feet.

I shrugged. He crossed the line and changed our relationship. "He slept on the couch."

Nikki stopped bouncing. "That's it?"

In direct words, yeah. But that's not what Nikki wanted. "There was…closeness, and then he ended up on the couch." And his lips, those plump, beautiful, tempting lips.

"Don't. Stop. Don't flip out."

"I want to kiss my best friend, and you expect me not to flip out?" My hand knocked over two kits from my outburst.

Nikki put them back on the shelf. "You admit it! Finally! Accept that, yes, you want to kiss someone you've been in love with for so long no one knows when it started. You should be overjoyed."

I sank to the floor, my knees no longer steady. "I can't lose him."

"You won't. You kiss him. In a few years, you'll get married. A few more, and you'll be complaining about kids messing with your sex life."

"We haven't kissed, and now we're married with kids?"

Nikki squatted in front of me. "You don't picture that future?"

I swallowed. "The future is fickle. It never pans out the way we hope." For that reason, I never envisioned a future beyond a few months. The only thing I yearned for was the bar; the rest, I left as a question mark. Less to lose.

"You are overdue for something good."

"And when it combusts?"

Nikki stood. "You two will fight, that's a definite. But you always go back together. No one can break you, like the yin yang. No one else stands a chance with either one of you." She collected the shopping basket, giving me a stern look. "Unless you're too much of a wimp?"

"I'm not a wimp."

"Then go kiss your best friend." She puckered her lips and pecked mine. "Wrong friend."

I laughed, then admitted a truth. "I'm scared."

"So talk to him."

I didn't sign anything else as I followed her to the checkout counter. I had another fear—maybe the way Dev and I had always been was no longer an option.

Chapter Fourteen

Devon

At the front of the classroom, my professor leaned against his desk, talking in a deep voice. I caught a few sounds here and there, mixed in with electrical noises, all background crap to me. Next to him stood one of my two interpreters, hands a blur as she did her job.

My focus too shot to pay attention.

Instead, I shifted my phone on my lap. To avoid any issues, I looked up, made eye contact with the interpreter, and wrote some nonsense on my notebook—I don't think I managed actual letters. All part of the drill. As the only Deaf student in the class, it was pretty darn obvious if I goofed off.

My head wasn't in my studies. My head was with my best friend. No texts from her, not that I had sent any.

I needed to figure out where to take her on our date—the main thing I still had a semblance of control over.

Only I had run into a problem: I'd inadvertently taken her on all my dates. There wasn't one thing I could think of that we hadn't already done together.

I flipped my phone and scrolled through my text messages until I came to Pete's contact.

Me: Where would you take Jas on a date?

And I was an idiot for leading with that. The tabletop needed to meet my head. Instead I wrote down something that had nothing to do with my class.

Pete: Why am I taking Jas on a date?
Me: You're not.
Me: I am.

Or, I hoped. I shoved my phone away and managed to focus for a few minutes before curiosity got the best of me and I checked my phone again.

Pete: WTF?
Pete: You serious?
Pete: Friend date or date date? Because you know there isn't much difference between the two.
Me: Nice. You should give yourself a pep talk.
Pete: We're talking about you. Not me.

Wimp.

Me: Serious. Date date. Not friend date.

Pete: Wow.

Helpful.

Me: I just took her to the movies, so that's out.

Pete: Well, that happens when you date someone you're not dating.

Me: And when was the last time you took Nikki to the movies?

Yeah, I called him on his shit. The only difference was that Pete had had this conversation with me before. On my side, this was brand new.

Pete: Nikki and I haven't been playing this game as long as you two have.

I glared at my phone, then remembered the interpreters would be watching me and made an effort to pay attention before responding. When I looked again, I found another message.

Pete: Take her to a restaurant. A nice one. She always eats cheap because she doesn't like handouts.

I turned the phone over. Pete was right. Jas and I ate together all the time but always at the casual-friend level. Dinner was the way to go.

I CLIMBED THE steps to my apartment, going back and forth between two restaurant ideas for the date, neither striking me as the perfect option. I unlocked the door and entered my apartment, only to find her on the other side, trench on, makeup prepped for the bar. I knew the type of work clothes she wore. With none of it visible, I couldn't stop the fantasy of her wearing nothing underneath. For me.

We both froze, staring at each other. So much passed between us, yet the wall was there, keeping us separate. Her hair was full of curls and loose. Either due to the light or something Jas had done, I swore her hair was brighter than before.

A different kind of tension arose. The shift had been unavoidable, a growing pressure, but this, this distance between us sucked.

Only one way to handle it: move on as if nothing was different. "What did you do to your hair?"

She raised an eyebrow. "My hair?"

I didn't stop myself when the urge to touch her locks popped up. I picked up a curl and ran it through my fingers. Definitely lighter.

Jas shook her head. "I told you I dyed my hair."

"You could dye it purple, and I would still like it."

A wry smile crossed her face. "I have to go, or I'll be late."

I nodded and stepped aside, giving her access to escape to the hall. Her gaze traveled to my lips and lingered. My pulse gave a good kick, but I remained where I was.

She took a step toward me, arm reaching past my shoulder to close the door. Her brown eyes were wide and full of want, an invitation present in them. My fingers itched to yank her to me, but I needed her words.

"Are we crazy to think about changing us?" she asked.

"You're the one thinking, not me." Not anymore. I hardly had enough blood left in my brain to think.

She bit her lip. A shaky smile crossed her face, bravado surfacing. "We can't go back. Can we?"

I shook my head as my pulse continued kicking. But she needed the out. "If you want me to, I will." I'd hate myself, but I'd do it.

I held my breath, waiting for her response. That shaky smile remained. "I don't want to." She rubbed the toe of her shoe against the floor. "Can I kiss you?"

I tugged her close, until she had to look up to meet my eyes. The urge to warn, to make sure we wanted to create this change, rang out. But the words were pointless. We knew them, and we both agreed to be here.

My hand brushed her cheek, cupped her chin. Hers scratched at my stubble. We knew each other so well and yet we tiptoed around each other like two awkward preteens at a parent-supervised dance.

The sudden ridiculousness of it made laughter bubble up inside before I could stop it. I stepped back and bent over.

"You're laughing? Seriously?" Sparks appeared in her eyes. "How can you even think of laughing when—"

I covered her hands, the feel of her skin a tease as she stopped signing. Her eyes grew wide, and before she had a chance to react, I tugged, sending her body into mine and crashing our lips together. We both froze, mouth to mouth, as a warmth grew. Then she melted into me. I wrapped an arm around her waist, holding her close while our lips brushed back and forth. Her hands dug into my hair, urging me closer. Heat, so much heat passed between us.

I broke it off, rested my forehead against hers. Any longer and I'd drag her into my bedroom. Her cheeks were pink, as were her lips from my kisses. "See you at the bar."

"Wait," she signed, halting my movement. I paused, and she flung herself at me, arms around my neck, mouth against mine. I collected her against me as her plump, sweet lips drove me beyond insane.

She opened for me, but I didn't dare push this any further. I slowed the kiss to gentle passes, then stopped. For a beat we looked at each other, arms still locked and out of signing range. Here was my best friend. Here was so much more than friendship.

And we both knew it.

Jas untangled herself. "I have to go to work."

I nodded. "I'll see you later." She slipped out the door, leaving me alone in the apartment.

I settled onto the couch wearing the stupidest grin ever in my life. Some change had to be good. If it felt like this, no way could it go wrong.

I PUSHED OPEN the doors and scanned the bar. I found Jas bent by a table, writing on her board to a mixed crowd.

Her ass stuck out, covered by short shorts that molded to her frame. Up top, she wore another black tank. I ate up the sight of her.

She straightened and met my gaze, catching me checking her out. It wasn't like I hadn't already made my intentions known. She propped a hand on her hip, cocking her head to one side. "Like what you see?"

I couldn't deny the weirdness of out-and-out chatting about this. "Always have."

She shook her head, but a smile broke out, one that would fool anyone into thinking it was just another night. I wasn't anyone.

She nodded toward the bar, and I met her there. She wiped her board as she arrived. She paused, looked at me, and attached the board to her hip. "Remember, no beer. What do you want?" Then she stuck her hip out.

This was strange. I'd never written on her board, never had to. I always gave her my order or spoke it to Len.

I bent over and quickly realized two things: the height of the barstool meant I was lined up with her perky breasts, and writing on a human was not an easy task.

Also, I found it damn hard to concentrate with my head so close to her rack. A few short shifts, and I could bury my face in her cleavage. I had to grip her hip to keep her steady and felt the inhale of air she took. When I finished, she bit her bottom lip and made no move to create distance between us.

Screw it. I had a taste, I wanted more.

I wrapped a hand around her waist and yanked her to me. Her body collided with mine as I claimed her mouth.

Her smell and taste devoured my senses, leaving me with only her.

Jas pulled back, a nervous grin on her face. Our eyes held, and sensations passed between us. But no words. I couldn't read her and bet she couldn't read me. Not anymore.

She unclipped her board and read my shaky handwriting, her shoulders shaking. "You are a brave man."

I was. My brain was fried by her breasts, so I'd written *surprise me*—not like I was getting a beer this week, anyways.

Jas moved off, slipping behind the bar, and I knew I was in trouble.

Someone clapped or stomped nearby, slow and rhythmic. I turned one way, then the other, before finding Pete two feet away. "That…wow, what a kiss. Shouldn't you date her first?"

I rolled my eyes, then glanced at Jas, noticing the flush to her cheeks. She didn't make eye contact.

Pete slapped the bar, no longer paying us any attention. His eyes were wide and directed over my shoulder. He stuck a finger out at Jas. "What did you do to Nikki?"

"You blame me? You know Nikki does what she wants."

I tuned them out, searching for Nikki, and passed right over her. She stood a few feet away, sporting a hair color that I never in a million years would've thought I'd see on her. I glanced back at Jas, then to Nikki. "You two have the same hair color now."

Nikki shook her head and joined us. "Not quite—different boxes." She fluffed her newly blond curls.

Pete reached out a tatted arm, dark only because of the ink, but didn't touch her hair. No one touched Nikki's hair unless they received explicit permission. He needed to man up and ask. "Why?"

"It's fun." She banged on the bar. "Bartender. Give me a drink. Make it fruity."

Jas slid an amber drink under my nose, nodded, and got busy working. I didn't investigate my drink, too caught up in Jas in her element. Her hips swayed in that little drink-making dance she had. Happiness radiated off her. Anyone could tell she was doing what she loved, what she was meant to do. And it was temporary until Len took over his bar again.

She needed her own place, deserved it. One day, she'd get it. If I could help her, I would. Anything to see her like this more often.

I picked up my drink, banked on her not trying to kill me, and took a sip. Strong and bitter, but good. "You trying to get me drunk?" I signed when she handed Nikki something with a cherry on top.

Jas cocked her head to one side. "It's true, you're easy when drunk."

I rested my elbows on the ledge. "So you admit you're trying to get me drunk."

She held my gaze. I knew Nikki and Pete watched. I didn't care. Not when this new sexual edge passed between us, filled with promise and potential. If she wanted me in her bed tonight, in any way, she'd have me.

Jas backed up and collected her board, returning to the other tables. She either didn't know what she wanted or was too afraid to find out.

Nikki pushed at my shoulder. "You two kissed, and I missed it?"

"It wasn't a show." I'd kissed her because I needed to feel her again.

Nikki shook her head, long swishes with blond curls adding to the effect. "You two can't do anything simple, can you?"

I sipped my drink. For once in my life, I liked the idea of complicated.

Chapter Fifteen

Jasmine

I KISSED HIM. He kissed me. I wanted to gush to him, like I did with any important event in my life. Silly since he was there. He knew.

Still, silly had some appeal.

Len stayed out back longer than usual; he must've been sucking his way through an entire cigarette pack. Only now I had to juggle the bar area as well as the tables. It kept me busy and reduced any further conversations about me and Dev or with Dev in general.

On my bathroom break, I needed five minutes to rest my weary feet. And a little silly went a long way to relieving aching toes. I went into the back room and plucked my phone from my jacket.

Me: You know that guy I hadn't told you I was crushing on?

I stared at the words, and my heart kicked in my chest. No more obvious than kissing him. Did I dare click Send?

I did. And then I buried my face in my hands until my phone vibrated.

Dev: I know. Something happen?

He wasn't in the room, but I could see his smile, that full and bright one he reserved for me.

Me: I sorta kissed him.
Dev: Sorta? That was much more than sorta.

I clamped my lips closed as I laughed.

Me: Then what was that?
Dev: Nice. Really nice.

Warmth spread from my chest down to my belly.

Me: Yes, it was.
Dev: The next night you're off, I'm taking you out.
Me: Did you just ask me on a date?
Dev: Yes.

My hands froze, and my breath backed up. It didn't make sense why those words affected me differently than our kiss, but they did. Everything became more real.

Dev: You going to answer me?

I swallowed past a dry throat.

Me: OK, next night I'm off.

My words weren't as cheery as I intended, but he didn't call me on it. Either he didn't catch it, or he played it low-key.

More than kissing my best friend, I was about to go on a date with him. Dates led to more kissing, and kissing led to sex. While the thought of being wrapped around Dev made me ache and yearn, I feared for what it would do to our friendship.

Back in the main area, I poured beer, mixed a few drinks, and handled the grumbling customers who were not too happy they couldn't voice their order. I had one simple and big rule: if someone became too drunk to write their drink, they were cut off.

By closing time, I was dead on my feet. Len had returned, but I suspected he had sneaked whisky along with his cigs, so he was a useless lump. At least all the tips were mine and the customers were happy. As dead as I was, I also felt alive. Nothing like the rush and the liquid and swaying happy drunks.

My friends left before closing, but I still had to see Dev back at home. I cranked my car and let the little engine rumble to life. Home. Was Dev's place really home? Would that remain if we continued the not-friends dance?

By the time I pulled up to his complex, my head wanted the night off as much as my feet did. I unzipped my boots in the living area. Dev's blanket and pillow remained on the couch, but there was no sign of him. Which meant he was waiting for me in his room. I cracked my neck. He'd watched me work; didn't he get I was too damn tired for anything right now?

I checked my phone, searching for any clues as to what waited for me. Nothing new from Dev. One unread message from my boss.

Len: Thanks for tonight. Take tomorrow off. You deserve it.

I frowned at my phone. Sure, the tips were great, but I worked my ass off because there was a better life than this waiting for me. Nights off didn't help, especially when they weren't warranted.

I didn't type any of that. He didn't want me to work; that was it. Maybe it was time to resume my search for a different job. Tomorrow I could worry about it. Tonight I had other things to deal with.

In Dev's room, I tossed my boots in the corner. He sat on the bed, above the covers, in plaid lounge pants and a fitted tee shirt. I wanted to curl up next to him and sleep. Just sleep. I unbuttoned my jacket and tossed it on a chair. "Before you start, I'm exhausted."

He patted the bed next to him. "Come over here."

I should have washed my face and prepped for bed first, but I did as he asked and sat stiffly next to him with my knees tucked close to my chest. My entire body felt sensitized to his presence, as if I'd either jump or be halfway to orgasm if he touched me.

"I don't want this," he gestured between us, "to destroy our friendship."

I let out a breath and dropped my head to his shoulder. I took in his comfort, the way he wrapped an arm around my waist and squeezed me to him. Being this close made my pulse kick and my breasts ache. As scary as this was, we were heading here, one way or another.

I picked my head up. "I can't lose you."

His hand tightened around me. "Not happening." His signing hand brushed back my hair and skimmed my cheek. I wanted to melt into him, always had.

I leaned into him, chest to chest. He cupped my chin. Everything was new even as it was old. A part of me reveled in this, while another part wanted to move forward or back and get out of murky waters.

Then our lips touched, and murky waters seemed just fine. I opened for him, and his tongue brushed against mine, shivers of heat spiking from the touch. An urge grew to straddle him and take and give until we were too spent to do anything else.

Kisses would forevermore belong to him. To us. Everything was new and scary and tentative. And solid. Which made the whole scary factor shoot up a thousand degrees.

Dev pulled back, resting his forehead on mine. Our breaths battled for higher ground. Then he straightened, creating room to talk. "Are we OK? You and me. Dating?"

His eyes were so serious, I couldn't help but take a jab. "We can't be best friends with benefits?"

The serious only intensified. He flipped us over so I was on my back and then hovered over me. I couldn't catch my breath and didn't want to. "Is that what you want?" He kissed the side of my mouth. My cheek. My jaw. My neck.

I arched into him, my body in control, yearning for anything he gave. I wrapped a leg around his waist and connected my pelvis with his hard length.

We broke apart—my ass pressed into the mattress as Dev held himself off of me. That was more than stolen kisses. Dev dropped his head, shoulders laughing. "You and me. We're trouble." But he smiled, eyes shining.

I nodded. "Truth. Always have been."

He stood, adjusted himself. I wanted those to be my hands on him. "You OK with staying here now that we're dating?"

"You haven't taken me out on a date yet." Although, with my changed work schedule, said date could be tomorrow.

He shook his head. "In reality, I think we've already been on plenty."

Humor and lust faded. I thought back to all the times we'd hung out, gone to the movies, bowling, mini golf. Alone. Together. With this thing simmering between us. "Damn, we've missed a few anniversaries."

Dev smiled. "I'll make it up to you. Answer my question."

There wasn't any other place I wanted to be. "I'm OK. I've got your bed." I snuggled down and wrapped myself around the pillow. "Len gave me tomorrow off."

Dev's smile grew to a lickable length. "Then tomorrow, you become mine."

I'd been his for a long time. "I'm not property." Damned if I'd admit it to a sexist line though. He'd figure it out soon enough.

"Fine, scratch that. Tomorrow we go out on an official date. You game?"

Bastard, he knew I couldn't back down from a challenge, not that I wanted to. "I'm game."

"Good."

Chapter Sixteen

Devon

ANA HELD THE screen door open, bouncing on her toes, yelling what I assumed were encouraging words as I shouldered in the last box I had managed to squeeze into my car. I dumped it in the living room of the narrow two-story apartment, along with many other boxes.

Today was moving day for Bea and her family. I blew off another day of classes in order to help, which included ignoring the incessant vibrating of my cell for the past hour.

Ana ran over and pet a box with her name on it. "So beautiful," she signed.

Her older brother entered, voicing to his sister with hands dangling at his side. Whatever he said, she wasn't happy. A scowl crossed her face, and then they erupted into a shouting match that had me turning my hearing aids off.

As far as I knew, Bea had no hearing at all, but her mother skills were spot-on, a lot like my own mom. She entered the room, stomping, and in a flurry of signs, she intercepted the fighting and sent both kids to their rooms.

They stomped up the stairs, but a secretive smile spread over Bea's face. Sure, her kids were being brats, but for the first time in almost a year, they had headed off to separate rooms, not one large bedroom shared by all three.

I couldn't deny my soul felt full after a day like this.

My phone went off again, and with no more boxes to lug in, I finally faced my next problem of the day.

Dad: Where the hell are you? Your last class finished over an hour ago.

Hell, I hadn't even realized he knew my schedule.

Me: Helping Bea and her family move.

I cringed after I clicked Send, but I wasn't here in any official capacity, and Dad knew the family. I wasn't violating any confidentiality.

Dad: The computers are all messed up. I need your help here.

I looked around at the small apartment. Nothing fancy, yet it meant the world to the family who now resided here. I was supposed to leave this to mess around with Dad's computer system?

Katherine waved. “What’s wrong?”

“I’m needed at the accounting firm.”

She nodded, but I caught the glint in her eyes; she knew they didn’t have me on board, not yet.

I was torn, like there was a crack ripping me apart. I had almost no time left and this huge problem hanging over my head.

At least tonight’s date with Jas gave me some much-needed happy feelings.

Still, I turned my attention to my phone, ready to tell Dad I had to stay, I was needed here.

I chickened out.

Me: Be there soon.

I said my good-byes, which took another twenty minutes, and accepted a cupcake from Bea for my help. I nearly ate it before remembering the matzo challenge. It pained me, but I deposited the cupcake in one of the trash bags littering my car. I drove away, knowing I had done good with my day.

And landed directly in hell.

Dad’s computers were fucked. Somehow, all the electronic filing had turned to shit. Since it was tax season, everyone was up to their elbows in work, and “normal” hours were a fallacy.

I had Jas at home waiting for me, an honest date planned, and a computer problem that would take me hours to solve. My good day was up in smoke.

At six, I sent her a text saying I had no clue when I'd be able to leave, and that grated. Yes, she knew me, she knew my situation and all the bullshit of my life. But that didn't mean I couldn't impress her.

Jas: Poor baby. Grow a pair and talk to your father.
Me: Not that easy.
Jas: Types the man whose father is still alive.

Sucker punch.

Me: And you wouldn't be arguing with your father if he lived?
Jas: Yeah, over which vodka to purchase and how much cleavage I had on display. Don't forget, I want to follow in his footsteps. You don't.
Jas: You're miserable and you haven't even graduated yet.

I stared at my phone, the work in front of me forgotten. I tried to picture her in a world where her father didn't die. She'd be working side by side with him, dueling for control, the spark I'd seen last night magnified tenfold. She'd be happy.

For her the answer was simple. For Blake too. Not for me. I got up, ready to tell my father once and for all that I wasn't working here in a few months. My hands were balled up and sweaty, knowing I'd be destroying a dream that had been brewing for over twenty years.

Dad burst in, hair messed up in multiple directions. "Why are you standing there?"

No time like the present, even if he looked ready to pop a lung. "I wanted to—"

"Not now. I need the papers finished, or we'll get even farther behind. Have you finished yet?"

"No. I need to talk with you."

Dad shook his head, already backing out of the room. "Later. We need to stay until we're caught up. All part of the fun." Then he was gone.

Fun my ass. This was torture. No way could I do this. I stood stiffly, my shoulders carrying far too much pressure. I had to have this conversation, more than ever. But during tax season it would be impossible.

I relaxed my shoulders, defeat winning. I picked up my phone.

Me: Talk postponed until after tax season.
Jas: Among other things.

Crap. I felt like used gum on the bottom of my shoe.

Me: I'm sorry.
Jas: Don't be on my account. This is your life.
Me: It was our date.
Jas: I'm not going anywhere.

That brought out a much-needed smile.

Me: I'll make it up to you.

Jas: You better.

I laughed and got back to work. I needed to see her, and the faster I finished this shit, the quicker I could.

Not ten minutes later, the door opened again and Blake walked in, halting in an almost comic manner when he saw me. "What are you doing here?"

I gestured to the work in front of me. "What do you think?"

He shook his head. "You had a date planned."

"Tell that to Dad."

Blake looked around, as if the answers to some mysterious question rested on the walls. "Go. See Jasmine. I'll finish up." He moved to take over, but I stuck a hand out to stop him.

"Don't you have a date of your own?"

"Yes. The difference being that this is my life, and Shawn knows it. If he can't handle tax season, we're going to have issues. This isn't your life, and Jasmine shouldn't suffer. Go."

I clamped a hand on Blake's shoulder and collected my stuff.

I sneaked out. No way around it. I didn't want to bump into Dad. Best let Blake handle it. The minute the cold night air hit my face, my day from hell ended. Freedom awaited me. Jas awaited me. Time to take the right woman on a date.

Chapter Seventeen

Jasmine

NIGHTS OFF WERE a rare commodity. So rare I didn't know what to do with myself. Tonight should have been spent with Dev, but his work had gotten in the way.

In some odd way, relief was the first emotion I had. I knew I should be excited to go on a date. And I was. I couldn't quite remember the last time I had been out on one. My work hours and ambitions made it difficult to meet anyone, never mind plan a date. But first dates equaled nerves, and being nervous around Dev felt plain wrong. I didn't think it was possible, but here I was, dealing with more nerves than I could count. Even now, with the date canceled.

This was why I needed work; too much time left to myself, and my brain couldn't be contained.

I flipped through the pages of my notebook. Instead of expanding on a concept, I read through everything, the words inspiring a familiar surge of energy. It was all here, waiting for me. The next step, getting myself to a point where I could execute my plans, would be tricky. Time and perseverance would be my strongest business partners.

Even all my hopes and dreams couldn't hold my attention from what my night should have been like. I tossed the notebook aside and stared up at Dev's ceiling, contemplating whether I wanted to change my nail polish or not. Not even Blake was home—proof of how crazy things were at their dad's firm.

If we kept this up, one day we'd have sex. I flashed back to this morning, when I had woken up just as Dev returned from the shower. His wet hair stuck to his forehead, water droplets clung to his chest, and a low-slung towel was wrapped around his waist. Nothing I hadn't seen before, yet I had clamped my eyelids shut, letting him change in peace, wondering what his happy trail led to. I wanted my best friend naked, and one day soon, I might have just that.

I closed my eyes and flung an arm across my hot cheeks as I remembered his lips on me, the way his body felt on top of mine, his hands digging into my hips—

A hand grasped my wrist and removed my arm from my face. I startled, only to find Dev leaning over me. My cheeks flamed, and I bit my lip, lost in a mix of confusion and lust.

Then reality hit, and I sat straight up, knocking him back a step. "What are you doing here?"

His face lit up. "Blake took over my work. You ready?"

The words took a moment to sink in. I looked down at the old tee shirt and tattered jeans I wore. "You're joking, right? I'm not dressed for a date."

He took me in from head to toe, a slow glide that touched me without contact. "You always look beautiful."

I stared. My heart swelled. I hadn't seen those words since Dad died. Emotion clogged my throat, and I did my best to ignore it. "Where are we going?"

"Out. Dinner."

Helpful. "Fancy. Casual. What?"

He narrowed his eyes and leaned over me. "What do you want?"

I bit my lip. Him, for starters. But I knew that wasn't the question. And a small dose of shock bubbled up; there was something he didn't know about me. "I like to dress up." Not that I had many fancy clothes, since I basically lived at the bar. But getting dressed up was fun, especially for a date.

"Then dress up. I'll leave. But first—" He wrapped a hand around my neck and pulled me in for a quick kiss. Just as I fell into the swelling heat, he backed up and left.

I stayed where I was, a bit dazed from the conversation and his mouth. Then I picked up my phone.

Me: You do know that I'm a woman and take forever.

Dev: Good thing my backpack's out here. I'll get work done. Take your time.

Was he for real? Even Dad used to get upset at how long it took Mom to get ready for a night out.

Me: Are you really this guy?
Dev: Get ready and find out.

That sent a little thrill through me. My nerves vanished. It was time to get to know my friend in this new light.

I opened up his closet and thumbed through my meager belongings until I came to the dress Nikki had insisted I buy. Girl was right. I'd need to pair it with a sweater and my boots, but it wasn't black, it wasn't old, and—bonus—Dev had never seen me in it. The tight red material hugged my curves and grazed my knees. I wondered if he'd touch me in this dress, if I'd feel his heat through the fabric. The last thread of nerves was replaced with hope. I took my hands off my hips and shook my head. No more delaying. I slipped across the hall to the bathroom to fix my hair and makeup.

My reflection held confidence, and I hoped it would knock Dev's socks off. Then I remembered the tee shirt he was wearing. I sneaked back into his room and went through his clothes, pulling out a navy button-down and pair of beige jeans. Not his usual first-date material, but that's what he got for dating his best friend.

In the living room, I found him bent over a textbook. I stood and waited, wondering if he'd shave first and almost hoping he didn't. The light stubble brought out his blue eyes and looked sexy as hell on him.

Those eyes glanced up, slowly climbing up my body, all but touching my skin. "Wow."

"You have to change too."

Dev's eyebrows furrowed, but he looked down at his shirt and nodded. "I'm gonna grab a quick shower too, spent my morning moving boxes." I didn't stop him as he headed to his room. I could have warned him about the clothes, but he'd figure it out soon enough.

I thumbed through my phone as I waited, and less than ten minutes later, he walked back out in the clothes I had picked. His hair was wet, he hadn't shaved, and he looked like a movie-star hunk. I wasn't used to seeing him somewhat dressed up—it stole my breath.

He held out his hands, looking down at himself. "You don't trust me to pick out my own clothes."

Shit. "I'm sorry, I didn't mean—"

He cut me off with a kiss. I grabbed onto his shoulders, unable to stop the fall into him.

"You can pick out my clothes, if you want to play mother. But I'm capable." It was hard to take him seriously with my red lipstick smeared across his lips.

I wiped part off. "Next time, prove it. Now, clean off your lips."

He sent me a wicked grin and meshed our lips together again. Goodness, we were never getting out of here. Not with those lips, not with his hands on my hips. Not with the feeling of him.

Dev pulled back. "Come on. We'll clean up, then I owe you a dinner."

A thrill traveled down my spine. Yes. He did.

DEV TOOK ME to a steak house. Nothing too fancy, but certainly not my usual fare. I'd never been to a place like this.

I stepped out of the car into the night air. It ruffled my curls and threatened to freeze my limbs, since I left my trench at the apartment. Dev came around to my side of the car as I wrapped my arms around myself. "I would have gotten the door for you."

I looked back at his car. "Why? You never have."

He stepped into my space, blocking the wind and sharing his body heat. "Tonight, you're my date. That's why." With an arm around my shoulders, he held me close as we made our way inside. I shook off the chill as the warmth of the establishment hit me. A bit of a rustic feel, lots of exposed wood and dark colors.

When I stopped checking out the decor, I noticed Dev already communicating with the hostess. He held up two fingers and tugged me to him, but the woman's mouth continued moving.

"Can you hear her?" I asked.

He shook his head. "No, there's a lot of background noise."

I turned back to the hostess, flashed her a smile, and held up two fingers. Her eyes darted between us, no doubt catching us signing and answering a few of her questions. She checked her listing of tables, shot us a worried glance, and opened her mouth before closing it. Even I knew she wasn't speaking.

Dev made a motion for writing, and the hostess nearly whacked herself in the forehead. She grabbed some paper and scribbled a note: *It will be five to ten minutes.*

I held up a thumb, and Dev pulled me over to the crowded bar. He took in the long dark grain counter, eyes flicking from bottles to cups to me.

"What?" I smoothed down my dress—was it bunched up somewhere?

"I can't see you in a bar like this."

I studied the area and the prim and proper bartender. "Too small. Too food related. People don't come here to get drunk."

"You like the drunks."

"I like the true bar vibe."

He picked up a bar menu and flipped through. "How does a bartender not drink?"

I rolled my eyes. "A sober one."

He put the menu down. "You're really that worried?"

I took in all the alcohol bottles lined up against a mirrored wall. Dull colors all but glittering in the lighting, an artistic array of temptation and addiction. "Yes and no. I want alcohol to be my business, not my pleasure."

"What about tonight?"

"What do you mean?"

"No pleasure when you're not at work?"

"Are you trying to get me drunk?"

He played with the end of one clump of curls. "Maybe I want you to have a good time." His eyes didn't meet mine.

"One, I can have a good time without alcohol. Two, I won't have a good time with you?"

He raised his baby blues to mine, a vulnerability shining through. I wanted to call him on it, to point out we were still who we were, but the hostess flagged us down. We followed her past filled tables to a small booth in the corner. She handed us our menus, opened her mouth to say something, then promptly left.

Dev picked up his menu, only to press it down to the table, knuckles white as he gripped the edges.

"Can we agree not to be all weird about this?" I asked, ignoring my menu completely.

He leaned forward. "This isn't weird?"

I took a deep breath, trying to find my own sense of calm. Dev's gaze dipped down to my chest, and damned if I didn't arch my back to give him a little more to look at. "Yes. It's weird. But we're still us, right? Because if this change is going to kill us, then you can take me home right now and we'll forget we like kissing each other."

"You signed *home*."

I fell back against the seat cushion. I had.

The waitress showed up, and once she figured out we were deaf, she knelt by the side of the table and wrote back and forth. We ordered our drinks—nonalcoholic—and promised to check the menu.

We had other things more important to discuss than the menu.

Dev rubbed the back of his neck. "I want this; I've made that clear. But don't we need time to see each other differently?"

I always was good at sniffing out the flaws in his logic. "So you having feelings for me is new?"

He narrowed his eyes to slits, and I couldn't help laughing. Patrons at other tables glanced our way, but who knew if I was too loud or if it was just the novelty of two people signing. Story of my life, so I paid it no mind.

"You know it's not new."

"So why do we need time to see each other differently?"

He rested his elbows on the table. "And you haven't been pretending you don't have feelings for me?"

A direct hit. "How long do you think this has been simmering?"

He didn't break eye contact, barely blinked. "A long time."

With a nod, I broke the contact and turned my attention to the menu. Food was a safer topic.

Chapter Eighteen

Devon

"REMEMBER, NO BREAD," Jas signed as the bread basket hit our table. She hooked a finger in the wicker, dragged it closer to her, and sniffed. "That smells delicious."

"If I can't have any bread, what about you?"

"I haven't kept Passover in almost ten years. This year is no different. You bought the matzo." She pulled apart a piece, steam rising from the soft filling. A healthy dose of butter later, and her eyes closed as she chewed. "Heaven. You are missing out."

Since I watched her eat, I missed out on nothing. "Not from my perspective." I nudged the basket closer to her.

Jas laughed as she chewed. "You sure you haven't cheated yet?"

Almost. "Not yet."

"You still have the rest of the week to go."

"I don't back down from challenges easily."

Her eyes lit with an invitation. One I wanted. I leaned forward, rising off the seat, aiming for those luscious lips. She held out a hand and stopped me. "No stealing bread from my mouth."

I plopped back onto the seat. "Seriously?"

Jas nodded. "I'm not keeping Passover, so I'm not kosher."

This was a whole new level I hadn't anticipated. "So I can't lick you?" My signs made it clear which part of her anatomy I referred to.

A strong pink color rose to Jas's cheeks. "Not today. Good thing I don't have sex on a first date."

I dropped my head and tried not to laugh. Once upon a time, I made sure Jas was this way, wanted her to get to know a guy before she slept with them. Now that *I* was that guy, I wanted to strangle myself. Even if it was right for us, we couldn't rush into anything.

"I'm still kissing you."

"When there's no bread in my mouth, sure."

I leaned back, relaxing into the cushion. "Ever have a first date like this?" Because I sure as hell hadn't.

Jas pulled off a small piece of bread and slowly closed her lips around it. Screw the bread, my dick was jealous. "Never. It's usually small talk, figuring out who the other is, even if you know them a bit."

I ticked through some usual first-date conversation fodder but couldn't come up with any questions I couldn't answer for her. "The weather, we can always talk about the weather."

"True. It's cold. Next topic?"

I placed my elbows on the table. "I can make it warmer."

"And now we're back to sex. Is that really the only area not explored?"

I dropped my gaze down to the two mouthwatering breasts molded by her dress. She waved and forced my eyes back on hers. "I've known you since before you've had those. Yes."

She shook her head. "Dirty mind."

"See, something new to learn."

I HAD THOUGHT it torturous to watch Jas eat bread, but that was nothing compared to when she closed those lips around a spoonful of chocolate cake. A very X-rated vision created in front of me, my mind and dick agreed: we wanted her lips on us. Sucking. Swallowing. My water glass was empty, so I chewed on a piece of ice that did nothing to cool me down. I almost dropped a cube into my pants, but Jas sent me a mischievous look.

She was baiting me.

I couldn't eat the cake—or her—but I did feed her the rest. Sure, I was hard as a rock in my pants; I knew I wasn't getting any that night. But it was worth the pink I saw tinting her cheeks. Wherever the night headed, we'd continue tempting each other.

On our way back to my car, I wanted to walk slow, enjoy the crisp night air. Cool the fuck down. But Jas shivered. I huddled her next to me, sharing my warmth—I had too much anyways—as I hurried her inside and cranked the heat.

"You need a warmer jacket."

"I'll wear my dad's coat anyways."

I gripped the steering wheel. I didn't want to go home. Sure, we'd still be together, and we could watch a movie or play some games. Dinner wasn't enough; she deserved more. An idea popped into my mind. I eyed Jas. It could work.

I drove onto the highway, heading in the opposite direction of home. It took Jas two minutes to figure out things weren't right. She flipped on the car light so we could communicate. "Where are we going?"

"You'll see."

I glanced in her direction to find her head against the seat, a warm smile on her face. "This could be very bad for you."

"I like risks."

Her cheeks curved along with her lips, and I tore my gaze back to the road—otherwise I'd get us into an accident. Not my idea of a fun night.

Twenty minutes later, I pulled into a parking lot. We had a bit of a walk, the only downside. "You won't freeze in two blocks, will you?"

Jas studied the area, recognition crossing her face. "It doesn't matter, I'll be sweating soon. You brought me to a club?"

I took my keys out of the ignition. "Yes."

"I haven't danced since our senior prom."

"Which we went to together. We're too slow."

She laughed and clasped my cheeks, bringing our faces close together. And it occurred to me that at our prom, this was all I had wanted to do. She brushed her lips against mine, somehow managing sweet and sexy as hell all at once.

"Should we have kissed back then?" I asked.

"Probably." Then she got out of the car.

I held her close to my side for warmth as we headed to our destination. I tried to move fast, but she slowed us down, leaning into me.

Once in the club, Jas took a moment, surveying the area. Music swelled, something connecting uncomfortably with my hearing aids. I flipped them off. Beats and sensations outdid any sound, a thrill vibrating through my veins.

She nodded to the beat, her whole face alive and happy. It killed me that I hadn't seen the need for this type of night for her. That it had taken until now to get this expression on her face. I had to do better. And I would.

We skipped drinks and headed to the dance floor. I pulled Jas to me, finding the beat as she wrapped her arms around my neck and placed her head on my shoulder. The song was much faster than we were, but I didn't give a damn. I had her in my arms, her body against me. Nothing else mattered.

Her hips swayed, bumping against mine. Everything about this held some normalcy, except in the past we'd managed to keep some air between us. Not this time. Things wouldn't go much further, not tonight. Probably not tomorrow night either. That didn't stop our bodies from knowing each other. I gripped her hips, shifted her closer. Her chest rose and fell in choppy spurts. If I didn't keep my head on straight, I'd throw the whole "first date" thing out the window.

Jas pulled back, enough so we could sign. She studied those around us. "Are they really able to communicate?"

The people around us mostly danced without attempting to talk, focusing on body language over spoken language. A few were angled to each other's ears and probably still had to yell to be heard. I shrugged. "Maybe, not as easily as we can."

"Deaf people can dance and communicate, shock!"

I grabbed her hips and connected us again, claiming her mouth with my own. She settled against me, opened for me, and I plumb forgot which beat was the music and which was my pulse. I licked into her mouth, stroking her tongue, all my senses on high alert. She turned me on in every which way, and with our bodies pressed together, she knew it. Then again, I had a good guess that her nipples weren't pointy due to coldness.

Someone bumped into me, either on purpose or by accident, and we broke apart. For a few beats we stood there, breathing heavily, watching each other. "Not so weird anymore, is it?" I asked.

Jas shook her head. "No." She stepped back into me, wrapped her arms around me, and continued swaying to the music. I tapped her shoulder, and she pulled back.

"Is this a good first date?"

She brushed my hair off my sweaty forehead. "The best."

I LOST TRACK of time on the dance floor, too caught up in the feel of Jas against me. The lack of space between us, the new closeness that came with touching each other just about everywhere. No lines were truly crossed, just body plastered against body. Dancing allowed us to press the limits, shift our relationship little by little until I felt ready to burst if I didn't have her.

I tried to cool off on the car ride home. But she was there, right there. Bare knees peeking out from the hem of her dress. And she was mine. Despite our discussion about taking it slow and not having sex, we ended up plastered to each other the minute I closed my apartment door. I didn't know who made the first move, just that Jas's back was against the door, her leg around my hip, and one of my hands in her hair, the other on her ass.

Everything burned and flamed to life. She arched into me, all those curves making it so I damn well didn't care about breathing. I started to fall down the hole, into the dark excitement of lust. With one last shred of sanity hanging on, I grabbed it and pulled back.

"I'm going to the couch." Otherwise she'd be naked on my bed in five minutes.

Jas took deep breaths, her body all but shaking. "No."

"You do realize my control is ready to snap, right?"

"Mine too. I want to sleep next to you."

I ran my hands through my hair. "I can't promise I won't touch you."

"I'm not asking you not to touch me."

Dammit. I collected her into my arms. Brain powered down, dick now in control. We stumbled through the hall and into my room. Mouths clung together as I backed her up to my bed, then followed her over. She broke the kiss, and I licked my way down to her neck.

Her body arched underneath me. My fingers gripped her hips, fabric bunching in my hands. She made me crazy. Everything about her fueled me like no one else ever had. I ground into her, unable to help myself. She wrapped one leg around my ass, grinding right back.

Jesus. She was hot as hell. I wanted to burn with her.

But her nails dug into my back, and I realized she wasn't just doing that out of enjoyment. My hand was halfway up her stomach, and even though I wanted it higher, I stopped. When I picked up my head and met her eyes, I knew I'd read her right, even with my eyes closed.

She shifted until she could sign. "Slow down. We should sleep."

I dropped my head, trying to get some blood flow back up. "I told you I couldn't promise."

She wiggled against me, and I had to clamp a hand on her hip before she blew my last thread of control. "I like this. But we should stop. You're Devon Walker; you won't be an asshole."

I rolled off her and stared at my ceiling. "Maybe I am."

She leaned over me. "You're not." She scrunched her nose and tilted her head. "Remember, my father was well over six feet. I'm sure his ghost would love to maim you."

I laughed and thought of Eddie Helmsman. I could almost picture him watching his daughter leave for a date. He'd stand to his full height, cross his arms, and give the glare, the same glare he gave to unruly customers. Eddie would have scared the crap out of Jas's dates.

Maybe not me, since he'd also let me taste test a few beers and help Jas wipe down tables. He'd given me one big secret to life: the most important ingredient was the happiness of the ones we loved.

He had looked at Jas when he signed that. I always assumed he meant her happiness was important to him. Now I wondered if he'd known, if he'd be happy.

I hoped so.

Which meant I had to do him good. And keeping my hands off his daughter was the right way to go.

I sat up and did my best not to notice how Jas's nipples pointed against the red fabric. "Sleep. But if you don't wear pants, I can't stay here."

Jas laughed, gave me a kiss, then collected some clothes and headed to the bathroom.

I changed into sweatpants and a tee shirt while she was gone, then stared at my wood pointing toward the door. I adjusted myself, but it refused to get the hint. Fuck it, not like Jas hadn't rubbed herself against me already. My hearing aids remained powered down, so I popped them out and set them to rest. I had a long night ahead of me. At least I'd be able to hold her.

Chapter Nineteen

Jasmine

MOST MORNINGS I woke up alone, even if I fell asleep with Dev. This morning I woke to find Dev sitting on the bed and Blake, dressed for work, standing with a phone to his ear.

My phone.

An uneasy feeling churned in my stomach and forced me into instant awake status. I sat up and touched Dev on his tee-shirt-clad shoulder, the same shirt he'd slept in. "Blake heard a phone ringing, turned out it was yours. No clue what's going on," he signed.

Blake noticed I was up and cushioned the phone between his shoulder and ear. "You know a woman named Tanya?"

I shook my head.

"She claims she's your mother's neighbor."

My heart leaped into my throat. "Unit 4B?"

Blake spoke into the phone, then nodded.

I scrambled out of bed to a standing position. I couldn't take the phone from him, but I had to do something. "What happened? What's wrong?" How did she even know my number?

Blake held up a hand, listened, then started signing. "An ambulance showed up early this morning. Your mom fell. She's being taken to the hospital."

Given how weak she was, a fall couldn't have been good. "Which hospital?"

Blake spoke, then interpreted. "I don't know. They just took her. She barely had the time to tell me to call Jasmine. I'm so grateful you answered; I had no idea how I was supposed to call a deaf person."

Dev squeezed my shoulders, and Blake rolled his eyes. He spoke to Tanya for a few more minutes but wasn't able to gather any new information. They hung up, and he handed me back my phone.

I paced, shoved my hands in my hair. I had to find my mother. Why hadn't whatever hospital she'd gone to called me? "How do I find her?"

Dev collected me into his arms and held me tight before signing. "We call around and ask for her." He eyed his brother.

Blake held up a hand and darted out of the room. He returned with his cell in hand and Bluetooth device in his ear. "Look up numbers. I'm ready."

They both turned to me. I wasn't alone, because I had the Walkers. "Don't you have to leave for work? And class?"

"Emergency," they signed simultaneously.

Dev sat on his bed, thumbing his phone. "I've got the closest hospital to her up. You want to talk, or should I?"

Blake waved. "They may only talk if Jasmine's signing."

Dev grinned. "They won't know the difference."

Again, both of them waited on me. I looked at Dev. This was what he did. He handled crises, figured out how to solve problems. He knew what to ask for more than I did. I just wanted to find my mother. "Go for it."

Dev rubbed his hands together. Blake handed over his phone, and Dev typed in the first number. The brothers worked as a well-oiled machine, neither needing to prep or explain anything to understand one another. Each place they called, Dev asked for Constance Helmsman. Each hospital informed us that no one by that name had been admitted.

He wanted to keep going after we finished with all the local hospitals. I stopped him. It made no sense that she would be transported that far away from her home or her doctors.

Blake took off his headset. "The information must be too new."

Dev nodded. "We can try again in a half hour. She's bound to show up somewhere by then."

I forced a smile I didn't feel. "Tonight. We'll call tonight. You two have to get going."

Blake collected his phone from Dev. "If you need me, text me. Tax season or not, I'll come running to help."

I gave him a hug, emotion clogging me. He left, and I knew the real trouble was about to start. "Go to class," I signed before Dev could.

He shook his head and pulled me to him. I wanted to push back. Instead I clutched onto him. My mother wasn't much of a mother, but she was still my family. Now she was MIA.

"I can stay. We can call again, track her down."

"No. We don't know how long it will take for her to show up in their system. Go."

He tangled one hand with mine. "I'm not leaving you."

"No. Go. I'll text you if I need you. Right now, you do me no good if you stay."

He wanted to fight me; the set to his jaw made that clear. But he knew I'd fight worse. We'd been at this impasse before. We'd be here again. Only instead of leaving, he moved to me, kissed me long and deep. Then he collected clothes for the day and left.

I collapsed on his bed, fiddled with my phone in my hands. I didn't know if Mom had hers or if Tanya had it in her possession. Reason stated if no hospital could claim her, Mom wouldn't be texting.

Still, I couldn't resist.

Me: Tanya called. Blake answered. Where are you? You OK?

The message sent, and I watched my words until my screen went black. My mind traveled to the phone call that had changed our lives, the one reporting Dad was in the hospital. The bar was on the same street as our home, yet no one notified us until he was already there.

By the time we arrived, it was too late.

I dropped my head into my hands. Would it be too late again? My mother checked out that day, but she was still my mother. If she died, I was truly on my own.

And since my residency consisted of sharing Dev's room, I belonged nowhere. A speck of dust floating in the wind—that was me.

Mom could be dead. If so, I prayed Dad had her smiling again. I had grown tired of trying years ago.

I wiped my cheeks. My hands came away wet. I hadn't cried since Dad died.

The tears spilled, and I had a very bad feeling in my gut. I had to find her. Surely even if she was dead, some hospital would claim her body? Right? I mean, Mom had to do all this shit to identify and take care of Dad.

All that would fall on me.

I wasn't ready to deal with that at twenty-one. Twenty-one, homeless, orphaned. Yeah, that sounded like a real catch.

I picked up my phone, searched for the hospital I suspected Mom would go to if she had a choice. Only I didn't want to connect to the interpreter relay service. I wasn't sure what to say, how to prove who I was.

I needed Dev.

My phone told me that somehow two hours had passed since Tanya called. Which meant I'd been sitting here like a lump for two hours.

Me: What's your schedule? I want to call around for Mom again but need your help.

Dev: You really think I left you alone?

I threw my phone on the bed and headed into the living room. Dev looked up from his spot at the kitchen table, books spread out. "You stayed?" I signed.

He crossed the room to me. "Of course I stayed. Blake almost did too, but I convinced him you'd kick both our asses."

I flung myself at him, burying my head into his chest. He held me tight, the way he always had.

When I pulled back, he brushed my cheeks. "Ready to call?"

I nodded.

"Good. Go get dressed."

"What?"

"Blake insisted he help. Get dressed. We're going into the office. I'll let him know we're on our way."

I blinked as the full impact hit me. They treated me like family. Even when I felt alone, they proved I wasn't. I flung my arms around Dev, kissed his cheek, then hurried off to get dressed.

Chapter Twenty

Devon

BLAKE CLOSED THE door behind us and settled in behind his desk. "How you holding up?" he asked Jas.

She had her flyaway curls pulled back in a ponytail, no makeup, and bloodshot eyes for the first time in eleven years. Worse, she didn't even attempt to placate him; instead she raised a noncommittal shoulder. Her spark was gone, and it killed me to see her like this and know there was nothing I could do. Except find her mother. I had to do something beyond that, anything, even make her crack a smile. Wrong time to try, though it didn't stop ideas from floating around in my head. The devastation on her face stopped me cold each time.

Blake popped in his Bluetooth and handed me his phone. I scrolled through the hospital listings on mine and began typing in one when Jas stopped me.

She shook her head and pointed to another on the list. I deleted what I had typed and reentered the number she chose.

This time, I had Blake start with the emergency department—a suggestion Katherine had sent me after I emailed her for advice. When someone answered, Blake explained we were trying to find out if a Constance Helmsman had been taken there.

"May I ask who's calling?"

I turned to Jas, who straightened in her chair. Without any prompting, she began signing. "Jasmine Helmsman, I'm her daughter."

"Yes, Constance arrived a short while ago. I don't have an update on her condition, but she's here."

Jas reached out and clutched my hand, eyes still on Blake for communication. "Thank you."

Blake disconnected, and Jas released her bone-crushing grip.

"We know where she is. We know she's alive—" I signed.

"We don't have an update." Jas bit her lip, blinked her watery eyes. "They didn't have an update when we called with my dad."

Shit. I pulled her to me, held her trembling body. Over her head, I caught Blake's eyes. "Go to the hospital. I can't leave to interpret, but maybe we can figure out who works with that hospital?"

I let go of Jas. "No, I'll write. It's faster. We'll be fine."

Jas scrunched up her face. "What's going on?"

"We're going to the hospital."

Eyes wide, she nodded.

I heard a bang and turned to Blake. "Dad's expecting you here today, better update him."

I rubbed my neck and contemplated asking Blake to handle my shit, but I knew better. "Give me five minutes." I left Jas with Blake and prayed five minutes would be accurate.

I found Dad in his office alone. No client. No interpreter. Small miracle. I toggled the light switch until he looked up. When he pulled off his glasses, I worried my five minutes didn't have a chance in hell. "You gave your work to Blake yesterday."

I all but saw the five minutes go up in smoke. "No, Blake volunteered. I had a date."

Dad's eyebrows raised. "A date is more important than your work?"

Yes. A date was more important than a job I really didn't give a damn about. And even if I had cared, Jas needed the date, deserved it, more than work needed me. But that wouldn't get me anywhere but stuck in his office for another hour. This conversation was going to shit quickly anyways, might as well toss another log on the fire with my real reason for being here. "I'm leaving now and won't be in later on today."

Dad steepled his pointer fingers, tapped them to his mouth, used those fingers to propel his sign. "Really?"

"Jasmine's mom is in the hospital. I'm going with her to help." *Like I want to do for a living.*

"Won't your new girlfriend think that's funny?"

I angled my head, trying to figure out what had happened to my father. If I ever dated anyone who put themselves before a hospital visit, that wasn't going to fly. "Jasmine's who I'm dating."

Dad's eyes opened wide. Part surprise, part preparation for attack. I intercepted before he had a chance. "We don't know if Constance is dead or alive. I have to go and help her. We can finish this conversation later."

"Yes, we'll finish this later."

I turned to leave, fighting the overwhelming urge to punch a wall or yell. We shouldn't even be having this conversation, not if Dad respected my actual wants. I faced him again, ready for battle.

He beat me to it. "You be careful with Jasmine."

That knocked me out. Battle won with one punch. "What do you mean?"

"She's had a lot of hurt in her short life, possibly more with her mom in the hospital. You've been there for her, helped her through those dark days. If dating doesn't work out, you could hurt her."

"I have no plans for dating not working out."

Dad cracked a smile, one filled with older wisdom and cynicism. "Dating can be wonderful or make things really sticky. And Blake said Jasmine's staying with you for the time being. I'm not naïve enough to not know what that means."

I rubbed my neck. We hadn't had sex yet, but I didn't dare sign that. Dad would focus on the *yet*.

"Make sure you always put her needs first. Nothing matters if she's not happy."

"Which means I should get her to the hospital to check on her mom."

"You like helping. Help her."

I nearly signed *I'd help a lot more than her* but curbed my hands. We'd have this conversation another day. Today was about Jas.

Chapter Twenty-One

Jasmine

I FOLLOWED DEV into the emergency room, past the many full chairs and somber faces, to the desk where two women in scrubs shuffled back and forth. Dev had the forethought to swipe a pad of paper from work. While we stood there, ignored, he bent over and wrote a message—*We're looking for Constance Helmsman*—before turning it in their direction.

It took another two minutes for them to pay attention to us. If it wasn't for the clock on the wall, I would have easily guessed ten. I focused on the second hand, noting how each shift took an eternity. A minute was always a minute. Sixty seconds. So why did it take so damn long for the black hand to make it all the way back to twelve again? I tried to look down the hall, where the patients would be, but no answers awaited me. The only patients visible were an older dude and a young female—not Mom.

A woman in light blue scrubs read Dev's note, then looked up and spoke to us. Dev leaned forward, clearly trying to hear, but he shook his head and pointed to his ear. Then he picked up the pen and paper and handed it to the nurse.

She gave us a look, like we'd bluff about this for fun, but picked up the pen and wrote. *Who are you to Constance?*

Dev gestured for me, and I took the pen. *I'm her daughter, Jasmine.*

The nurse nodded and held up a finger. She clicked on her computer before responding. *Let me call back, see if she can have visitors.*

Dev grasped my hand as the nurse picked up a phone and spoke to someone. After another really long period that was probably only thirty seconds, she nodded. Dev collected the paper and pen, and we followed the visual directions from the nurse.

I had to identify myself again at a nursing station before being allowed through an automatic set of double doors. We found Mom two rooms down on the right, blocked off by a flimsy curtain closure.

Mom lay in a hospital bed, wearing a blue and white hospital gown, a white blanket covering her. An IV had been hooked up. Her distant blue eyes stared at the corner of the room. She was alive. She breathed. I had no clue what was wrong, but she lived.

I stepped into the room and caught the television in the corner she stared at. I waved until her eyes met mine. I expected them to light up, look relieved, anything.

Nothing.

Instead she glanced behind me to Dev, giving him a look that said *What are you doing here?*

I intercepted. "What happened? Are you OK?"

"I fell." She signed one-handed, not moving the one with the IV, white ID bracelet sliding down her arm.

"Are you OK?"

"I'm here. No."

I'd been worried about her, and she barely gave me a few words. I wondered if somewhere beneath her cold exterior, she thought of Dad. I wondered if the hospital scared her or if she was ready to see him again.

The last thought scared me, felt too close to becoming real.

"Why here?" Mom signed.

"Tanya called, told me you were taken to a hospital. Why wouldn't I be here?"

"You don't care. Your new life is too important. You're not here to help."

"I'm sorry."

Dev's hand clasped my shoulder. I hadn't been good enough to Mom since Dad died. Possibly ever. He was the nurturer, not her.

"She was worried about you. We had to track you down," Dev signed.

Mom shifted, eyes to the television. "Doesn't matter. I'm stuck here now. One more problem in this no-good life. Been this way since Dad died."

The lighting of the hospital, the white walls and floors, the bustle of nurses in scrubs all brought back memories. Of me standing in the hall, trying to figure out what was going on, where my father was. I had studied the body language of the nurses, their lips moving, but couldn't figure out a thing. Then Mom had collapsed, sobbing, and I knew whatever had happened was bad.

It had taken until Dev and his mom picked me up to understand how bad. I should have figured it out, after a half hour of watching Mom cry. But I had been stuck without communication, without my mother's support.

She'd been this way since that day. Cold. Closed off. Unhelpful. She'd left me to raise myself. Sure, life had sent a ton of crap. But we didn't band together to fight through it.

She gave up.

"It wasn't Dad's fault he had a heart attack." I signed small. Because it was the truth. The debt he left the bar in, that was his fault. The attack was not. I wanted to tell Mom she wouldn't die, not yet, not now after all this time. I feared she'd argue with me.

A small flame of emotion flared to Mom's eyes; I should have known she didn't need much incentive to argue. "Yes. It was. He carried all that stress, worked himself to the bone, piled on the debt that destroyed our lives."

"He tried to save us."

"He tried to save his bar. Not us. Never us. Always the bar. I hated that damn bar."

"Of course you did. That's why you got rid of it the first chance you had."

Mom shifted, then winced in pain, and I felt bad. I shouldn't be arguing with her. We could have this conversation another day, not today. "I did what I had to, to keep food on the table."

I held myself back. Now was not the time to call her out on her depression and the meager meals it created. I needed to stop this fight, but I couldn't, not yet. "I wanted your love, not food."

Mom's eyes traveled to Dev, and even with all the changes between us, my stomach clenched. "You always did get what you needed elsewhere."

Dev was the one who told me Dad had died. His mom was writing and working on communication, but Dev heard it. My own mother couldn't give me two signs to let me know why my world was falling apart. Although I guessed she had been the reason Gail and Dev had shown up in the first place.

"She's your daughter. Did you ever think about that? She came here because she cares. I don't know why you can't express anything positive for her."

I grabbed Dev's arm and shook my head. Not the time. Not the place. Not when my head was buried in the past and I couldn't find my way back up.

Mom looked at me, and I swore I saw remorse. Did she see the parallel? Did she feel the hurt? I'd leave her again, leave with Dev, stay with Dev, while she continued to shut me out. "Leave me alone."

"The last time I left a parent in the hospital, one died." I had to blink back tears.

So did Mom. "A broken hip won't kill me."

"You promise?"

Mom brushed me off. Couldn't blame her. I wanted to fling myself at her, feel her arms around me. Dad's death should have brought us closer. Instead, I couldn't remember the last time she'd hugged me.

Dev tugged on my hand, stepping toward the hall. Mom turned to the television. I willed her to look at me again, give me something, anything.

"If you don't give up that bar dream, you'll end up like him. And I can't stand by while you destroy your life like he did."

Dev squeezed my hand, but I pulled it free. "Dad's the only parent I ever truly had. You don't want me following in his footsteps? Give me someone else to look up to."

Then I turned and hightailed it out of there. I made my way down the hall, past the double doors, and into the waiting room. My feet propelled me forward, into the icy spring air.

I stopped before I hit the street, breathing in, freezing my lungs. Dev wrapped me in his arms. No words necessary. I needed him. His strength, his warmth, his scent. Comfort. Anything to eradicate the chill left behind by Mom.

SOMETIME AROUND THE second exit on the highway, the overwhelming urge to be alone, to get away, hit me like a bug on the windshield. I instructed Dev to drop me off and go to work.

He shot me a look but signed nothing. I did my Connie impression, shutting others out, because like it or not, I did a few things the same as my mother.

I fought my battles alone.

He didn't push, didn't rock the boat of my fragile state. My breaking point was way too close for comfort. At the apartment, he idled in front of the building. I reached for the handle, but he touched my arm. I steadied my breathing and faced him.

"You going to be OK?"

I forced a smile. "Always."

He didn't sign anymore, and after a moment, I could no longer look at him. If I did, I'd collapse, or beg him to stay, or kiss him, and I needed to be alone.

He let me go. A part of me wanted to pound on him. But I recognized it was what I wanted, what I asked for. And whatever distance Dev granted, it came with a time limit.

I needed to get my shit together fast.

Unfortunately, wandering his apartment alone didn't give me any clarity. I stood in his place, with his belongings, here because I accepted a handout. The story of my life, always needing something from someone. I had to turn my brain off and stop thinking for five fucking minutes.

I left for work early. Requiring something, anything, to do. The early departure meant I didn't have to worry about seeing Dev at the apartment.

He'd find me soon, and then I'd have to deal with it all. As I considered the growing number of text messages from Dev that I was ignoring, everything felt like it was crowding in on me.

An hour into my shift, he arrived. I did my best rendition of our fifth-grade fight: I ignored him. It worked for ten minutes, until he snatched my wrist as I walked past. "Why are you upset with me?" His touch was no longer tentative.

I shrugged free. "I'm not. I want to be alone. Why can't you understand that?" Then I hid behind my work, giving him a wide berth. Hoping he'd get frustrated enough to leave.

I should have known better. Devon Walker stuck to his principles the more frustrated he grew. Which meant that an hour later, I had a bigger section to avoid, as Nikki and Pete had arrived.

I couldn't avoid my two friends. They didn't know the shit that had gone down. I greeted them on the other side of the bar, needing as much distance as I could get.

"Your mom's in the hospital?" Nikki signed as soon as I got close.

I dropped my board down and locked eyes with Dev. "You haven't finished updating them? You brought them here; you deal with it."

I went to hand my board to Len, but Dev reached over the bar and grabbed my arm. "Stop running from me."

I faced Nikki. "Want a sleepover tonight?"

Dev dropped my arm, ran two hands through his hair. "You don't need to play these games."

"You don't need to help me. Find someone who wants it. I'm on my own."

Nikki banged on the counter. "Again. Yin. Yang. You two have never been alone."

I shrugged it off and handed my board to Len. No smile from him—something was in the air, turning everyone to shit. I grabbed my marker, added a line to my list of orders. *I can make these if you want a break.*

He erased my words. *Not your job.*

It could be, if anyone had any faith in me. I stayed nearby as he completed my drinks, kept my eyes trained away from my friends. How had I not noticed how sloppy Len was until now? The mixes were off, the beer over-foamed. Not good, not good at all.

I wanted to talk with him, but he shoved my tray toward me. And I got it; I was the waitress, a kid playing bartender. Even if I could do a better job than him.

I delivered my drinks. The other tables didn't need me, and I wasn't ready to see my friends, so I escaped to the bathroom, a single-stall unisex room near the back office. I kicked at the door, not bothering to ensure it latched closed, and leaned over the sink, staring at myself. My smile was nonexistent. My eyes were devoid of spark. I looked as bad as Mom and Len.

The door opened, and through the mirror I saw Dev enter. I rolled my neck. "Bathroom means privacy."

"Then you should have locked the door." He came up behind me, for which I was grateful, as it felt a little less personal with us both facing the mirror. "Talk to me."

I wanted to laugh but was too afraid it would turn into a cry. "What for? You were there. You know what happened."

I kept my gaze on his chin; his blues held too much emotion for my present state. "And I know you're acting too much like your mother right now."

I spun around and pushed my hands against his chest. "What do you expect me to do? Pretend nothing happened? Discuss all the little details of how I feel?"

His hands balled into fists before he started signing. "And what do you expect me to do? Watch you in pain and do nothing? How can I help? Tell me what to do." He flung his arms out wide, and for the first time, I saw it. My pain on him. It was there in the shine of his eyes, the stiffness of his jaw and shoulder. If I bled, he bled.

I always was alone until Dev got involved. And if I was honest, vice versa. Nikki's yin-yang comment pinged back to mind. He was there when my dad died. I was there when his dog got hit by a car. I made him laugh after Tiffany Stone dumped him in eighth grade. He helped me study after bombing a history test.

And now I fought against that very same help. Double so for Dev, who had a life calling to butt into people's lives and try to flip a magic switch. Only I had no switch to flip. My pain didn't go away. It had grown roots to become a part of me.

My gaze traveled to his lips. There was one way to make him feel better. To make me feel better. I darted across the narrow space and kissed him. His soft lips turned a shitty day upside down. He pulled me close, and I shoved my hands in his hair. The day disappeared until only the two of us remained.

He backed me up until my ass hit the sink. I wrapped one leg around him, and his hands played with the strip of skin exposed between my short skirt and tank top. Our lips clung, tongues teased. Pressure built. I arched into him, connecting with a definite erection. This time we didn't break apart. This time we melted further together.

The lights flashed, and we broke apart. I opened my eyes to a very amused Nikki and Pete. I quickly fixed my skirt as Dev dropped his head to my shoulder, laughing.

"That was hot," Nikki signed, fanning herself. "You really don't want to sleep over with me."

I tried to get my head on straight. One minute we were fighting, the next, ready to devour each other. With the door unlocked.

Pete nudged Nikki as Dev picked his head up. "Told you they were hot."

"No kidding. I thought we were going to need to hose them down."

"You finished?" Dev asked.

"Depends. You done fighting?" Nikki's retort had all three looking at me.

"For now."

Dev arched an eyebrow, and I couldn't help myself; I kissed his cheek.

Nikki turned to Pete. "Mark it down. Ways to make Jasmine feel better: kissing Devon."

"I suspect that goes both ways." Pete followed her into the hall.

Dev faced me. "You OK?"

I took a deep breath. My world still felt a little topsy-turvy, but one thing was certain. "I'm better."

Chapter Twenty-Two

Devon

One downside of diffusing Jas's anger: without it, her bravado faltered, leaving her exhausted. By the end of the night, she yawned and shifted on her feet. And still told me to go home as closing time approached.

"No. You're too tired. I'll drive you."

She yawned. "I'm fine."

I leaned on the bar and stared her down. Besides two others, I was the only one left. Nikki and Pete had gone home hours ago.

Len came over and picked up Jas's board. He wrote a message, then plopped it in front of her before returning to his usual spot. The guy was not on his A-game, not even close.

Jas read the board, then sighed. "Fine. Drive me home."

I glanced at the message Len left telling her to leave for the night. With the small crowd, he had this covered. Jas needed rest.

By the time I pulled up to my apartment complex, she leaned against the seat, fast asleep. The streetlight illuminated her face, her closed eyelids, and those lips I had robbed of lipstick earlier. I finally got the chance to open the car door for her. She didn't budge, deep into slumberland.

I undid her belt and collected her into my arms. It took a little maneuvering to use my keys to get us into the apartment, but I managed.

I laid her down in my bed, and she curled right up like usual. I undid her boots and managed to slide her trench off. She'd want to wash up or change into pajamas. I didn't dare change her myself; we weren't at that point in our relationship yet.

Did I wake her or not?

I leaned over her, brushed her hair back, and shook her shoulder. She shifted and stayed asleep. I kissed her temple. "Sleep." With the day she'd had, she deserved it.

After a trip to the bathroom, I changed into my pajamas and curled up behind her, wrapping us both in a blanket. The exhaustion of the day must have hit me as well, and I conked right out with her.

I WOKE FIRST. Not a surprise on Jas's part, as her job had truly made her a night owl. It was a bit of a surprise on Blake's part, until I recognized the second jacket hanging by our door—Shawn's. I brewed a large enough pot of coffee for everyone, although who knew when the guys would be up and around.

As the brown liquid dripped into the pot, a light flashed. Our doorbell. I glanced at the time. It was too early for guests. It might have been an electrical interference, but even so, I checked the peephole.

Mom and Dad stood on the other side.

Not how I wanted to start my day. I pulled out my phone and warned Blake. Whatever his plans were on introducing Shawn, they were shot now. I opened the door. "What are you doing here?"

Mom patted my cheek. "That's not how you welcome your parents."

I rolled my eyes and stepped back. Dad signed nothing. Since our conversation at work about Jas, things had not been smooth between us.

Mom placed a bag from a local bagel place in the center of the kitchen table. I hoped she'd gotten a half dozen to accommodate the extra person. She brushed her hands on her jean-clad hips. "How's Jasmine?"

I turned to Dad, and he gave me a curt nod. Realization dawned, and a warmth encompassed my chest. They were here because of Jas. "She had a rough night but is sleeping now."

Mom placed a hand on her heart. "That poor dear. I always worried about Connie after Eddie died. Jasmine put on too good of a front at school, never letting us know if we could help." Mom was one of the Deaf teachers at the school Jas and I had gone to.

I shook my head and reached into the bagel bag. Jas and I knew getting her mom in trouble would be ten times worse on Jas. As long as she could crash with my family when needed, she'd be fine.

I pulled out an everything bagel and popped it in the toaster. My phone vibrated, and I checked the display.

Blake: They staying?

Me: They brought bagels. They're here for Jas, but she's still asleep.

Blake: Shit.

Me: You can't hide Shawn forever.

Blake: Going to be obvious when he comes out of my room.

Me: Hide the hickeys.

Blake: Do Mom and Dad know you're dating Jas now?

I put my phone away. Dad knew. It all depended on how much he'd told Mom.

Dad glanced around. "Where's Blake?"

Sleeping. With his boyfriend. "Don't know, haven't seen him yet." Best answer—the two could hide out in his room for hours if they wanted to.

...Or face the music. Blake dragged one hand through his bedhead hair. The other held Shawn's. I needed to teach them the act of subtlety. "Good morning," Blake signed. Then, without giving my parents a beat to be shocked, he continued. "This is my boyfriend, Shawn. He's hearing but is learning ASL."

Dad's eyebrows shot up. His sons were giving him a hell of a week. Mom beamed, eyes darting back and forth between the couple. In contrast to Dad, she was probably envisioning wedding invitations. "Nice to meet you." She slowed down her signs so Shawn could follow and stuck a hand out to him.

Shawn shook it. "Nice to meet you too." He shot Blake a look, clearly thinking things weren't as bad as anticipated. But Blake held firm. Mom wasn't the problem.

Dad rubbed his neck. I wanted to sign *not a phase*, but the man would figure it out eventually. With any luck he'd see how good a man Shawn was for Blake.

I backed away. "I'll see if Jasmine's awake." I hoped some of the tension would be defused by the time we returned.

I slipped into my room, closing the door behind me. Her legs were tangled in the blankets, all long limbs and smooth skin. I hated waking her, but Blake and Shawn needed the distraction. Besides, Mom and Dad were here for her. I shook Jas's shoulder until she stirred. She rolled over and went back to sleep.

I laughed; waking her was always a challenge. However, I did have a new trick up my sleeve. I kissed her.

It started as brushes against still lips, but then her lips began to move with mine. Slow, but like each time when I kissed Jas, the rest of the world faded. Her lips took on more urgency. I pulled her body to mine. And when the last shred of sanity threatened to leave, I remembered the party in the kitchen.

I pulled back, and her eyes popped open. A lazy smile crossed her face. “Good morning.”

That made one of us. “Sorry to wake you, but my parents stopped by. To check on you.”

Jas sat up. “What?” She checked the time. “It’s too early. You people are not normal.”

“Shawn’s here.”

Her eyes widened. “Oh. Blake hiding him?”

“They’re in the kitchen.”

She swung her legs over the bed. “Now that I want to see.”

I stomped until she turned. “Your makeup.” She looked fine to me, but with the smudged mascara and messed-up hair, not to mention last night’s bar clothes, she looked like we’d had sex.

Her hand flew to her hair. “I have to wash up.” She grabbed some clothes and sneaked out of my room, down the hall to the bathroom.

I returned to the kitchen, where Blake handed me my forgotten bagel. Shawn and Mom chatted in slow signs. Dad leaned against the counter, arms crossed, closed off from everyone in the room. If I couldn’t get his support on something as simple as this, I had no chance in hell of him supporting my career.

Jas entered as I took a bite of my bagel, her face free of any makeup, her hair pulled back into a messy bun. She wore jeans and a tee shirt, nothing like the sexy-as-hell vision I had encountered in my bed, yet every bit as enticing. My hands itched to touch her. I would have, if it wasn't for the present company. Her eyebrows shot up, and she pointed at me with an accusatory finger. I opened my mouth to take another bite, then promptly put the bagel down. Shit. I forgot about the matzo thing. I signed, "Sorry," as Mom excused herself from Shawn and greeted Jas.

"I'm so sorry," Mom signed as she pulled Jas into a hug.

Over Mom's shoulder, Jas sent me a glare. "You failed."

"It was a mistake."

"Later." She let go of Mom and faced her. "Thank you."

Mom asked a few questions about Connie. Jas responded with vague answers, since we knew very little. "What's her diagnosis?"

"Broken hip."

"What's the treatment plan?"

"No clue." Tension stiffened her shoulders with each answer. Without thinking, I pulled her to me and pressed a kiss to her temple.

Everyone froze. All eyes were on us, taking in my action and our closeness. Even Blake and Shawn, who knew we were dating, hadn't seen us together, not like this.

I backed away. "Bagel?" I asked Jas.

Pink spotted her cheeks. She nodded, and I went to hand her my mistake bagel, only to have her shake her head and pull out a cinnamon raisin instead.

Mom waved for attention. "You two... boyfriend/girlfriend now?"

I glanced at Jas. We hadn't established any labels; there hadn't been a need. "We're dating," I signed.

Mom studied us both, then a smile crossed her face. "About time." She faced Dad. "I told you they'd end up together."

Jas turned and focused on her bagel. This was all new, and Mom was already acting like us being together was permanent. The wedding-planning wheels in her mind were probably working double time on us. But Jas was used to relationships messing things up. I had to let her know that whatever happened, we'd always be family.

It took some time, but eventually Mom and Dad left, and Blake and Shawn retreated to Blake's room. Jas and I remained at the table, sipping our second coffees. "Your dad really didn't say much."

"I suspect this was Mom's idea."

"Definitely. She liked Shawn."

I nodded. They'd hit it off, language barrier and all. Of course, Mom's teaching side meant she could be much more patient with communication than others.

"I'm sorry about the bagel. With everything going on, I forgot." I hadn't finished it—only that one bite escaped me.

"I only challenged you because it's hard to eat only that for food. It's no big deal." Yet tension lingered. I damn well knew it wasn't just the matzo, but it all rolled up together.

"I was enjoying the food." I had. A little dry, but a nice break from normal.

"Then you've been sneaking food in elsewhere." A tiny smile crossed her face.

"You told me no bread. I haven't been eating bread."

She ran a finger across the top of her mug. "Popcorn? I just remembered, you can't have popcorn either, nothing that expands."

I rolled my head back and laughed at the ceiling. I had grabbed a bag of popcorn with lunch the previous day. "How the hell was I supposed to know that?"

Jas shrugged.

"How can I make it up to you? Want me to eat it for two weeks?"

The sad smile played at her lips again. "It's fine. Forget it."

"No. I made a mistake with the bagel. I told you I'd stick to it, and I will."

Her sad smile morphed into a real one, and it tugged at my heartstrings. While I had always been there for her, she was too used to her mother letting her down. The challenge might have started because I'd bought the matzo that she hadn't wanted, but I suspected it meant something more to her now.

"Don't be silly." The smile left, replaced by the lingering unease. Jas rotated her mug, her focus on the liquid inside. She'd been like this ever since Mom brought up our relationship. This wasn't how I wanted us to be. Ever.

I tapped the table until she looked up at me. Time to lay out some cards. The more air we cleared, the better off we'd be. Even if the change in our relationship meant there were risks. "How soon after a date can I ask if you want to be my girlfriend?"

Her lips tipped up, and color bloomed on her cheeks. "I thought we were talking about matzo?"

"You told me to forget it." I'd prove myself with actions, not words.

Her wide eyes held mine captive. "I don't think there are any rules."

"So…now?"

Jas raised her hands and hesitated. "You've never done that before."

"Established rules?"

"Asked someone to be your girlfriend."

I moved to respond, then froze. I hadn't; she was right. And yet now, with her, there wasn't a question in my mind. "I'm asking you."

"Don't change yourself because of me." She held herself stiff, and I smelled a trap.

"I'm not." My jaw tightened. If anything, I finally had a reason not to force myself to be what I wasn't. "It's a label. That's it. The change is already there."

"And if the change doesn't work? That will destroy our friendship."

I shook my head. "Nothing will destroy our friendship. I don't know where this change will go, but you and me, we're family."

"You don't date family."

I stopped myself from signing the obvious answer, that one did date family if they were married. But that was way too soon and scared even me.

I rested my elbows on the table, tapped my hands together. I glanced at my wrist as Nikki's words came into mind. "Yin yang. Nikki's right: that's us, always a part of each other. We'll get it tattooed." I made the yin-yang sign again and broke it up, half for Jas, half for me, on our wrists.

"You're crazy," Jas signed, but she laughed.

I leaned forward. "You like it."

She pressed her lips together, but that only fueled me. I knew I had her. She always talked about getting a tattoo someday. Why shouldn't that distant day be now?

"I'll contact Pete, find out who he uses." I pulled out my phone, but Jas banged on the table.

"You're serious?"

"About you? Yes."

She held my eyes captive, emotion swirling in hers. "You want me to be your first girlfriend?"

Since I was twelve. "Yes."

A smile crossed her face. I leaned across the table to kiss her, but she stopped me. "You have to keep eating the matzo though."

Chapter Twenty-Three

Jasmine

OF ALL THE things I could do on a day off, I never suspected I'd be at a tattoo parlor. It had always been a desire of mine that I didn't often talk about—one Dev was well aware of. Something I'd thought I'd be able to afford after getting my bar established. I couldn't deny the little thrill it created. What better way to commemorate my youth than with something bold and brash? Pete hooked us up with his guy, who turned out to be a woman with availability, and suddenly my *one day I'll do this* became *today.*

I was getting a tattoo. And after this, I'd be forever marked in a way that connected me to Dev.

He brushed my hair out of my face. "You sure about this? We can change our minds if you aren't sure."

Nervous? Yes. Wanting to back out? No. "I'm sure."

He rubbed the back of his neck.

"Are you sure?"

"Yes. Of course." A little too much bravado, but hey, needles weren't exactly his thing.

Pete had come along, either for moral support or entertainment. He worked with the artist, Kit, who knew a little ASL. She had a nose piercing, dyed pink hair, and tattoos up and down her arms and peeking out from the V-neck of her shirt. She put down her pencil and held one thumb up. Pete looked at the sheet, nodded, and turned the paper our way.

I had assumed we'd just do a simple version. But Kit had drawn one with a flowery leaf feel. She let us study it for a minute, then held up a hand. "Or simple." And flipped the page over to a bold plain version.

I turned to Dev, a bubble of excitement threatening to break free. I tried to imagine each design on his wrist, but I couldn't focus. What would it feel like to run my fingers over a marking that matched mine? To have this little physical representation of the connection we'd always had?

"Which one do you prefer?" Dev asked.

I held up a finger to Kit and Pete and pulled Dev aside. My hand brushed at his wrist, sending a tingle straight through me. "I have no idea." I held out my wrist. "Which do you think will look best?"

His thumb pressed against my overactive pulse point. He stared as if the answer to world hunger resided on my wrist. The pressure of his hand made me tighten my thighs to try to combat the growing need inside me. Even thoughts of needles didn't help.

Still holding my wrist, he let his eyes travel up my arm and over my face. The little half smile showed he caught the goose bumps and was damn proud of it. "I'm thinking simple. Your strength and beauty doesn't need flourish."

And now my heart melted along with my core. "Simple it is."

He let go of my wrist to tilt up my chin, giving me a quick kiss that nearly set my panties on fire. When we parted, I had to blink the world back into focus. Not Dev; he'd already let Kit know our choice.

She rubbed her hands together. Through gesturing she inquired which half we each got. When we didn't have an answer, Pete looked up the symbol. The black side, the yin, represented femininity. And darkness. It fit me.

And Dev was my light.

I went first. Kit prepped my wrist and then punctured my skin with ink. It wasn't comfortable, and pain followed the pricking. But it was about time pain meant something good was being added to my life.

Pete and Dev kept me entertained. I couldn't really respond because I signed with my whole body, but I managed a simple word or two in response.

Kit wiped away ink and blood from my wrist. The blood made sense, but I would never have expected it, for whatever reason. I faced Pete. "You do this often?"

He grinned and flexed the eagle on his arm. "Worth it. You'll see."

I guess I had no other option.

When Kit finished, the skin around my tattoo was red and angry, but in the center the yin represented peace.

Yes, it would match up with Dev, but it also epitomized what I'd been through and where I was headed.

For some odd reason, it represented hope.

With my arm bandaged, I hopped off the table. "Your turn."

Dev settled in as I joined Pete. "Think he can handle it?" Pete asked.

"You ask me that now? I need a partner for my yin yang."

He flashed me a million-dollar smile. "I'll match you."

The floor vibrated, and we turned to Dev. "Over my dead body."

I smiled, couldn't help it. There was something about Dev being possessive over me.

Then Kit began her work, and Dev closed his eyes, tight.

Pete doubled over in laughter. "He can't handle it, I love it."

Dev flipped Pete off. He must have heard the laughter.

I was close to laughing myself, as Dev's free hand tightened into a fist. He definitely wasn't reveling in the pain like I had. I ran my hand down his free arm and laced my fingers with his. He cracked open an eye, but Kit must have done something, because he snapped it closed again.

I turned to Pete. "And the award for bravery goes to Jasmine Helmsman, good job."

I caught Kit's eye. "He cry?" I asked, gesturing to Pete.

She glanced back at him. "Little bit."

Pete insisted on taking us to dinner to celebrate. I suspected it was in part a stall tactic to keep us from removing the bandages. Our usual pizza place didn't leave Dev with many options due to the whole matzo challenge. I contemplated letting him off the hook, but he'd already rejected my attempt to let him free. Beyond that, a part of me reveled in his commitment. He kept it because it was important to me. Dev the friend would have accepted my way out. Dev the boyfriend wasn't letting go.

He had to know how much that meant to me.

He ate his chicken fingers and fries, and I didn't bring up the fact that chicken fingers were battered in flour. I was also distracted by my bandage and what lay underneath. I may have handled the pain better, but Dev had the waiting game down. I wanted to see what the tattoos looked like in action.

As soon as we got back to his apartment, I made a beeline for the bathroom, ready to get the bandage off and clean my skin. I stepped into the hall before Dev stopped me. "You have to wait an hour."

I checked the time. "Close enough." The whole situation had me antsy. I rarely did anything like this—spontaneous and for myself. I felt free and alive, and I wanted it to continue.

"Patience," Dev signed. "I can keep you busy." Before his words fully registered, he kissed me, and all my antsy energy found another outlet.

I put my arms around him, pulling my left wrist back when the bandage pressed against my sore skin. Dev wrapped one arm around my waist and yanked me to him, and I didn't miss the fact that he'd only used one arm. Yet I didn't care, not with his lips pressing against mine, not with his tongue teasing me with slow strokes. Not when I was more than ready to take this one step further.

As if the tattoos weren't enough.

We stumbled into his room, and he trapped me against his closed door, his hard body holding me in place, ratcheting up the heat until I melted into him. I wanted to climb him, meld us together until I couldn't tell where I ended and he began. The need grew, and I knew I wasn't stopping until he was inside of me.

I broke the kiss, head back against the door, struggling to catch my breath. Dev kissed my chin, my neck, his hand traveling up my stomach and wrapping around my breast. His large hand covered me, a possessiveness in his movements and his gaze, each setting me off more than the other. I tightened my grip on his shoulders, otherwise I'd fall to the floor. In all our kissing, we hadn't made it this far, and I wondered why. Dev touched me through my clothes, and my body lit on fire for him. Every nerve ending woke up and begged for more, more, more.

More I could take. I released one hand from his neck and trailed down his tight chest, to his hard abs, to the end of his jeans. He stopped kissing me, his hand stilled, as I caressed up and down his hard length. I wanted to feel all of him. In my hand. My mouth. Me. I didn't think I had ever wanted someone the way I wanted Devon Walker.

He lifted his head and leveled me with a serious gaze. "You ready?"

I brushed my fingers up him again. He sucked in a breath. "You are."

He pressed our pelvises together, and I forgot to breathe. "You answer my question, or this stops right here."

"Yes. I want you, in me." I signed that last part slow, graphic, torturing him for all my worth.

"You'll pay for that." He spun me away from the door, and the next thing I knew I was flat on my back on the bed, with him on top. If this was paying, then I was all for it.

His hand snaked up my shirt and pulled down my bra cup. Then we were skin against skin. My breast ached for more. The area between my legs throbbed. I squirmed as he teased, and my body gave itself over to him.

But I wasn't a passive player. I tugged at his shirt, then helped him get it off without rubbing his bandage. My eyes traveled down his body, all those hard planes I could now explore. My hand followed my eyes, his skin warm and welcoming to my touch.

He pulled at my shirt, and we repeated the process around my bandage. Once my shirt was gone, he kissed down my neck, over my collarbone, not stopping until he sucked my cotton-covered nipple into his mouth. My body tightened. And while I had liked his tongue in my mouth, his tongue on me was much better.

I needed to touch him. I ran my hand down his abs and dipped inside his jeans. He picked his head up, those abs expanding and contracting, but it didn't stop me. I slid my hand down until I grasped his hard, smooth skin.

Oh, yeah, this was what I wanted. My hands on him, moving against him. Everything new and old at once, like this was meant to be.

I shook those crazy thoughts aside and went to sit up and really get down to work, only Dev pushed me back. A heart-stopping wicked smile crossed his face as his hand slipped inside my jeans. One stroke of his finger and I nearly jolted at the contact. The second I arched into him. The third he slipped inside.

I closed my eyes, lost in his movement. My hand was still in his pants, though no longer moving. He had me all but incapacitated.

I didn't like that. I tried to push myself up but ended up pressing my sore wrist against the bed. I let go of him and grabbed my wrist.

He took it from me. "You OK?"

I winced and pulled it back. "Yes, just stupid. I leaned on it."

He kissed the skin around my bandage, pressing a light one to the center. "Maybe I should help you with your clothes."

I was aiming for his clothes, but when he looked at me like that, as though I was an overflowing bowl of ice cream, I'd let him do just about anything.

Dev kissed down my body and popped my jeans open with his teeth. He slid the zipper down. I raised my hips so he could pull off my pants, leaving me in a bra, thong, and socks. His gaze touched on every inch of my exposed skin. But he'd seen most of this whenever we went swimming. So I removed the rest of my clothes.

Naked in front of him, I tried to catch my breath but figured breathing was overrated at a time like this. His eyes raked up and down my body, caressing without touch. Somehow I continued to burn up and refused to do so alone. "Your turn."

His smile, I could lick it. He got onto his feet, and when his hands went to his jeans, I got on my knees. "No. Me." I leaned over him, popped his button with my teeth, then pressed a kiss to the bulge underneath.

"You're killing me," he signed, before taking over and removing the rest of his clothes.

I sat back on my heels, taking in his happy trail and an impressive body part pointing at me. I licked my lips, wanting a taste, only to have my chin raised until I met his face. "Not this time, later."

"Why not now?" He looked better than ice cream.

Dev dropped his head, then held up his hand. It shook. A sure sign his control was ready to snap.

I settled back onto his bed. "Fine. Later. You got a condom?" But he was already searching in his bedside drawer, uncovering a foil wrapper.

I snatched it from him and tore it open. Then I sheathed him.

We settled back down onto his bed. Flesh to flesh. Our bodies had been lined up similarly before, but always platonically. There was nothing platonic about this moment. Not when Dev hovered over me. Not when I wrapped my legs around him. And certainly not when he pushed inside. Slowly, inch by inch. I wanted fast but was powerless to do anything but feel.

Once fully seated, he brushed my hair off my sweaty forehead. "Beautiful," he signed.

"Of course I'm beautiful. You're in me."

He shut me up with a thrust of his hips, claiming my lips once again. I scraped my nails up and down his back as I moved with him, in and out, wanting it faster and, at the same time, to never end.

The pressure built as we continued moving. Dev hitched my leg higher, shifted his angle, and everything in me burst. Sparks of light dotted my closed eyelids as I felt every little twitch of him fueling me over and over.

I dug my nails into his ass, needing him with me. It worked. He thrust one last time before burying his head in my shoulder. Our breaths battled and my head swam, because that was amazing.

Dev picked up his head. "No going back after that."

I smiled and shook my head, because there wasn't.

"You OK?"

"What do you think?"

He checked out our still-connected bodies. "I hope so."

I laughed, and he pulled out, disposing of the condom before climbing back into bed beside me. I snuggled in, the friends barrier no longer between us. I hadn't thought of it holding us back before. But Dev's arms like this were so much better.

My wrist shifted, reminding me of the bandages. "We've got to get these off." I hopped out of bed and reached for some clothes.

"I can distract you again."

I looked at his groin, expecting it to be less happy than before. It wasn't. I raised my eyebrows. No. Tattoo. "Prove it to me later. Get dressed."

He got up and wrapped his arms around me from behind, kissing the spot where my shoulder met my neck. Then he pulled on some clothes. We'd changed things. I could only pray it wouldn't backfire.

Chapter Twenty-Four

Devon

JAS STARED AT her wrist as I finished applying cream to my skin. She caught my eyes in the mirror. "I can't believe we did this."

I held up my wrist, black yang outline, white filling, black circle. "We've proved it doesn't wash off."

Jas laughed, then held our wrists together, uniting the yin-yang symbol. Hers had been bandaged while mine was being done, so we hadn't seen them together until now. Somehow, the lines matched up, the two symbols belonging together.

Like Jas and me. We both took in our wrists for longer than necessary, the connection an escalation to our already escalating relationship. I wouldn't have it any other way.

"Wow," Jas signed, dropping her wrist to her side.

"Don't freak out on me now." I saw it brewing. Maybe this was the real reason why Jas and I had remained friends only for so long; our change came with a lot of baggage. We could never be two people casually dating. Our bond catapulted us to a serious relationship at the start.

She glanced at her wrist. "Too late, right? I can't afford to have it removed." She bit her lip, but I wasn't touching this one. I paid for the tattoos. My idea, my money. She needed her savings more than I did. It was the way things worked between us. Jas paid when she could, and I took care of the rest.

Our new relationship should've made it easier, but Jas wasn't one who assumed a guy would pay for her. I grasped her hand and tugged until her balance sent her into me. I ran my fingers over her smooth cheek, then my thumb over her tempting bottom lip. She opened up and bit me, not enough to hurt, but enough that I wanted more.

I claimed her lips with my own, noting another difference as my hands wandered over her body. A new closeness existed after having sex, after knowing a body intimately. Distance and barriers were no longer needed, not with my hands on her ass, pressing her into me.

Of course, there were still a few things left to explore.

I nudged her until she sat on the counter, then settled myself between her legs. All the while our lips clung. Here was Jas, available to my touch. I cupped her breasts, molding my hand to the weight and size of her. A perfect fit. Granted, I had never been picky. I liked a wide variety of boobs. But hers, hers were made for me. I ran my thumbs over her nipples, brushing against her hard points. She had fueled my fantasies for years, but nothing compared to the woman squirming against me. Everything about her blew my fantasies to shit.

She broke the kiss, breathing heavily. I continued down her neck, moving one hand to skim down her body and into her pants. Jas gasped as I slid into her wet warmth, and I was glad I still had my hearing aids on. Before, I couldn't hear anything beyond the whooshing of blood leaving my head. Now I heard a little high-pitched rumble of noise from her.

I picked my head up. "I haven't heard your voice since fifth grade." An occasional laugh, sure, but otherwise she kept her voice off.

Her hand left my back and went to her throat. "Really?"

I nibbled at her neck. She made another squeak. "No one's ever told you that you make noise?"

"You're the only one with some hearing who knows ASL."

I shook my head. We weren't going there, not with my hand in her pants. We knew enough about each other's pasts, no need to rehash it. "Let's see what other noises you make."

Before I could do anything, she plucked my aids from my ears and placed them on the counter. "Now you're deaf, same as me."

I hooked my fingers inside her and grazed her neck again. She made more noise, the vibrations rumbling through her body. "Can still hear you." I removed my coated fingers and licked them. I needed more of her. "Taste you too. Take off your pants."

"Bossy." But she did as I asked.

I positioned her on the counter and knelt, pressing kisses to her inner thighs. She gripped my hair. I set my mouth on her and licked, loving her taste in my mouth, the way she squirmed against me, and the soft murmurs from her.

Which meant she was actually rather loud. With any luck Blake wasn't home.

I continued until she shook, until her hand tightened then released and her body relaxed against the mirror. I slowed down, kissed her thigh again, and stood.

Her chest rose and fell in fast spurts. "You need a license for that thing."

"All yours now." Perhaps that revealed a bit too much, but I hated there to be any secrets between us. Especially when our current relationship proved this one secret might not have been needed.

She pointed to where I strained against my jeans. "Lose the pants."

I patted my pockets. "I don't have a condom."

Her lips curved to Cheshire level. "You don't need one." Those eyes promised naughty things, and I nearly lost it in my pants like I was much younger.

I shucked my jeans. I hadn't bothered with boxers. Jas licked her lips as I twitched in anticipation, which just expanded her grin.

She slid off the counter pantsless, and knelt in front of me this time. Before I could fix my stance, her lips wrapped around me, all warm, wet mouth. She sucked me right in, and I had to lean forward and brace myself on the counter. I did not want to think where she learned that.

I watched as she continued to suck and lick. Most of my view was her wild hair, but I got some glimpses of myself going into her mouth, and it was just about the best thing I'd seen.

She picked up her pace, and I had to brace a second hand on the counter. Tingling started at the base of my balls. I tapped her shoulder to warn her, but she brushed me off, increased her suction, and had me coming right into her mouth.

Hottest fucking thing ever.

Jas let me go and leaned back against the counter, grinning like she had won a prize. I was pretty sure my smile matched hers.

IN ALL THE times Jas had shared my bed, I'd never woken up spooning her. Granted, we'd never been naked, and we both needed to keep our tattoos from sticking to fabric.

Our tats were almost lined up in this position, even if in the reverse order. Never thought I'd be a branding guy, but I was. I'd claimed Jas once and for all.

And I really needed my head on straight. We'd just started dating, and my brain wanted to skip down the path toward the future. I needed to chill and have a good round with a punching bag. Jas was a here-and-now type of person. If I started talking about the future, I'd scare her off. Best to give her time and space to come to the same conclusions on her own.

I slipped out of bed and got ready for the day. In the kitchen, I found Blake and his usual morning setup: coffee and a book. He looked up when I approached. "I guess taking it slow with Jasmine is out the window?"

Shit. He was home. "Sorry if we were too loud."

Blake laughed. "You showed her a good time. I'm impressed."

I rubbed the back of my neck. Blake stopped laughing. "What's on your wrist?"

I held it out to him. His eyes grew wide and then searched my face. "Tell me this is not a tattoo?"

"Fine, I won't tell you." I moved to grab the matzo box, purposely ignoring the still-full bag of bagels, but Blake grabbed my arm.

"I can't believe you did that."

"Why not? It's my body."

"How many professionals do you know with visible tattoos?"

Many probably had them, but the statement still gave me pause. I hadn't given one damn about the practicalities of having a tattoo. Mine could be easily covered by a long-sleeved shirt once it healed, but that also meant I'd be stuck in long-sleeved shirts in a professional environment.

How could I have been so careless? Pete was a hands-on factory-type guy—tattoos worked for him. Jas in a bar would be fine. But me, maybe not so fine.

Then I thought of my volunteer job and the relaxed environment. As far as I knew, no one there had a visible tattoo, but they didn't seem like the type to care about a simple yang symbol. "I'm sure it'll be fine."

"Dad's going to flip." Yet Blake continued to eye my tat.

"Same as any day." I wouldn't be able to hide this from him, not unless I magically hid my wrist or didn't go to work for a few weeks.

"Why half a yin yang?"

"Jasmine has the other half."

Blake leaned back in his chair, the front legs leaving the floor. "Really?"

"Yes, really."

"That's huge! You just started dating and already have matching tattoos."

"We're not temporary."

His chair returned to all four legs with a bang. "She doesn't have a long-term plan."

"You mean her bar?"

"I mean where she's living. She's welcome here, but nothing has been established. Right now, she's just staying and you're footing the bill. That's not her or you."

I fell back into a chair. Blake was right, of course he was right. I ran on the assumption that Jas was with me and everything was fine. But I knew that while she might be okay for now, soon the gears would click and she'd need to establish something.

Not what I wanted. I had been so focused on our relationship that I hadn't focused on her stability. And now I had more than likely fucked it all up.

"Shit, she's going to think I'm giving her a handout."

"Does she want one?"

I glared at him.

"Wait before you react. She's been taking care of herself since her mom checked out. Maybe it would be a good thing to be taken care of for a change?"

I shook my head. "She doesn't want that. She'll freak out." Even if I wanted that. That was all I ever really wanted—to take care of her.

"Then you need to have a conversation with her. Figure out where she plans on living and how." Blake rubbed his neck. "You might need a new roommate, anyways. Since Shawn's met Mom and Dad, he wants me to move in."

"That's great." I expected Blake to smile, but the only tilt to his mouth was a nervous one. "Aren't you excited?"

Blake sat up straighter. "To live with Shawn? Of course. But…"

In the silence, I figured out the problem. "Have you talked with Dad?"

"Not yet. But soon."

Yeah, soon; I knew that sentiment.

"You will talk with Jasmine, right?"

I nodded. "Yes, but I need to figure out how." Her upbringing made a discussion about any sort of living situation or money a trigger for her.

Blake stood. "Good luck." He patted my shoulder and rinsed his mug out.

Luck? What I needed was a time machine. Because this was a conversation we should've had before sex and matching tattoos.

Chapter Twenty-Five

Jasmine

I WOKE EARLY, a rare occurrence. In my defense, my wrist ached and had become plastered to the sheet. I pried it free and stared up at the ceiling, blinking in the bright light. The morning was somehow colder than the ones before—at least that's what I thought before shifting and having the cool sheets brush against my bare skin.

I curled into a ball, a sickeningly wide grin stretching my face. Sex with Dev, definitely something I should have considered long before now. Perhaps part of that was the whole best-friend thing. Even if the sex itself was new, we understood each other, could read one another. A bit of a well-oiled machine. In and out of bed.

And now I was warm instead of cold. I reached over to his bedside table and plucked my phone off the charger. I smiled at the text message notification. Dev couldn't even wait, could he?

But the text wasn't from him.

Mom: I'm going to need rehab.

Clothes, clothes would be good before dealing with this. Foolish, but there it was. I pulled on a tee shirt and jeans and settled back on the bed with my phone.

Me: I'm sorry.

I didn't expect an immediate response. I hadn't checked the time stamp. Mom could have sent that yesterday for all I knew.

Mom: I'm too young for rehab.

Young? Yes. Healthy enough? No. I took in a deep breath, not liking my next words but not having any other choice.

Me: Want me to visit?
Mom: Yes.
Me: Will you be nice?
Mom: Yes.
Me: I'll see you later.

Not how I wanted to spend my day before work, but somehow bits and pieces of the dutiful daughter remained.

I left Dev's room in a desperate need of caffeine. He sat at the table, his phone in front of him while he bit into a piece of jam-covered matzo. My unease left, and I wanted to laugh even as the sight warmed my insides.

He took another bite and made a face as the matzo broke into three pieces in his hand. I let the laugh free, and he turned, blue eyes locking in on me. "You think this is funny?" he signed with a piece of cracker stuck to the corner of his mouth.

I walked over and brushed the food away. "Little bit." I snatched a small broken piece and popped it in my mouth.

He leaned back and gestured to the bagel bag. "What? No bagel?"

"Oh, I plan on having one. I thought I'd be nice and wait until you leave." I flashed him my most innocent smile.

"Brat." Dev finished off the last piece and brought his plate to the sink. "I have to get going anyways. Enjoy your yeast." He bent and gave me a kiss. I'm sure he meant it to be quick, but I wrapped my arms around his neck and held on. Nothing like the taste of Dev first thing in the morning, mixed in with some sweet jam and a hint of coffee.

MOM GAVE ME her room number at the hospital, so I took the elevator up to the fifth floor and followed the colored dots down the long, sterile hallway. I had no clue what the dots referenced, and a part of me wanted to play hopscotch with them, but at least some color lightened up the gloom.

The room numbers led me past the nurses' desk to get to her room. Before I reached the open doorway, movement caught my attention. I turned to a not-so-pleasant-looking woman, mouth flapping my way.

I pointed to my ear and shook my head. Not-so-pleasant morphed into confusion. I gestured for writing, since clearly she meant to interrogate me.

She pulled a piece of paper from behind a tall shelf and placed it on top. I approached as she wrote.

Who are you here to see?

Didn't realize we needed to sign in. I took the pen.

Constance Helmsman. My mother.

The nurse introduced herself as the one on Mom's case and mentioned they were worried about her. I debated my next line but in the end knew I had to do it.

She's been battling depression since my dad died ten years ago. She's not in a good place.

The nurse nodded, and I prayed I hadn't made a mistake. Mom didn't need things to get worse, but I wanted something to become better for a change.

I entered her room. She lay as she had in the ER, eyes almost glazed over, staring at a television. I waved, and she looked my way. A small spark came to her eyes. I couldn't remember the last time she appeared happy to see me.

"You look so much like your father."

Maybe not so happy. Looking like Dad wasn't a good thing. "How are you feeling?"

She looked at the ceiling. "Awful. Pain. Can't move."

"I'm sorry."

I stood there in awkward silence. No clue what to sign.

"Can you fix the volume?" She pointed to the television. "I can't get it to work."

I looked at her. "You want your deaf daughter to adjust the sound?"

The barest hint of a smile crossed her lips. "I'll guide you."

I couldn't take my eyes off her to follow orders. She hadn't done shit for me in years, and yet the little girl inside me wanted to run over and wrap her arms around Mom.

I reached up, toggled the button up, then raised my thumb, "Up or down?" Only Mom didn't respond. Her eyes landed on my left wrist.

"What did you do?" A pained expression crossed her face, and I didn't think it had to do with her hip.

I looked at my wrist. "What do you mean?"

"When did you get a tattoo?"

Proof of how bad our relationship was: I could have told her I'd gotten it years ago, and she'd believe me. "Yesterday."

"Why?"

"Because I wanted one."

Mom blinked, her eyes suspiciously watery.

"Does it really upset you that I have a tattoo?"

"I never thought I'd see you with one. It's against our religion."

"What?"

"Why do you think they branded us in the Holocaust?"

I absorbed her words as a slow anger grew in my gut. "How was I supposed to know this?" I signed large and forceful. "You've taught me nothing of my religion. Nothing. And you expect me to know this?"

"I never thought..." Her hands fell back to her side.

"You never taught. You stopped everything when Dad died." Tears threatened to form in my eyes. I backed up. I had more to sign, but words wouldn't come. Only hurt. Only anger.

She didn't move her hands. I didn't move mine. The fragile bridge connecting us dismantled. I turned and left, following the blue dots back to the corridor. Once there, I leaned against a wall, trying to swallow my anger and tears.

I looked at my tattoo, resisted the urge to brush my thumb against it. Last night, I loved everything about it. Today, it was an unforeseen complication in my life.

So much for spontaneity.

AFTER I LEFT Mom, I sat in my car with the engine off, since I didn't dare waste any gas. With the sun setting, there wasn't much warmth. At least I wasn't in my bar clothes yet.

I needed a moment to digest what Mom had told me and decide what I wanted to do about it. Well, that wasn't exactly true; the tattoo was permanent. I couldn't change it easily if I wanted to. The question was, would I have changed it if I'd known?

I rolled up my sleeve and looked at the dark ink. Less than a day with the tattoo, and already it was a part of me. Just like Dev. Maybe I would have done things differently with more knowledge. But I couldn't deny this was who I was now. And I kinda liked her.

My phone vibrated. I fixed my sleeve before accessing the screen.

Dev: Want dinner before work?

My stomach rumbled, reminding me I'd skipped lunch.

Me: What did you have in mind?
Dev: Where are you?
Me: Hospital, visited Mom.
Dev: You OK?

Proof of how well he knew me and my mother. She was the one hurt, and yet Dev knew the mental damage a few minutes with her could cause.

Me: I will be.
Dev: Meet me at the bar, then we'll grab something to eat.
Me: OK.

I turned the key, and my beat-up car stuttered to life. After giving it a few minutes to warm up, I headed to the bar. Dev was already there when I arrived, and I hurried through the cold breeze to get into his warm car.

Instead of shifting gears and driving off, he took my face in his hands, studying me, making my heart ache for his concern. One hand trailed down my cheek. "How are you doing?"

I shifted and buckled my seat belt. "I'm fine."

He didn't budge; only his eyes narrowed.

With a sigh, I settled against the seat. "Can we, for once in our lives, not talk about it?"

His lips curved. "You never want to talk about it."

"Fine. But please? I was having a good day. I want to go back to that."

Dev faced forward. "That I think I can do." He shifted into Drive, and for the next twenty minutes I relaxed, taking in the scenery. He gave me this time to be, without questions or pestering. I suspected it would stop soon but took in the peace while I could.

I didn't expect him to pull up to a park and shut off the car.

"What the fuck? Where are we going to eat?" A few houses were nearby, maybe a restaurant, but there was no obvious reason to park here.

Dev reached into the back and pulled out a large paper bag and a blanket.

"It's barely forty degrees outside."

He reached back again and grabbed a portable space heater.

"Are you thinking clearly?"

He leaned forward and claimed my lips, making me forget about his crazy plan. "Maybe," he signed, more of a gesture with both hands full. Then he got out of the car.

I followed, stomping and waving until he looked my way. "It's not picnic weather!"

"Live a little."

"Not having heat means I'm having a bad day."

Dev dropped the bag and blanket in a patch of grass that clearly stated spring wasn't quite upon us. "I'll keep you warm." He opened the bag. "I have Chinese."

I kicked at a patch of dirt but joined him on the blanket, fixing my trench to try to cut the chill. Dev set up the heater, and a minute later hot air fought back the cold breeze. He handed me the box of lo mein.

"OK, maybe this isn't so bad." I dug my fork in and twirled.

Dev stabbed at some chicken. "That's high praise, coming from you."

I pushed his shoulder, and he laughed. And even though I didn't have a home and Mom was upset with me, I felt good. "So this is how Devon Walker dates?"

He shifted until our legs touched. "As my best friend, I think you know the answer to that."

I shook my head and shoved some food in my mouth before signing. "No. Only secondhand information. What you or your dates have been willing to share."

He put the chicken down. "None of those girls have been you."

"I'm well aware of that."

He shook his head. "I mean, they didn't mean what this does." His face held such a serious expression that I had trouble swallowing.

"And what's that?" Not my best move leading with that. I wiped my hands over an imaginary slate. "Never mind. Forget about that. I really don't want to know." I reached for the chicken, but he stopped me.

"Are you really afraid of me answering that?"

I looked at my wrist and the imaginary watch. "We've been on one date. And I know sex doesn't bring out the commitment freak inside you."

"So the answer is yes."

I glanced up at the darkening sky and let out a laugh. "Do us both a favor, and don't do anything differently because we know each other so well. I need a little fun in my life. Be that person." I didn't give him a chance to rebuff me. I straddled his lap, running my fingers into his hair before bringing my mouth down to his.

Dev was going to stop me, the tension running through his body all the proof I needed. My lips stopped him. He crushed me to him, taking the kiss deeper, and I no longer cared about the cold wind outside of the heater's range.

He leaned back far enough to sign. "Is this going to be your new answer for everything you don't want to discuss?"

I glanced over his shoulder, pretending to give it some thought. "If it works? Yes."

His arms went around me again, but instead of feeling his lips against mine, I ended up flat on my back, the heater warming my side as Dev hovered over me. "You don't play fair."

I brushed a piece of hair out of his eyes. "Never have."

He lowered his head to mine, and I arched up to meet his lips. The food was probably getting cold, but I didn't care, not when I had him against me. I wanted more days like this. As much as I didn't want Dev talking about deep personal shit, I knew he'd do his best to give them to me.

His hands were in my hair, every inch of him pressed against me, holding me down and keeping me warm. I shifted my hips, rubbing against the bulge behind his fly. A rumble occurred in Dev's chest, and he licked into my mouth, taking our kiss darker.

Then his hands slid down to my hips. When he angled me into him, I had to break our kiss and gasp for air, not that I really cared about such a simple thing as breathing. He kissed a path down my neck, taking a nibble of my collarbone. I spread my legs to get better friction, friction I desperately needed, but my knee bumped into something.

The lo mein.

I nudged Dev off me and picked up what remained of my dinner. Not much had fallen, but still—lo mein.

"I see where your priorities lie," Dev teased from a sitting position.

I brushed the fork on a napkin and stuck it back in the container. "I never play games with food. I never know when I'm getting more."

Humor fell from his face. "You don't have to—"

I cut him off. "I know. But I also don't have a ton of time before I need to get to work." I shoved more in my mouth. Definitely cold. Still delicious.

Dev leaned forward and pressed a lingering kiss to my temple before gathering up his dinner.

"What was that for?" I asked.

"I figured you'd yell at me if I kissed your lips while you were eating."

I choked on a laugh and a noodle. "Smart man."

Chapter Twenty-Six

Devon

"WHERE ARE WE going? Don't you have class?" Jas asked as I turned off the car.

"I do have class. Later."

Jas rubbed her eyes. "You woke me up early. You better have a good reason."

I leaned across the console and kissed her. She may have been tired and cranky, but none of that registered on her lips. Of course, one kiss from her and my own plans faded from consideration. I had to force myself to pull away. "Come on."

I opened my door and stepped out into the morning air. Jas did the same, squinting at the store names. "Either you're way too early for pizza, which you still can't eat, or we're...painting?" Her eyebrows rose high.

"Pottery." I moved to enter the store, but she dug in her heels.

"Seriously?"

I turned to face her. "Yes. Seriously. You need fun and to have more belongings that can't be shoved in a bag in five seconds."

I waited, taking in her face for any hint as to what she was feeling. Jas was good at the blank face, at keeping even me out when she wanted to. One corner of her mouth curved, and she placed a hand on my cheek. "But I can just leave it with you." Then she left me to enter the pottery place.

I caught up with her inside, the smells of plaster and paint filling the air. "Only if you stay as well." I held her gaze, letting her know I was serious. I couldn't imagine life without her, not now that I had her.

She inhaled sharply. I waited for some confirmation. She took a step back. "So how does this work?"

Through gesturing, some writing, and some listening on my part, we worked with the staff and learned how to prep our pottery and the proper way to paint. Once we had the rules down, we browsed the many white ceramic options, ranging from dragons and princesses to dishware and vases, and many options in between.

I caught up with Jas taking a wine goblet down from a high shelf.

"The woman who doesn't drink wants to paint a wineglass?"

She placed it on a near shelf to sign. "I work in a bar."

"But what will you drink out of it?"

She eyed the pottery, a devilish grin curving her lips. "Soda. Maybe an ice cream float."

I swallowed my laughter, not wanting her to think I was laughing at her. I was constantly amused by who she was. I reached up and grabbed a second goblet. "Maybe I'll put beer in mine."

She collected hers in one hand. "Depends on what I decide to serve you." With a swish of blond curls, she sashayed over to a table. I stood there like an idiot, eyes on her hips as they swayed. I had the urge to come up behind her, bend her over, and…

I shook my head. Wrong place. Not somewhere that had tooth fairy boxes for little kids.

With one last glance around for another project that could grab me, I settled on the goblet. Something to match Jas's.

"What are you going to put on yours?" she asked when I joined her at the table.

I inspected the inspiration ideas on the walls, hoping for something to click. "Don't know."

We got up to examine the different stencil and stamp options. I rummaged through one bin, looking for anything since my artistic skills were not the best, and pulled out a yin-yang symbol. I held it up in Jas's view.

She tossed her head back and laughed. "What? The tattoo wasn't enough?"

I shrugged. "It could be our theme. We'll blame Nikki."

She studied the stencil, our goblets, and then the stencil again. "OK, I like it." Then she snatched the yin yang from my hands and headed back to the table. I collected black and white paints, but some color was needed. So I picked up two different greens, dark for me, teal for Jas.

When I placed the paints on the table, Jas nodded and grabbed the teal. "Good thinking."

We settled in, not signing as we began working. There were only two other people in the place, a mother and a young child. Otherwise it was empty.

Jas finished her first coat, then got up and returned with two more colors: purple and blue. I snatched the blue. "What's this for?"

She settled back down. "The inside. A little more color. Why come to a place like this and make something boring?"

I lost myself in her face, the one that held none of the stress it usually did. "To have fun?"

She glanced at the ceiling. "Fun? *Fun*...what a strange word. What does that mean?"

"I've failed you as a friend." I placed my elbows on the table and leaned forward. "I can make it up to you."

"While I agree that sex can be fun, I don't think that's appropriate here." She glanced at the little kid. "Don't want to corrupt the younger generation."

"Then it's a good thing our language is different."

"I don't know...some signs can be pretty graphic." Her eyebrows rose in a tease, and I knew I was in trouble.

"Then you'll have to be creative."

She snorted and turned back to her brush, meanwhile I had to shift and adjust myself. I was aroused while painting pottery. Never would've guessed that one.

When the base was finished, Jas snatched the stencil.

"What am I supposed to do?"

She lifted a shoulder. "Don't know. We can't share, not this way."

I got up and went searching for another, not missing the laughter that came from her. I suspected it was evil too. In the second bin I searched, I found another stencil, identical to the one she had claimed.

I waved it in front of her as I sat back down.

Her eyes narrowed. "Let's do this like our tattoos were done. Separately."

"But they might not match."

She picked up her goblet. "That's a risk I'm willing to take." Then she settled down at the next table, her back to me.

"Brat," I signed to her back. Then I pulled out my phone.

Me: I'm not responsible if this doesn't match up to whatever vision you have.

Jas: Think of it as a test. We're using the same stencil. How different will it look?

I stared at the back of her head, sensing there was a deeper meaning here, like the matzo challenge. I shook it off. Even if there was, she wasn't baiting me to be a mind reader. That wasn't who Jas was.

It took a little studying of the template, but eventually I knew what I wanted to do. I didn't want the symbol complete, because it wasn't on our wrists. But I also didn't want it to appear broken. Because we weren't. I made each part separated from its match, but still lined up and easy to visually put together. The white didn't go on as smoothly as the black did, hindsight and all that crap, but it looked like it might work.

I was finishing the last coat when my phone vibrated.

Jas: You done?

Me: Just about, give me a minute.

I rinsed out my brush and had to adjust to the room after staring at an up-close object for such a long time. When my eyes focused, I caught Jas watching.

"No cheating," I signed.

She picked up her wine goblet and set it down next to mine, lips pressed together. I took in hers, then mine, and caught the amusement in her eyes. We'd done the exact same thing.

"I think we've known each other too long," I signed.

Jas doubled over in laughter and fell into the chair next to me. "You think?"

I slid my fingers between her hair and neck in order to tug her toward me. Her lips met mine. We belonged together, like the yin yang, like the goblets we'd made. We matched. And that was my only excuse for what I signed next.

"You're planning on living with me, right? I'd hate to separate the wine goblets."

Jas pulled back with a jerk. "We just started dating."

I eyed the matching pieces of ceramic. "I think we know each other quite well."

She shook her head, then got up to return her paints. I stayed where I was, noting the tension in her shoulders, and wanted to kick myself. *Way to go, Dev.*

"I'm sorry. Forget it. You know you can stay as long as you like."

"No, you're right. I should probably look for my own place anyways."

"Stop that. What's so wrong with staying with me?"

"I'm not a charity project. I'm not another little thing you can help rather than help yourself."

I balled up my hands. Low blow, but I deserved it. "I know that. But I happen to like you sharing my bed." Jas shifted as though to turn, and I caught her wrist. "That came out wrong."

"No. You're right." She glanced around, clearly looking for an escape. "Don't you have a class to get to?"

Like I gave a shit about my classes right now. "Let me explain."

She shook her head, her eyes glassy and causing my gut to clench. "No. I need to figure things out for myself. As I always do." She collected her jacket and left.

I prayed she wouldn't try walking off as I gathered up our projects and brought them to the front to pay and find out the schedule for them to be fired and ready. By the time I made it outside, she was standing by my car. I wanted to gather her in my arms, tell her to forget everything. I almost did, until she sent me a look that froze my balls.

Jas was going to need some time before she'd listen to me.

Chapter Twenty-Seven

Jasmine

WHAT WAS I going to do with a painted wine goblet?

Not that it was bad to have nice things—I couldn't wait to have it finished and glazed and filled with a drink—but I still had nowhere to put it.

I walked through Dev's kitchen. He'd already left for class, and I had the place to myself. I could all but see both of our goblets sitting side by side on a shelf. The thought tugged at my heartstrings, and I couldn't figure out if it was because living here was temporary or because I wanted to gaze at the goblets and know they represented home.

Didn't matter. I wasn't one to mooch, and I'd been here long enough. I settled on the couch and pulled out my phone to check on apartment listings. Craigslist was out after my last experience, but everything else was more than double the cost. My entire check would go toward my living arrangements, giving me nothing to put aside for savings.

Story of my life. Nothing went my way, ever.

I closed my eyes and leaned back against the cushion, wishing to go back to childhood. Before housing even became an issue. I'd been worried about my living arrangements for nearly a decade. It was tiring and frustrating and not fair. Why couldn't I stay here, with Dev? Why couldn't I accept what I knew he'd give me?

Life.

Every time I let down my guard, got too comfortable, something else happened to mess it up. I knew Dev wouldn't hurt me, not on purpose, but I also knew I couldn't tempt fate or I'd be back on my ass for who knew what reason.

I checked the listings a second time. Dev might be the mathematician out of the two of us, but even I knew living alone was a lose-lose situation. The balance of income and expenses meant I'd need to utilize my savings, not increase it, and once that ran out, I'd be screwed.

Unless I stayed.

I sent a text to Nikki.

Me: How soon after dating someone would you consider living with them?

Nikki: Me? No clue, haven't dated anyone I'd consider placing my toothbrush next to. But you're not asking about me. You're referring to the person you're currently living with.

I threw my head back against the cushions, only moving it when my phone vibrated again.

Nikki: And you two know each other better than anyone I've dated. What's the problem?
Me: Hello? He'd be supporting me.
Nikki: Good, let his little helper complex have an outlet. You know you keep him from bugging the rest of us, right?
Me: You could take on some of that and give me a breather.
Nikki: You love it and you know it so stop complaining.

I took a deep breath and typed the next part with my eyes closed.

Me: And what happens when it crashes and burns?
Nikki: You fight it out, make up, and keep going.
Nikki: Dev isn't your parents. He won't let you down.

I wanted to believe that, but rooted deep in my subconscious lived a little girl who, no matter what she did, could never get her parents back. I feared I'd ruin us if I stayed.

I hadn't messaged him by the time I made it to work. And he hadn't messaged me. I wasn't strong enough to bring this up on my own, too afraid of where the pieces would fall. That didn't stop me from checking for him each time the door opened. I knew he'd show up sooner or later, and like a middle schooler with a crush, I kept checking. Even though I'd just tell him to go home.

It took an hour, but he arrived. I stood by a table, some chick getting a kick out of writing on my board. My eyes locked on Dev. I thought for sure he'd get some sort of thrill out of the position I was in. He never took in the table or anything below my neck, only my face.

My traitorous body warmed up a few degrees.

My customers finished, and I headed to the bar to drop off my orders, only to find Len MIA. Again. I wanted to tell Dev to leave, but the words wouldn't come. Or maybe I didn't want to sign them.

Before I could slip behind the bar, he grasped my elbow. His short sleeves showed off his tat, which hit me with an influx of emotions.

If I drank, now would be the time to drown myself for some serenity.

"I'm working," I signed.

He looked around the place. We had two tables and three people at the bar—that was it. "They can wait." Even with all my walls and back-off vibe in place, Dev wrapped his arms around me, held me tight. My eyes stung, and I blinked to keep them clear.

I kept my hands at my side, and eventually Dev pulled away. "I'm not stopping until you hug me."

I rolled my eyes but put my arms around him. The feel of him seeped through all my defenses, as he damn well knew it would. Instead of letting him go, I pressed in further, breathed him in. Accepted one moment of him before pulling back. "I looked up apartment listings today."

"You don't have to leave."

I couldn't, really. Life didn't give me options. "Maybe it would be better." I cursed myself. I had my answer and still couldn't share it, couldn't put myself out there.

He banged on the bar top, and I closed my eyes, feeling everyone in the bar looking our way. When I opened them, he was ready to pounce. "Bullshit. You're scared. Of us. Of needing help."

"I don't need anything."

"We all need something."

I swallowed, but my throat was dry. I rounded the bar and blindly went about creating a drink that no one had ordered. When I was finished, I set it down and backed away until I bumped into the wall where all the alcohol was kept.

I hadn't made it just to make something. I'd made it for me.

Dev studied me, but he didn't need any explanation. He knew. He leaned over the bar and plucked the drink out of my reach. "What you need does not involve alcohol. It involves people. And you've shut them out for ten years."

I shook my head. “I don’t—”

He held up a hand. “It’s true. I think I’m in a position to know this better than you. Name one friend you have that you met after your dad died.”

My world was small. I kept it small. Dev, Nikki, Pete. And we’d been friends since elementary school. “Maybe you three are already too much to handle.”

“Or maybe…” He trailed off. “Maybe you’ve lost so much you’re too afraid of losing more.” He reached out, brushed a hand just under my tattoo. “I don’t know how else to prove it to you.”

I caught shifting at one of the tables and grabbed my tray, not explaining to Dev what I was doing. I didn’t know which end was up or which end I wanted to be up. The only thing I knew was that I really wanted that drink.

Chapter Twenty-Eight

Devon

I KEPT MY eyes on Jasmine. Her stiff shoulders were the only indication a war raged inside her. She needed this, needed to break through these issues holding her back.

The timing sucked.

I fiddled with my phone but didn't dare drag Pete and Nikki into this. This was our battle.

I picked up her drink, letting the liquid swirl around. I had always supported her decision not to drink and thought it was precautionary if not odd.

The look in her eyes said otherwise.

For the first time, I got it, truly got it. If she kept her distance, she'd be fine. This was her world as she wanted it. As long as what happened tonight didn't repeat.

I took a sip and nearly sputtered. It was some of the strongest shit I'd ever tasted, like a messed-up Long Island iced tea. She would have been drunk halfway through.

Heck, I could be drunk halfway through. I put it aside, leaned back against the bar, and couldn't find Jas. Len was missing, and she had disappeared. I was about to get up to check the back room when she returned to the area, her tough-girl exterior shaken up. To everyone else, she looked normal. A bit frazzled, sure, the frizz to her hair adding to the effect. But others wouldn't see the vulnerability glistening in her eyes or catch the way her fingers brushed at her thighs. I did. And I knew she could mask even that much unless she wanted me to see.

She came right over to me and put her head on my shoulder. I breathed out, as if I had been holding it, and wrapped her close. I wanted to thank some higher power that she still came to me, because I was not ready to lose her. I'd never be ready.

She pulled back, eyes on my drink. Her hands shook when she signed. "I can't believe I did that."

I squeezed her shoulder. Signed nothing.

"That's strong. Don't drink it."

"I have a few more sips before you have to drive me home."

A light laugh came to her lips and vanished. "I should find my own place."

"You won't be my roommate when Blake moves out?"

"Seriously? They're making it official?"

I nodded, and Jas's smile fell.

"I can't afford his rent. I can't afford any rent."

"We can find a small one-bedroom somewhere."

Her eyes opened wide, and she stepped out of my grasp. "We've been dating for less than a week, and you want to live with me?"

"I've wanted to live with my best friend for years. Now we don't need a second room."

The door opened, and a new crowd came in. "I have to work."

"I'm not leaving without you."

She hesitated but nodded. I relaxed against the bar. Took another sip of my drink that burned a hole straight through my stomach, then pushed it aside. That drink needed a label: *drunk in one gulp.*

Before things went any further, we needed to solve her living situation. She could contribute to my part of the rent, that would be no problem, maybe split a utility bill. But Jas was used to living on her own.

I thought of my volunteer job. This was the type of situation they helped with. A problem arose, like housing, and options were researched and presented. I wanted Jas with me, yes, but I could research her options, let her decide what was best for her.

She tried to ignore me, but the bar remained slow, and even doing both waitress and bartender duties didn't save her from me. Therefore she cleaned. And when that failed, she finally came over.

"How bad?" She pointed to the drink, about a fourth gone. She hadn't offered me anything else, but I suspected that was due more to her head not being in the game.

"Strong."

She eyed the drink as if it had challenged her to a duel. "I need to know how bad." She took the drink, brought it to her lips, and took the smallest sip ever. Her eyes grew wide, and she pulled it away. "Wow."

She turned and poured it down the sink. "And you drank some of that?"

I held my hands out to the empty area in front of me. "That's all you gave me."

She shook her head and leaned forward, resting it on the counter. I smoothed down her hair, anything to touch her.

Jas stood up. "I'm sorry. You want a drink?"

"I'm fine."

She nodded, then left to do more unnecessary work. On nights like this, I usually stayed as her support. Tonight I wasn't helping her. For all the benefits of us dating, there were some things friends could do that boyfriends couldn't. Therefore I forced her to look at me when she came back around. "Are you coming home with me tonight? Yes or no?"

This should have been one of those no-brainer questions. It wasn't.

She took her time, nibbling her lip before nodding.

I got up. "I'll see you there. You can have the bed."

A small smile lit her face. "Funny, like we can stay apart."

Once home, I paced the damn apartment, waiting. I couldn't sit, couldn't watch a movie or play a game. Nothing. I needed to be active. I grabbed my loop headset and phone and headed down into the basement.

The small room held a washer and dryer for the building, and someone had hung a punching bag in the corner. I felt the machines and checked the dials, but nothing was in use. Which meant unless someone wanted to start their laundry at eleven at night, I had the place to myself.

I switched my hearing aids onto the t-coil mode, the slight rumbling of pipes or just mechanical shit fading to a light buzzing noise. I slipped the loop around my neck and plugged it into my phone. Then I scrolled through my music until I found some heavy metal.

When I pressed Play, the sound traveled up to my aids. I toggled it up to a level Blake once called *deaf* when I forgot to plug my headset in. Then we both laughed, because yeah, it was deaf level.

Anything less was nonexistent.

I shoved my phone in my pocket, then rotated my shoulders and swung my arms. I approached the bag and imagined transferring all the stress weighing me down. Fists up, we studied each other.

Then I swung.

Right, then left. Left ached a bit due to shifting skin near the tattoo, so I began a one-two-three, leading with my right.

I punched until my fists hurt, until my breath came in fast spurts. My shirt clung to my back and chest from sweat. I pried it from my skin and yanked it over my head, then kept going, needing a release that wouldn't come.

I wanted Jas safe and happy and feared I'd only fuck it up.

I knew her better than anyone else, yet I still didn't know how to be what she needed. It all boiled down to one word: help. My desire to help her would always be in conflict with her desire to not accept it from anyone else. She'd interpret my help as control, not realizing my true intentions were her happiness.

If she never accepted help, she'd never be part of a team. And even though she carried the loner vibe to her core, she wanted a family—one I'd given her willingly long before her father died.

Someone touched my shoulder. I grabbed the bag, steadying its movement, and turned. Jas stood there, taking in my bare chest with a secret little smile. I hadn't told her where I was, but she'd found me. She wore her bar clothes, nothing else, so she'd been to the apartment.

The relief I couldn't get hit me like a one-two punch.

"Bad day?" she signed.

I clenched and released my sore fists. "Something like that."

She approached the bag, running a hand down the material. The blood coursing through me from the activity all ran south. "You know, I've seen you do this before but never tried myself."

"It's fun."

She eyed me, then the bag. "What do I do?"

"Punch it."

"That's it."

I shrugged. "Yes."

She faced the bag. Sized it up and pulled one arm back, then tapped it. The bag barely shifted.

I flicked my hearing aids back to regular to stop the music, removing the cord headset around my neck and shoving it into my pocket. Then I came up beside her. "*This* represents all the shit going on in your life. You don't tap it. You punch the hell out of it." I moved behind her, picked up her wrist, and rammed it into the bag.

When I stepped back, Jas shook out her hands, studied the bag, then balled up her fists and flung. The bag jerked. She glanced at me.

"Nice. Again."

Determination crossed her brow. She went at it again. And again. And again. Getting into it and looking sexy as hell in her skimpy outfit and high-heeled boots.

I grabbed the bag and stopped her before she hurt herself. Before I could sign anything, she wrapped her arms around me, her lips devouring my mouth.

My hands curled into her hips as I took the kiss deeper, darker. So much had happened since our last kiss, and it hadn't been that long. She could be upstairs, locking me out of my room. Instead she was here, rubbing her body against mine, driving me out of my goddamn mind.

I broke the kiss. "Let's go upstairs."

She glanced behind her at the closed door, then back at me with her eyebrows twitching. Her lips grazed my chin and neck before I pulled back.

"Upstairs."

She reached into the front of her tube top and pulled out a condom.

I checked the door. It was locked. "You sure you're thinking clearly?"

"No!" She flung her hands out. "I'm not thinking clearly. Everything in my life is upside down. I have no home. I'm dating my best friend. Now, make me feel good."

I kissed her. Short and sweet, but she ratcheted up the volume, pulling me under into a drug-induced haze in mere seconds. I backed her up to the washer or dryer, I wasn't really sure which. She scooted back, and that short skirt did nothing to hide that I was a dead man the moment she'd walked into the room; she wasn't wearing underwear.

"You trying to kill me?"

She squirmed, her skirt shifting up higher, and I nearly missed her signs. "Maybe." She placed the condom beside her and folded her top down, exposing two perfect breasts.

I took in all of her. Her skirt and top both bunched around her waist. The erotic visual of her, like this, on the washer. Legs spread and body arched in complete invitation. I was going to die a very happy man. I claimed her mouth with my own as one hand caressed her nipple. Her hands went to my pants, and two seconds later they were around my ankles, and her hand was on me.

Control shattered. I would have slowed down, but then my hand trailed up her inner thigh to find her wet and ready. My fingers slid around and pushed easily inside, her muscles contracting against me. A high-pitched moan hit my ears as she pressed into my hand, and for one moment, I had her. I gave, and she received. Then she took the reins and ripped open the condom with a little hum that made me even harder before sliding the condom down my throbbing erection, one slow inch at a time that had me ready to burst.

I shifted her forward and pushed inside in one hard thrust. Too fast. I focused on her face, ready to apologize, but her eyes were closed, her mouth half open, and every inch of her screamed pleasure.

When I didn't move, she popped open an eye, sent me one devil of a smile, and squirmed against me. "Fast?" I asked.

"And hard." She hooked her ankle against my lower back.

I gave in. Fast and hard thrusts that she met with her own, fueling a euphoria like no other. I wouldn't last long, but she already trembled in my arms and clenched around my dick. I wanted to feel her without that latex barrier.

One day. If I was a lucky man.

For now, I brushed my tongue against hers, rubbed a nipple, helped prolong her enjoyment as much as possible, until I lost it. I stood there in her arms, spent and mostly naked in the laundry room.

I picked my head up to find Jas wearing a large grin. "I needed that."

I kissed her before pulling out. "Good." I disposed of the condom in the trash, hating that I needed to bring shit back up. "We need to talk about things."

She nodded. "Not tonight. I've hit my limit for the day." She hopped down and fixed her skirt and top.

"Tomorrow," I agreed. Words threatened to break free, words she deserved to see. But until things were settled between us, I didn't dare.

I DIDN'T WAKE Jas in the morning, so we didn't talk. Which was fine, I didn't want to start the day with that shit and then have to go our separate ways. I went to class, then to my volunteer job. Jas and housing weighed heavily on my mind, to the point where I snagged Katherine when I found her alone.

"Can I ask you a question?" I asked.

"Of course."

"Remember my friend with the eviction notice? She lost her housing and can't afford much. What do you suggest she do?"

She frowned. "That was fast. Doesn't sound right."

"It's not."

"I have a homeless client coming in fifteen minutes. Why don't you observe?"

"You sure?" Since my internship, I'd sat in on a random appointment here and there, but mostly I helped with paperwork and other stuff.

She nodded. "What happened to your friend?"

"They changed her locks."

"They can't do that."

"She didn't have a contract."

"Doesn't matter. She can fight them if she wants to. You could refer her to the pro bono lawyer place we use, see if they'll help."

My instinct did not want to go this route. But was that what Jas would want, or me?

Katherine's gaze shifted to my wrist. "That's cool. Is that part of a yin yang?"

I breathed a little easier. She wasn't upset. "Yes." I held out my wrist, and she examined it.

"New?"

"Yes."

"I heard they hurt."

I finger-spelled yes for emphasis.

"You know, I have a client who wants one. I could use your advice."

Pete was the expert, not me, but I could always ask him what I didn't know.

We chatted for a few minutes before her appointment joined us. I took mental notes as Katherine went over his options. Shelter—no way was Jas going there. Craigslist—that hadn't done her any good in the past. And subsidized housing—waiting list, would take time.

Mostly I studied how Katherine interacted. No blame, just facts and options. Deep in my gut, I felt myself sitting in her seat, dealing with my own clients in a similar gentle manner. This was the right path for me, and I knew I could do it.

One way or another, I had to talk to Dad.

Chapter Twenty-Nine

Jasmine

THE PROBLEM WITH difficult conversations was that they were easier to push off and harder to have hanging over your head. I woke up with a weight on my shoulders, one I had hoped the sex would eradicate.

It hadn't. Not even the second time, slow, in Dev's bed.

I needed a plan, a goal, some way to figure my shit out. And yes, Dev wanted to have this conversation with me to help me. I needed to know what I wanted first.

But that was unknown. I'd been living day to day with saving money the only goal. And in that vein, saving money worked best if I lived with Dev.

As much as living with him felt good, I didn't want to live with him because I had to. I wanted to do it because I wanted to. Big difference.

Which was foolish. Why was it any different now that sex was involved? We should be closer than ever, not having to deal with all these new issues.

Tonight. We'd talk tonight. And between now and then, I needed to know what Jasmine Helmsman would do, Dev or no Dev.

I dressed in warm layers—one a sweatshirt of Dev's—and pulled on my trench. I needed some time to think and had a place I went to when life pushed me to my limits. The thirty-minute drive to the south shore alone gave me a little breathing room, as there was nothing but the road to deal with. I turned off the highway, down a residential street lined with trees, until I arrived at a large green area: the Jewish cemetery where my father's body lived. The place was huge, lots of lush green mounts with trees dispersed. If I went left, I'd find most of Mom's side of the family. If I went right, I'd find Dad and his. I assumed Mom would eventually be buried on this side, but I didn't know what her plans were.

With any luck, I wouldn't find out soon.

I followed the winding roads until I arrived at the large stone that reminded me of a nose. I parked along the side and walked down the grass. The headstones were part of the ground, nothing sticking up. If it wasn't for the markers, I'd never know where I was.

I passed my grandparents and turned at the tree, then headed to the shady spot where Dad lay. In the center the name Helmsman appeared in large letters, flanked on either side by Jewish stars. It listed Dad's details, including the words *Loving husband, father, son.*

I sat in front of him, brushing some scraps of grass off his plaque. "Hi." I felt silly signing to nothing, but I did it anyways. "Mom's in the hospital. She fell and broke her hip, but she'll be OK."

I fixed my trench when a breeze fluttered the ends. "I lost my apartment, but Devon let me stay with him." I smiled in spite of myself. "We're dating now, so it's complicated. And I need to find a new place or commit to being with him."

I looked up at the clear sky, shaking my head at myself. "I don't know what to do. I want a bar, but saving money and living seem to contradict each other. And I know I'm young, but there's been so much hurt and pain, and I want to settle down and be happy for a change. Is that really too much to ask? For a little happiness and stability in this awful life?"

With my hands out wide, tears streaked my cheeks. I really hated that I was suddenly crying at everything after crying at nothing for years. "The only stability I have is Devon, and now that's changed."

I looked at my wrist. Stability remained. Different, complicated, but there for the taking. I couldn't imagine life without him. When I was alone, he made me not alone.

"I should just live with him, shouldn't I? I mean, that's what you do when you love someone: you want to be with them. And when they're gone, it hurts like a bitch."

Mom loved Dad. I refused to turn into her if I ever lost Dev, but the thought of losing him permanently made giving up on everything seem warranted.

"What do you think? Should I stay on my own or move in with Devon?"

The trees rustled, but no answer came. No answer would. I'd done this before, sat here, asked Dad a question, hoping for some divine intervention to change my life. The answer wasn't going to come from him; it had to start with me.

And yet, being alone was overrated. I'd done that since I moved out of Mom's apartment at eighteen. And I hadn't enjoyed being "home" until this past week with Dev.

"Yes, I think I will live with him. He makes me happy." I glanced at my wrist. "Oh, and we got matching tattoos. Mom flipped. You probably would too."

With the breeze still rustling, though not as cool as before, I stood and brushed grass off my coat. "Thanks for the coat. It's awful at keeping me warm though. Didn't you freeze while wearing it?"

I stared down at him, a man I'd still have to look up to see if he lived. "I love you. I miss you. And one day, I will run a bar in a way that will make you proud."

I wrestled my phone from my back pocket, ready to text Dev and have this talk once and for all. Only there was a text waiting for me from Len. Another one telling me not to come into work tonight.

I understood the last time. And yeah, I had filled in for him the night before, but the bar was dead, it was a breeze. I wanted to question him, but he'd been so moody lately, he'd fire my ass.

I switched to my text thread with Dev.

Me: I'm off tonight. Plenty of time to talk.
Dev: I've got work, then I'm all yours.
Me: And if talk bad?
Dev: We'll figure it out. I'm not losing my yin.

My heart warmed even as the breeze cooled me. I wanted these types of conversations. Discussion about dinner and when we'd be home and who paid the electricity bill. It wouldn't be easy, but life rarely was.

THANKS TO TRAFFIC, Dev arrived home before I did. His homework was spread out before him on the table. He looked up, those light eyes striking against disheveled shaggy hair. For an awkward moment, we stared at each other. I didn't think either one of us even breathed. Before the tension mounted, I inhaled deeply. It broke the spell. I removed my coat and joined him at the table. Earlier I'd had all the answers, but now I hesitated. I had never hesitated with Dev before.

He held up a finger and took control. "Before we start, I learned about different housing options at my volunteer job today. Options that may help you."

Options. I figured out what I wanted, regardless of finances, and he gives me options. When I needed the man, he gave me the social worker. The straightness of his spine, the serious expression—he was in work mode. I didn't want work mode, I wanted him and his emotions.

"Your old landlord is in the wrong for changing your locks. You can fight them, maybe even get money from the situation."

On what planet would they owe me money? As tempting as this was, I doubted it would pan out.

"One, there are shelters, and shelters can give homeless certificates, but I don't like this option for you, so don't even think about it."

I rolled my eyes. So Dev's work mode blurred when it related to me.

"Two, subsidized housing. There are applications you can fill out, and your rent will be based on your income. Three, section eight for reduced rent, but I'm not sure this is any better than Craigslist, and that hasn't been good to you."

"Half of what you're telling me you don't want me to take." Social workers weren't supposed to be this personal. If I pointed it out, maybe he'd stop treating me like a client.

"I don't want you to take any of these. I'm letting you know what's available for you."

"Why?"

Dev rubbed his neck. His expression lost its serious edge, and his shoulders slouched back to normal. "How else am I supposed to help?"

Help. It always boiled down to help with him. "I don't know. You want me to stay with you, then you give me other options that involve me living elsewhere. How about you telling me what you want for a change?"

His chest was heaving as if he'd run a marathon. "What I want? I want you living with me. I thought I made that clear."

"Why?"

"Why?" he repeated. "Because I…" His hands, balled into fists, came close to crossing into the sign for love before they fell to his sides.

He froze. I froze. The unfinished sign hung between us, scary and wonderful and threatening to heal or destroy us. This was what I had wanted, even if he'd almost given me a boatload more than I'd expected. This wasn't the social worker talking; this was Dev, the man.

"Stop overthinking," Dev signed. "I know you caught that."

"Caught what?" I didn't give him a chance to respond; I just steamrolled forward. "We don't need to talk. I'll stay. There. Conversation finished."

"Are we ignoring that last slip?" I tried to overlook the sudden sadness in his eyes, but it was too damn hard not to.

"Yes. You don't commit."

"You ever ask why?"

No, he couldn't go there. I couldn't handle seeing any more of him exposed. I poked him in the chest. "Don't you dare pin your past failed relationships on me."

He shoved both hands into his hair, leaving the ends sticking out. "I'm not. That was my problem, because I was too much of a wimp to say anything to you. But if you don't feel the same…" His hands trailed off, and he shook his head. Then he leveled me with a piercing blue-eyed gaze. "No. I know you. We wouldn't be dating if you didn't feel something. Maybe I'm too early—"

"Of course you're too early. We just started dating. There isn't enough time—"

"And fifteen years of friendship means nothing?"

I tried to corral my breathing, but it was pointless at a time like this.

"What do you want? If there were no limits, no restrictions. What would Jasmine Helmsman want?"

Him. We were going around in circles when we both wanted the same thing. "This is scary."

"I'm not going anywhere." The sincerity of his words was written across his face and in his body language as he held his hands out to the side. I felt so much for this man, it ached.

"Do I drive you crazy?"

A small smile played at his lips. "All the time."

"Good. That makes two of us."

He crossed the room to me, tapped my forehead. "What's going on in here? You're keeping yourself hidden."

"I want to live with you. If you want—"

He collected my hands in his. "The offer is there, always there."

"I don't want a handout."

"I know. I think I can work out a deal." He leaned in and kissed my neck.

I grasped his hair and pulled his head up. "My part of the rent does not relate to sex."

He laughed. "Just whatever you paid at your last place. Blake and I have this covered. We'll figure things out when we move."

Move. Together. On purpose. A twinge traveled up my spine, and Dev rubbed my shoulder. "Don't worry about that yet. Blake still has to make it official with Shawn."

I relaxed. "We're in a real relationship, aren't we?"

He kissed my forehead. "We've always been real."

Chapter Thirty

Jasmine

THE SETTING SUN dotted the sky in purples and oranges as I made my way to the bar. I figured either the sight depicted a beautiful masterpiece or warned of an impending storm.

I parked my car in the empty lot, another slow night surely in my future. The wind chilled my bare legs as I hurried to the door, ready to get into the warm environment.

My fingers wrapped around the handle and pulled, my shoulder jerking when it didn't budge. I tried again. Nothing. A far-too-familiar déjà vu settled into my stomach as I cupped my hands and looked through the dirty side window.

The inside was dark. I made out a table, with the chairs turned upside down from closing. One thing was clear: no one was here.

Huddled into myself for warmth, I fumbled in my pocket for my phone and set up a text message for Len.

Me: I'm at work. You're not. What's up?

Waiting was pointless, so I hurried back to my car. At least the wind no longer added to the cold factor. My phone vibrated.

Len: The bar is closed.
Me: I got that. What's up?
Len: Closed. Finished. Done.

The words took time to fully sink into my veins, weighing me down like lead. My job, my livelihood, gone.

No. I wouldn't give up that quickly.

Me: I can run it.

I bit my lip as my pulse beat against my neck. He had to know I'd do a better job than he would.

Len: No.
Me: What do you have to lose? Give me a few days and then decide.
Len: No.

I gripped my phone, frustrated vibrations building in my chest. Responding was pointless. He wouldn't budge.

I tossed my phone on the passenger seat and banged my head on the steering wheel. For years I had searched for another job, unable to find one. It wouldn't be any different now that I was out of work.

I cranked the engine but didn't shift gears out of Park. I had no place else to go. Home. But now that Dev and I had finally worked things out, I wouldn't be able to contribute to the rent.

I refused to have him take care of me. I wasn't his problem. I was my own problem. There had to be another way. Maybe it was time to put this bar dream behind me. Clearly the universe was against me.

One thing remained certain: nothing good ever happened to Jasmine Helmsman.

I drove around aimlessly for a while, not ready to share this latest shit storm with anyone. Dev's words from the other day came to mind, about other housing options that didn't involve him. It physically hurt to contemplate them, but I was no one's burden.

An hour later I ended up back at the Walkers' apartment building. I parked but didn't get out of the car. Not yet. With any luck, Dev wouldn't be planning on visiting me at work. Although if he did, he'd save me any explanations.

I leaned back against the headrest. This sucked. Life sucked. Whenever something good came my way, something else got ripped away. I should have known better. Dev and I were friends. This relationship, this happy-couple shit that could morph into more, that wasn't who I was. My life showed me time and time again that happiness wasn't for me. And the harder I tried to hold onto it, the worse the situation became.

And my moping was making me sick. I needed to be strong and independent. But the only way out of the current arrangement would break my boyfriend's heart.

And mine, but this was my life. I became immune years ago.

My jumbled thoughts and emotions no longer made sense. And I was tired, so very, very tired. Maybe he wouldn't be home and I could curl up in his bed and will the world away.

Of course, his car parked not too far away killed that idea. Time to face him.

I didn't move.

I could drive around instead, maybe find a bar in need of help for the night, prove myself. But that was stupid, no one wanted a deaf cocktail waitress or bartender. And if they did, they wouldn't want me walking in off the street.

Still, I pulled out my phone, checked a few job listings. Two had potential, but one wanted phone calls only. The other had an email address, and I sent them a message.

It didn't feel right. Nothing felt right.

Time to wave the white flag. I clicked on my text folder and found Dev's thread.

Me: Change in plans. Another bar in my life has closed down.

Dev: You're shitting me?

Me: Would I joke about this?

Dev: Where are you?

I looked up at the building. I could see Blake's window from this angle, not Dev's.

Me: Parking lot.

My fingers hovered over the keys, wanting to tell him to leave me alone and let me handle this on my own. Instead I sent the text.

I didn't know which parking lot he thought I was in, but he found me five minutes later, his eyes so full of worry that I had the urge to crawl into him. But that was someone else's story, not mine.

"Come upstairs," he signed from two cars away.

"Why?" I couldn't stay in the car forever, but the minute I left, everything would become more real.

"So I can hold you."

Amid all the desire to flee and not be his burden, a hug sounded good. Damn good. By the time I collected my stuff and reached for my door, he was there, opening it from the other side. I stood, the cold air wrapping around me seconds before Dev did.

I buried into his shoulder, clutching his shirt. I was weak for him. Tough girl Jas was MIA.

In that moment, I didn't care.

He pulled back and brushed at my dry cheeks. "Come upstairs, it's cold."

That's when I noticed he didn't even have a jacket on. He wore short sleeves in thirty-degree weather and couldn't have known I was here and not still at the bar.

That did something funny to my insides. Not that I expected much different from Dev, but not even bothering with a jacket to get to me…

No, I couldn't go there. We were two separate people, end of story. Our yin-yang tattoos be damned.

In his apartment, he instructed me to sit on the couch, then went to the kitchen, opening cabinets and the refrigerator, before snatching something off the counter. "Want?" He held out the chocolate chip macaroons that I had completely forgotten about.

I held out my hands. "Gimme."

He tossed the package, and I had the first macaroon in my mouth before the cushion shifted from his weight. The coconut taste mixed in with chocolate, reminding me of my youth, of those happy Passover gatherings when everyone was still alive.

I handed the package to Dev, and he took a bite. "Not bad."

I leaned back against the couch, hugging the macaroons to my chest. Unable to shake the feeling my entire life was in quicksand.

Dev finished another macaroon and wiped his hands on his pants. "You want to have some fun or figure out a new game plan?"

Wallow. I wanted to wallow. I shrugged and stuffed my mouth with a macaroon.

"You're not getting any crazy ideas, right? You're staying. No question."

I nodded, hoping he wouldn't see the false emotion behind it. Truth was, I had no direction or plans. All I knew was that I needed to fight this latest battle on my own. As long as I remained responsible for only myself, I'd somehow find a way out.

Of course, I hadn't anticipated the hurt that thought would create while looking at him. I wanted to memorize him, from the shaggy hair, to the thick eyebrows, to those long eyelashes that made his blue eyes pop, to the tiny dip in his cheek that had come from a wrestling match with his brother.

I wasn't ready to lose this new bond between us. I needed a moment out of the quicksand, where nothing else mattered. No money or jobs or life. Just me and my yang.

I put the macaroons down and straddled him, sliding my body up next to his. He sucked in a breath, and I kissed him. His lips and tongue created that soothing excitement exclusive to him. And all my emotion boiled up and tumbled out, from my mouth to his, my heart to his.

His hands tightened around my waist as I fought against the emotional overload. At this moment, he was the quicksand, and I feared I'd never come out on top. I attempted to extricate myself from him, but his hands slipped under my shirt, brushed against my bare skin, and I was lost in him.

He gave what he took. Somehow in his lips and his hand sliding up to cup my breast, warmth not related to sex consumed me. I felt loved, accepted. I felt how much he wanted me.

But it had nothing to do with his hard length I rubbed against. This wasn't us having fun for the sake of having fun. This was us being close, connected, giving to each other.

I pulled back. Too much, and my body hated my movement. Dev grinned, that naughty grin that made me want to push his face into my chest, or lower. “Good idea. Blake could come home.” Then he swooped me into his arms and carried me into his room.

He carried me. That had never happened before. I kissed him before my eyes could tear up.

Something my father had told me resurfaced. “Love means taking care of another person. Not because they need it but because you want to.” Dev always took care of me. Even though that was him to the core, with me it was always about want, never need.

He laid me on his bed, covering my body with his. There was far too much emotion in every look, every touch. I couldn’t leave if I wanted to since Dev had my heart.

This was sweet lovemaking. I needed hard sex. I needed us to be downstairs in the laundry room again, banging on top of a machine. Anything to prevent this fall.

I flipped Dev over. None of my turmoil was on his face. “You want control?” Then he folded his hands behind his head.

I didn’t know if I could look at him. Maybe I needed a different position, one in which I wouldn’t be able to look at him and wouldn’t see how much he cared. But him beneath me, handing over all control, had both my heart and libido enraptured.

His shirt hit the floor. Followed by his pants. I wasted no time, desperate to get out of my head for five fucking minutes. I needed the passion, the all-consuming heat. I needed my brain powered down so I could feel without consequence. He was hard, gloriously so, and I couldn't help myself; I wrapped my lips around him, let his smooth skin slip back and forth between my lips.

His chest rose and fell with frequent breaths, eyes shut tight. This man could do things to me with hardly a glance. And as much as I loved tasting him, I needed mindless, and I needed it now.

I released him and practically tore my bar clothes off, then grabbed the condom. I licked my lips as he rolled the latex down his length, already envisioning how it would feel when he plunged into me. The moment he finished, I straddled him, anticipation rattling my calm. Eyes locked, I slid down, taking him all in.

Instead of looking away, I watched him as I began to move. The pleasure on his face, the grip of his hands on my hips, it was everything I could ever want. Dev wasn't a man out for his own pleasure alone. Every touch, every kiss, meant something. He could twitch, and I'd somehow climb higher.

His face held all the emotions that battled inside me. But unlike me, he let it show. He wore his passion and heart and gave it all to me. The control I had spiraled, my thoughts spiraled, until it was only us, and nothing else in the world mattered. We were in that blissful place where reality didn't matter, because Dev was in me. He shifted up, took a breast into his mouth. I could only feel, all my nerves pooled to those two spots where we connected. When his tongue brushed me, everything burst in a fistful of confetti, my orgasm shaking me to my core as I pumped through, prolonging every last drop of enjoyment.

He joined me. I came back to reality plastered to him, his breath teasing my hair. I closed my eyes, breathed him in. I wanted to keep him. Like this, with me, forever.

I just had no idea how.

Chapter Thirty-One

Devon

I STAYED AWAKE long after Jas fell asleep. Reminiscent of those nights in the past when my hormones had made it difficult to sleep so close to her. Now worry kept me awake. Worry about how this new turn of events would affect her.

Worry about how it would affect us.

Jas wouldn't lean on me. She wouldn't let me care for her. And the reality of being unemployed for a while was huge. Which meant she really needed to get over it and let us work through this together.

But she wouldn't.

I had a fine line to walk in order to keep her here. Not that she had many other options. If we were a true couple, we'd get through this together. It didn't matter that we were just starting to date; we'd been an *us* for over a decade.

Thoughts battled, but no answers came before I fell asleep. In the morning I moved on autopilot—which included making myself a matzo sandwich I was growing damn sick of—got ready for the day, went to class, then work.

I couldn't tell you what I worked on or even if I did it right. Everything was as bland as the matzo Jas had me eating. I did what I had to do until I could return to Jas and figure out a way to help her.

Dad interrupted me at one point, tapping the table and causing the numbers under my nose to jumble together. "You OK?" he signed once I looked up from the numerical mess.

I looked at him, head spinning in too many directions, back and forth between Jas's problems and mine. Part of me wanted to share, to lay it all out on the table. Dad had excellent problem-solving skills, if the issues weren't too close to home. Unfortunately for me, my issue was home. I gave a fleeting thought to him having some magical answer to her employment issues, when I knew he wouldn't. And who was I to bring up my own job-related woes when Jas's dream might be dead in the water? How could I push forward when she was stuck?

Another idea added to the chaos: if I sucked it up and stayed here, I could help her with her dream. The stability and income of working for Dad would generate a surplus, one that could be used to help Jas open her bar. I'd be miserable, but seeing her smile would be worth it. She deserved her happiness far more than I did, since being with her gave me part of mine.

"I'm fine," I eventually signed.

Dad studied me, not buying my signs. The truth was, I kept a lot from him; I had to. "We need more information from Charlie. He doesn't do well with phone calls. Feel up to visiting?"

It got me out of here. "Sure." I stood and grabbed the papers Dad held out. Only he didn't let go. He eyed my wrist, the same way he'd been doing for a few days now. That far-too-familiar look of parental disapproval. A reminder of how much this wasn't a match for me. A flash of guilt crawled into my veins, and I hesitated. If not for this job, I'd have no means of helping Jas. But it didn't change my dreams, dreams which Jas supported.

I let go of the papers. "I don't want this job." My hands moved small, and the minute I finished I wanted to take it back.

"Because of a tattoo?" Dad nearly laughed.

"Because I'm a social worker."

"That's why I have you visit Charlie." He dropped the papers on the desk, then turned and left, as if I had let him know I didn't like broccoli, not his job. Whenever I brought up anything related to social work, Dad changed the subject. He didn't want to acknowledge that my wants differed from his. And I was growing damn tired of letting him call the shots.

I moved to go after him, but a door slammed down the hall, and I bet it was his. I had half a mind to walk out and not come back. But then both Jas and I would be out of work, and I didn't want to burden Blake with the both of us.

So I collected the papers and headed to my car. At least visiting Charlie was work I enjoyed, even if it was for the wrong reasons.

I cranked the radio as loud as it would go, the vibrations and heavy bass soothing as they jumped along my skin and tickled my ears. I wanted fresh air on my face, but the damn noise was loud enough as it was for hearing people. At least the radio did the trick, calming me down so that I wouldn't bring any shit into Charlie's home. I shook off the rest of my aggression on the walkway to his home and rang the bell.

This time, when he opened the door, he smiled. "Good to see you again," he signed.

I held up the packet of papers. "Don't tell me that before you find out why I'm here."

Still, Charlie smiled, and I followed him to his kitchen table once again. In all my anger, I hadn't taken one look at the papers and realized I was not prepared at all for the visit. I opened up the folder and started sorting through, noting he had a lot more investments than I anticipated.

Charlie tapped the table. "Tattoo?" he asked, white eyebrows raised high as he pointed to my wrist.

Shit. "Yes, I got it recently."

I didn't know what to expect, not with the way everyone was on my case for a little ink. Charlie proved once again to not be what I anticipated. He nodded and grinned, then pushed up his sleeve to the eagle on his upper arm.

It was a beautiful black job, a little faded from time, but it still looked damn good. "Nice."

"I thought you were a straightlaced kid."

I laughed at that. "Not really."

Charlie settled back in his chair. "Good. I don't like the uptight ones. Life's too precious to be uptight."

Probably why my girlfriend wanted to own a bar rather than work a nine-to-five job. "You want to tell that to my father?"

Charlie shook his head. "Not at all. Part of growing up is fighting your own battles."

I froze at that, thought of Jas. Only difference was she'd been fighting her own battles for years now. "Sometimes it's nice to have help."

"Yes, but when it's important to you, only you can make it right."

I pointed to the papers in between us, but Charlie brushed me off. "You want to solve your IRS issue?" I asked.

"You don't want to do this job."

Shit. I was screwed if I was that obvious. "Want and real life are two different things."

"I've been there. Some days you play the game to get ahead. Other days you realize the game sucks and you need to be happy."

"Which one did you do at twenty-two?"

Charlie laughed. "At twenty-two I was awful. I didn't know what I wanted, had too much anger at the world. Later, around thirty, I figured it out. You don't seem that clueless."

I wasn't—at least I hoped I wasn't.

"The more you ignore your wants, the worse it becomes. I know that now." He rubbed his hands together. "What do you have for me?"

A healthy dose of respect. If all my accounting clients were like this guy, I'd be happy. But I knew that wouldn't be the case. And there was still all that paperwork shit. Together we dug in, found the missing pieces. I got everything I needed, then stayed and chatted awhile longer.

When I collected the papers and got ready to go, Charlie surprised me again. "Who has the other half? Boy? Girl?"

I nearly laughed. "Girl. My best friend."

Charlie's eyebrows rose high. "Friend only?"

"No."

"She special?"

How had we gotten here? "Very."

Charlie nodded, long and slow. I hadn't known him long, but I suspected another little token of wisdom would follow. "Her happiness comes first. There's plenty of time in life to make something of yourself. But if you lose her, the success might not be worth it."

He rose and walked over to a row of pictures, fingers brushing a faded one in black and white of a young woman with long, wavy hair and a big smile. I searched the other photos but saw none that looked like her.

I wanted to ask who she was, but the pain on Charlie's face was unmistakable. I didn't know if she was alive or not, though it was clear he loved someone long gone.

He wore no wedding band, and I didn't see his face in any of the photos. They all appeared to be friends rather than family. This guy was alone.

I didn't want that. I wanted pictures of Jas and me, children with her, long hours spent at whatever bar she eventually owned. I wanted a crazy and full life, where one day some young guy would visit me and have to listen to stories of my kids and grandkids and what my wife was up to.

Charlie had a story to tell, but it wasn't a happy one.

Chapter Thirty-Two

Jasmine

I WANDERED AIMLESSLY around Dev and Blake's living room with nothing to do and nowhere to go. Stupid life. The only thing I had left to lose was Dev, and I feared that would be my ultimate rock bottom.

I needed a good week of wallowing, at least. I knew I was being melodramatic as shit, but life hadn't shown me anything better. I wanted a parent to go to, a shoulder to lean on. A part of me knew I had that right here with Dev, but it was too complicated, too new.

I wanted my mother.

Not the mother I knew now, the mother I'd had once upon a time. Whose lap I'd sat on as she struggled to sign me a story, who'd tucked me in at night while Dad worked. I wanted that woman back. The woman who'd died with Dad.

I knew all this yet pulled out my phone, ready to send her a text, only to find she had sent me one and my damn phone hadn't notified me.

Mom: Being moved to Burrows Rehab.

Burrows, where the hell was that? I did a quick search, then responded.

Me: Sorry, my phone didn't notify me. You OK? Can I visit?

Mom: Lot of pain. Can't move. Yes.

Well, it gave me something to do. An hour and a half later, I entered the rehab facility. Or, rather, nursing home. I cringed at the thought. Didn't they have rehab centers for younger people? Or was that some weird age phobia society had?

I wasn't in the mood to attempt communication, so I slipped past the main area, doing my best to look like I knew where I was headed. The place was separated into wings. The first wing had the wrong numbers. The second wing took a few trips up and down, but I found Mom near the end. Her hair was pulled back into a messy ponytail, and she wore a hospital gown. Shit. Did she need her belongings?

She put down the magazine in her hands, her face almost relieved to see me. "Did you need stuff from home? I should have asked."

A small smile crossed her face. "Yes. Maybe next time?"

Wow, did she actually want to get along? "Text me what you need."

She nodded. The room was warm, but I kept my trench on, not wanting her to latch onto my tattoo again. I took in the floral wallpaper and old tube television, at a loss for what to say.

Mom waved. "What's wrong?"

I stared at her. The last time she asked me a question like that was… "Nothing."

"Don't lie to me." Her hands moved more fluidly than they had in a long time, even if her transitions were still choppy.

Was I nine again? Did this place come with a time warp? "You know the bar I work at? They closed down."

She sucked in a breath, and I nearly rubbed my eyes in disbelief when she signed, "I'm sorry."

"Really? You hate everything to do with bars."

"The bar situation with Dad was complicated."

I settled into the large green chair next to her bed. "I've got nothing to do."

Mom placed her hands beside her, shifted, and winced. "I wanted to go back to school. Art history. But we needed the money for Dad to open the bar. The goal was that once the bar was up and running, and finances stabilized, then I'd go back to school. We got close—I even began to apply—but I got pregnant with you."

I squirmed, and Mom waved. "Unexpected, but wonderful. Only now I couldn't go to school in the evenings, because Dad worked. I needed to stay home with you. So my dream got delayed. You'd start school eventually, and then I could go to classes at the same time."

"What happened when I started school?"

Mom shook her head. "The timing of classes didn't work. Dad couldn't shift the hours to accommodate what I needed. I found a few that worked, but then it was too expensive, or the car needed repairs, or wouldn't it be better to fit you with hearing aids. Always one thing after another.

"I hit my breaking point. We fought. Every day he went and did his dream, and every day I stayed at home deprived of mine. I hated him for it."

Mom's strong words took me off guard. These were not words from a woman who still mourned the loss of her husband. "I never knew this."

A wry smile came out. "Perk of having a deaf child: as long as you were out of the room, we could keep you in the dark. I suspect we did a lot of that. I don't know if it was for good or not."

"So you were upset with Dad?"

She turned to the window, looked out at the blue skies. "I loved him. He drove me crazy, but I loved him. He kept all the financial struggles of the bar to himself, and it wore on both of us. I wouldn't have demanded to go to college if I knew. I could have helped him. But instead..." She leveled me with her blue eyes. "We fought that morning, after you left for school. Fought long and hard. I mentioned divorce. He thought it would be better for me. I told him I hated him. He left." A tear trailed down her cheek. "And he never came back. Those were the last words I said to him. Not that I loved him. Not that I never wanted a divorce. Hate was how our marriage ended."

Tears clogged my throat. I got out of my chair and wrapped my mother in a hug. Foreign, so foreign, and yet she held me back. We cried together, like we should have done right after Dad died.

Mom pulled back. She grabbed a tissue and held the box out for me. "I'm sorry I'm not more supportive of you wanting to follow Dad's footsteps. Bars come with a lot of baggage for me. That's not your fault."

"I understand." And for the first time, I did. "Doesn't matter anyways. I can't afford to live and still save money."

Mom blew her nose. "I'm sorry. Life is not easy. I wish you didn't know that so well."

I STAYED AWHILE longer, until Mom grew sleepy, then I left. My feet moved slowly as I traveled down the hall, my mind still processing all the new information. Something caught my peripheral, and I turned to see a nurse looking at me, her mouth moving and a not-so-pleasant expression on her face. I pointed to my ear and shook my head.

Her expression lifted, and she held up a finger. She grabbed some paper and appeared at my side. *I'm sorry, you must be Jasmine, Connie's daughter.*

Mom told them about me? I nodded and read over the nurse's shoulder as she wrote.

I'm Barb, her nurse. I know she hasn't been here long, but she's on pain medication for her hip, and her new antidepressant medication seems to be helping.

I stared at the words after she handed them to me. My hand almost shook when I took the pen.

I don't know if Mom's ever had depression meds before. She always refused.

Come to think of it, she looked like she had more color to her face than I'd seen in a long time.

Her transfer papers from the hospital said it was a new diagnosis. Without these meds, her recovery would be much harder.

I thanked her and answered a few questions before heading back to my car. I had let the hospital know about her depression. I had no idea if the new medication would really work. Mom hadn't been in a good place for years, but even this brief window of having her back meant the world to me.

THE AFTERNOON FOUND me in a coffee shop, nursing a simple black coffee in exchange for free Wi-Fi. I searched for any bar jobs available, but the pickings were slim, and I knew even fewer would accept someone deaf.

Dammit, I wanted my old job back. It wasn't ideal, but it worked for the time being. If I could take control and make it my own, I could turn it into something special. I did a mental tally of my savings. It wouldn't be enough, but perhaps I could strike a deal. I set up a text to Len.

Me: If you won't let me run the bar, sell it to me.

I held my breath. He'd have to sell it to me for dirt cheap, and I'd probably inherit a huge amount of debt.

But the bar was stocked; no way would I find another deal this good.

Len: You can't afford it.
Me: Try me.
Len: Kid, it's over. You want it? Talk to the bank.

I banged my head into the table. Of course the bar couldn't be sold to me, no matter how much begging I did. It really was over.

Time for a new plan. My waitress skills had to be good for something. I broadened my search to restaurants and sent out a few more feelers, including one call with the interpreter video relay service. The call didn't go so well, as I suspected this whole job search thing wouldn't.

I sent a text message to Pete.

Me: How did you find a job that hires deaf?

Dev and Nikki were students. Pete and I were the workers.

Pete: As long as I lift boxes, they don't care. What happened?

Huh, Dev didn't share like he usually did.

Me: Bar closed.
Pete: Shit. You don't want to lift boxes.
Me: Want and need are different.

Pete: Those thin arms strong enough?

Me: How much do you think beer weighs?

Pete: Good point. Think about it. I can set you up, but this isn't for you.

Me: Then what is?

Pete: Serving me beer after I lift boxes.

Me: Can't do that without money.

Pete: Maybe Dev can support you.

Me: Sexist. I support myself.

Pete: Poor Dev, he wants to help, and you won't let him.

Me: Poor me, I have to put up with Dev.

Pete: LOL.

Sure, that was a little mean, and I didn't mean it, not completely. But there were certain things I had to do on my own.

I tossed my long-empty coffee cup into the trash. At the time of day when I usually began getting dressed for work, I headed back to the apartment. Time on my hands wasn't good for me. I was itchy and twitchy and needed to work.

And according to my gas gauge, I also needed gas. This no-income thing was going to get old real quick. I fueled up, then grabbed an overpriced cookies and cream ice cream from the convenience store. Because I had my priorities straight.

For the first time since I moved in with Dev, I wished I hadn't. Then I could be alone with my ice cream carton without anyone to interfere, a complete world shutout.

Instead I had two roommates to deal with, one of whom was my overbearing boyfriend.

I took a deep breath and tried to shake some sense into myself. What an ungrateful bitch I had turned into. What did it matter if Dev was overbearing? His heart was always in the right place.

I scanned the parking lot, hoping for a few more hours of peace. No such luck. With my ice cream clutched to my chest, I made my way inside the building and into the apartment, where a small crowd waited—Dev, Blake, and Shawn.

I turned to Blake. "I'm not used to seeing you. The sun's still out. I'm confused."

"I have to prove I'm not a vampire, otherwise I might change."

I laughed. Maybe company wasn't so bad.

Dev took the ice cream from me and checked the label. "Great minds think alike." Then he showed me the other two he bought—raspberry chip and caramel fudge.

"That's too much! I'll eat them all," I signed, worried I really would. And also fighting the urge to throw my arms around him for being my personal ice cream fairy.

"We'll help," Shawn signed.

All three men stared at me, questions written across their faces. They waited me out, and I had no intentions of playing along. I held up my hands. "I don't want to talk about it."

Blake rubbed his hands together. "OK. Game time. Pick your preference."

Shawn bent and picked up four boxes, placing them on the coffee table. Trivial Pursuit, Scattergories, Apples to Apples, and Monopoly.

"Do you want to work as a team or beat the shit out of the rest of us?" Blake asked.

A small smile fought its way to my face. I reached forward and tapped the Monopoly box, not missing the visual groan on the guys' faces. I was ruthless with the game, and not because I usually made drinks for the others as we played.

Blake and Shawn cleared the table and set up the game. I moved to sit on the floor, but Dev stopped me. "You OK?" He ran one hand down my arm and laced our fingers together.

"For now." I held his eyes, begged him to leave it at that. I wanted a few days of ignoring being a burden to anyone but myself.

He squeezed my hand—message received. The delay should have been a relief; it wasn't.

Chapter Thirty-Three

Devon

JAS PULLED AWAY. Slow, invisible steps as she retreated into herself. I knew it. I'd anticipated it, part of the reason why I'd begged Blake and Shawn to hang out with us. Distraction. Anything to keep Jas out of her head for a while.

Because once Jas got to thinking, the game was over. Not that her life was a game, but she'd been put through so much shit, her reactions had grown predictable. And each shit storm meant she retreated faster and stronger.

I'd always known one day she'd react so quickly that no one could help her. And I was deathly afraid that day was now. So I'd pull anything out of my ass to give myself a few extra minutes to problem solve an answer.

It hurt to see her this way, to know one wrong move could take her away from me, to feel the utter helplessness of not being able to help the woman I loved. I was right not to share how I felt about her—she proved it—but holding it in didn't change what I knew in my heart. I did so much for so many people, and the main person who mattered blocked me.

Unless I found an answer.

Until then, I gave her space. Jas was used to me knocking down her door and harassing her with text messages, not living with me. Messages and calls were irrelevant when I saw her face every day and held her at night. All the more reason to be extra cautious, because she'd been known to avoid me when things got rough. The more room I gave her, the better.

My phone vibrated in my back pocket as I made my way off campus for the day. I stopped walking when I found a text from Mom.

Mom: Visit before you go to work.

It said a lot that I was grateful for the reprieve, even if I should be worried about Mom's true intentions. I drove to the small school I had attended, where Mom still worked. Small white buildings dotted the campus. I never realized how small it was until I attended a hearing college and had lecture halls with over a hundred students in attendance.

I parked outside the middle-school building. Classes were over for the day, but I was used to being here at odd hours. I would stay and go home with Mom, and sometimes we would drop Jas off on our way.

Inside, the halls looked the same as when I'd been a student, only smaller. I didn't know if it was my size or the comparison with my college, but the building felt quaint, and if I signed that to Mom, she'd whap me on the head.

Her room was as I remembered it, a handful of desks in a semicircle so everyone could see each other and participate. Mom sat at her desk, discussing something with a student. I didn't want to eavesdrop, so I let her chat with the brunette until they caught my attention, and I realized the brunette wasn't a student at all, but the new math teacher, Carli, only a few years older than myself.

"Sorry, I didn't mean to delay you," Carli signed to both of us, two spots of color dotting her cheeks.

Mom brushed her off. "Don't worry. It's fine. I didn't know when he'd arrive."

I rolled my eyes. No skin off my back. The more time I stayed here, the less I had at work.

"Thank you for your help. I had no clue how to express that in ASL." Carli gathered her papers, holding them with one hand. "I should go collect my husband from his classroom, anyways. If not, he'll stay until the sun sets. Have a good night."

I waved as she left and took a seat close to Mom. "What's up?"

"That," she signed in the direction of my left wrist. "I thought your father was going crazy, tax-induced hallucinations, but there it is, ink on my son."

"It's only half of a yin-yang symbol."

"That you will have for the rest of your life. You weren't a rebellious kid—you understand the ramifications, don't you?"

I hadn't thought it through, but it didn't change that I wanted it. "Yes."

She gestured for me to come over, and I held out my wrist to her. She rubbed her thumb around the symbol. "And Jasmine has the other half?"

"Yes."

She gazed at her door. "You know, those two," she signed, indicating Carli and her husband, Reed, "remind me of you and Jasmine. Reed jumped on the job opening for her when it became available last year. There are some people you can just tell truly care for each other and will do anything for one another."

She turned to me and laced her fingers on her desk. Done with her part, she waited for me to fill in the pieces.

"What's your point?"

A smile crossed her face. "You're restless, about to graduate, and now dating your best friend. I smell trouble."

I rubbed the back of my neck. Mom did have a nose for trouble. "You don't like us dating?"

"You kidding me? I love it, been wanting it for years. Though thank you for waiting until you were adults. Those teen years, I did not sleep well." She laughed. "Blake informs me her bar closed down?"

Fucking family. "Yes."

Mom nodded, eyes trailing around her room. "If one of you goes into crisis, you both do. Always been that way. Worked when you were friends, but not now that you are a couple. In a relationship, one needs to be sturdy when the other weakens. You need to support each other differently than you are used to. Why are you still working for Dad?"

I blinked as I tried to follow the sudden shift in conversation. "What?" I didn't know which way to go and contemplated rubbing my eyes for clarity.

"Blake and your father, two peas, one pod. You, you were always mine. But your father had dreams, and you expressed honest interest when you were younger. But now? Now you know what you want."

"He's not listening."

"Sign louder."

I looked up at the drop tile ceiling. "But if I stay where I am, I can help support Jasmine."

When I dared lower my eyes, I found Mom nodding slowly. "But is that the right support? You've always been her partner in crime. Don't rock the boat when the waters are already unstable."

"Is this why you wanted me to visit?"

Mom leaned back in her chair. "I want to make sure that when you've graduated, you're happy with your life decision. And yes, that includes Jasmine. All I want is for my children to be happy."

Her words stayed with me through work, which I did on autopilot again, and as I returned home. I found Jasmine on my bed watching a movie. She looked my way and smiled, but it fell flat. I wanted to make her really smile again.

I'd been doing that since I was eleven.

I climbed onto the bed with her and kissed her. My hand tangled in her hair. She kissed me back, open and full. She never kissed me any differently. No matter the tension between us, when I had her like this, I had all of her.

She tangled her legs with mine, rubbed her body against mine. I dug my hands into her hips and forced myself to slow down before I did some basic, human interaction. I broke the kiss. "How are you doing?"

Her body stiffened, and she untangled her legs. "Fine."

Shit. I hovered over her, forcing her onto her back, her curls splayed out on my comforter. "Don't lie. It's an honest question."

"I dropped off some of Mom's belongings. She wasn't in the mood for company. Then I threw out the matzo box. You managed a week; you sure you didn't cheat?"

I felt like she'd either thrown a curveball at me or set a trap, even as I was relieved I could stop eating that crap. "I didn't cheat. I told you I'd last a week."

She rolled her eyes.

"I'll do anything for you, don't you realize that? I'd eat matzo for another week if you want. Where's the box?" My insides may have been screaming at me to stop this nonsense, but I still moved as if I was ready to save the cardboard from the trash.

"Don't be silly. How does eating matzo prove anything?"

"How else do I get through your stubbornness?"

"That kind of stubbornness is reserved for family."

Didn't she realize she was part of mine? "Family is only blood?"

Jas froze. She had to know I thought of her as family, had for years. "You know what I mean." She pushed me back and sat up, adjusting her tee shirt, a sure sign she intended to cut me off.

"You sure you want to build that wall?"

"I'm not building a wall." Yet the air cooled around us.

"Just laying the foundation." I never should have stopped kissing her.

She shoved her hands into her hair, blond curls fanning out around her. "I don't want to do this."

Good, something we agreed on. Except for one fact. "We'll just circle around and get back here later."

"Maybe later I'll feel like handling it."

Fat chance. "Maybe later you'll feel worse."

She blew out a frustrated breath. "Not now. Please."

We stared at each other as a barrier grew. If we drew attention to it, it would only expand faster. We knew each other so well, and yet there were no answers. The pivotal point in our relationship had arrived. Too soon. I wasn't ready. And there wasn't a damn thing I could do about it.

Jas climbed onto my lap, brushed her lips against mine. We used to talk things out; now we fed emotions with sex. Didn't stop me from kissing her back, taking what she gave.

Only neither one of us pushed it further. The kisses retained innocence, as if our relationship reversed. That should have brought some comfort. If we reversed, we'd go back to our friendship.

I didn't want that. I wanted everything that went along with being in love. I didn't care if some other guy would call me a wuss for that behavior. I knew what I felt and what I wanted. Which meant I needed to give Jas time and space.

And pray.

Chapter Thirty-Four

Jasmine

A CLEAR SIGN things weren't right between Dev and me: we slept in our pajamas. Sure, we'd done so countless times in the past, but since we'd started having sex, we were always intimate. Now the lack of it sat like a boulder between us.

I faked sleep when he got out of bed, eyes open just enough to get a blurry image. I had hoped for a little skin to start my day, but Dev took his clothes with him to the bathroom. Nothing like the man who curled his naked body around mine to sleep.

Unsettled as I was, I fell back to sleep. Easier to sleep part of the day away than deal with reality. When I woke, he was gone and I had the apartment to myself. I could stare at the ceiling or finish an ice cream carton. What I needed required a connection.

I got out of bed and collected my box with Dad's belongings. The familiar pain tugged at my chest, only now it morphed, tinged with a new sensation after my conversation with Mom. I shuffled to the bottom and pulled out the stack of pictures. A few of him, a lot of him and me, and a few of my parents together.

I stopped on one. Nothing special about the event. They stood in front of a store, Mom cuddled under Dad's arm, Dad bent to rest his chin on the top of her head. They looked happy. I'd never stopped to think about that before now; they looked like a typical couple who loved each other. And yet, they fought. They had their issues. But even with their last fight, they never stopped loving each other.

I went over to Dev's desk, where he had a picture of us framed. It had been taken before we'd started dating. Our arms around each other, we were smiling like two hams for the camera. We looked happy too.

No, we looked more than happy; we looked permanent.

I tried to imagine what the future could look like, but with my own employment up in smoke, I couldn't form a picture. Too many questions, too many unknowns. And without those answers, I wouldn't know how Dev would be affected.

I returned to my box, picked up the pictures of Dad and me. Stopped at the one from the bar. We each held an empty beer mug, corny smiles on our faces. Dad had one arm around me. Just a happy family picture, except for the fact it took place in a bar.

The bar that caused problems with my parents. I put the pictures back in the box, thumbed through the recipes. Dad loved his bar. Did I want to run one like he had because *I* wanted to? Or because of some foolish kid logic that I'd get him back?

I leaned back and closed my eyes. Pictured the smells of the bar. The finicky customers, the spilled beer. The smile nearly broke my face. Yes. It was still my answer, even if it was not exactly plausible.

My phone rumbled next to me, and I picked it up.

Nikki: You didn't tell me you lost your job!
Me: Not exactly fun to share.
Nikki: Friends don't care about fun.

I blew out a breath.

Nikki: Don't turn into a turtle unless we come into that shell with you.

I laughed, even as it hurt.

Me: I'm trying to figure out my next step.
Nikki: Great! I'll come over and help.
Me: Don't you have class?

I tapped my thumb to my phone, but no response came.

Me: I'm waiting for an answer!

I suspected I'd be waiting until she showed up outside Dev's door. And I was still in my pajamas. Well, if she arrived too quickly, she'd have to wait.

I managed to shower and run some gel through my hair before the doorbell flashed. Sure enough, Nikki stood on the other side. She barged in the minute I opened the door and paced the area, hands on hips. When she didn't come at me with anything right away, I realized I had been a shitty friend.

Nikki had her own issues on her mind.

"What's wrong?" I asked.

Nikki halted her pacing and dropped her hands. "What do you mean?"

"There's something bothering you. What is it?"

"Men suck."

"That's supposed to be a good thing."

Nikki's jaw dropped, and she stared at me. "You've never had that reaction before."

My cheeks flamed, and I tried very hard not to imagine Dev's mouth on me.

"Oh my God, I think I officially know too much about Devon."

I covered my burning cheeks; how had I dug this hole? "Forget I said that."

"You barely said anything. Details." She plopped on the couch.

"First you said you know too much, and now you want details?"

"Yes," she laughed. "Your love life is much more interesting than mine."

My eyes opened wide. "Wait, wait a minute, what's happening with your love life?"

Nikki bit her plump lip.

"Come on! You know too much about mine, spill."

"Pete came over last night…" Nikki's hands trailed off. I waited for her to get to her point, only to realize she had.

I slapped the couch cushion between us. "Pete? You and Pete?"

Nikki's shoulders stiffened. "Why is that so hard to believe? You and Dev are dating."

I shook my head to try to descramble this new information. "I'm sorry. I hadn't noticed it before." And if that didn't make me feel like a horrible friend…

Nikki slouched back against the cushions. "I hadn't either."

I blinked, but nothing made sense. "Explain. Now."

"As I said, Pete came over. And we chatted like normal, everything was great. Then he kissed me."

My eyes bugged out. "And?"

She played with an imaginary piece of lint on her jeans. "And I was shocked. I didn't kiss him back. I didn't respond. He left."

"Pete's an idiot."

Nikki stiffened.

"You're shocked because you liked it."

She pressed her lips together, signed nothing.

I whipped out my phone, set up a quick text to Dev.

Me: Nikki's here. Invite Pete over tonight. Do NOT tell Pete about Nikki.

Dev: I don't trust you.

Me: Good.
Dev: What's going on?
Me: I'm fixing a relationship.

I clicked Send before my words registered. Shit. We both knew things weren't right between us, and here I was behaving as if nothing had changed.

Dev: Ours?

Pain slashed at me from that one, and my stomach felt queasy.

Me: Pete and Nikki, but you don't know that.
Dev: OK.

The man made me crazy. I threw my phone on the cushion, only to realize Nikki had read every word.

"What's wrong with you two?"

"I'm unemployed."

"So?"

"Dev has a helping complex."

"So?"

I stopped signing, not wanting to get into this further.

Unfortunately, Nikki clearly wasn't going to consider my wants, not with the way she tapped her fingers to her knees. "I think you're scared. And rather than reaching out to others for support, you've already hid in that shell without us."

I shook my head. "I'm not trying to shut you out."

"Of course not, because you already have. Or do you not remember that we lost you, all of us, when your father died?"

I stood. "I'll make up some drinks for tonight."

Nikki stomped on the floor until I turned. "Stop hiding behind alcohol or anything else you can find. We like you as you are. Flaws, pain, and all. You don't have to prove anything—just be yourself. Can you? Can you let Jasmine Helmsman outside of her shell?"

I stared at her, dark skin, blond hair, focusing on details instead of myself. "I don't know."

"Well, you better figure it out. Because Devon needs all of you, or it won't work." Nikki settled into the couch and pulled out her phone. I stood rooted to my spot. Everything she signed was the truth. Truth I didn't know what to do with.

Chapter Thirty-Five

Devon

I ARRIVED HOME to a party in progress. Snacks in brightly colored bowls covered the coffee table. Nikki was mixing some sort of dip or something, and Jas stood in the kitchen, her hair pulled back into a thick mass of curls. I trailed my eyes down her snug powder-blue top and skinny jeans, which teased me with the threadbare spots on her thighs. Her tattoo was visible as she reached for something, a spot of black ink claiming her as mine. She moved with confidence, a lighthearted stance I'd been missing. Then her actions came into focus, namely the alcohol on the counter and in her hands.

That explained part of the happiness. I wanted to walk over to her, wrap my arms around her, and kiss her until she dropped a glass. My hesitation had nothing to do with Nikki.

I flicked the lights, and both women looked my way. Nikki waved. Jas's smile morphed, no longer carefree, but warm and only for me. Screw it.

I crossed the room and took her into my arms, bending her backward as I feasted on her mouth. Her lips parted in shock against mine, but I still felt that smile. She wound her arms behind my neck and gave into the kiss, into everything we were. But we couldn't fully give in, not with company. It would be enough for now. I set her back on her feet. Her pink cheeks all but glowed as she picked up the glass she had managed to leave on the counter.

Nikki fanned herself. "Hot."

I shook my head and wondered how much Nikki knew. Jas and I always shared more with each other, but Nikki and Pete were never that far behind. Would Jas start sharing more with them now that she and I were in this awkward place? That sucked, because I still wanted Jas as my best friend.

The doorbell flashed, and I didn't check the peephole, just let Pete in. I had forgotten Jas was playing matchmaker until Pete froze. For a long moment, he stared at Nikki and she stared back. I closed the door, nudging Pete out of the way in the process. Jas continued working. None of this distracted them.

I caught Jas's eyes over their heads. "What did I miss?"

She gestured infinitesimally to Nikki and Pete and puckered her lips. *Oh.* I studied my other two friends and noted the sexual tension in the air.

They continued their staring match, so I responded to Jas, signing "finally," my hands barely moving.

"You knew?" she whispered back.

I pulled out my phone.

Me: Pete's had a crush for a while.

Jas: And you didn't tell me?

Me: Wasn't my story.

We both put our phones away, having our own staring match. Because we'd settled one puzzle between us: we had no secrets, and yet when it came to romance, we closed ourselves off. We didn't share our feelings for each other, and that extended to how we treated our friends.

Jas shook her head and stomped on the floor, breaking both stares. "Sit. Drink. Eat. Friends hang out, right?"

Pete scratched his head and took a seat. Nikki stayed in the kitchen. Jas collected drinks, three different kinds, and handed them out.

"We haven't had dinner yet," Pete signed.

Jas shrugged. "So?"

I checked the food. Munchies, no meal. "Pizza?" After a week of no bread, I needed pizza. And every form of flour present in the munchies. After everyone nodded, I pulled out my phone and went through the online checkout for the local pizza place. Then it was back to awkward silence. I fiddled with my drink and took a sip, the alcohol tingling against my tongue and burning a path down my throat. "You trying to get us drunk?" I asked Jas.

"Each drink is different. Maybe she just wants you drunk?" Nikki signed.

Jas blew me a kiss, refusing to answer.

Pete put his drink down; if he'd tried any of his, it wasn't visible. He faced Jas. "I talked with my boss. We do have some openings, but I still think you can do better."

I shot my eyes to Jas, who nodded like this wasn't some new piece of information. It wasn't to her. I banged on the table, Pete's drink sloshing into a bowl of chips. "What are you talking about?"

Nikki took the bowl and cleaned up the mess. Pete collected his drink. I held Jas captive and waited. Her back stiff, she met my intensity, then breathed out. "You know it's hard for deaf to find work."

"I know."

She exhaled again. "It's another option for me. Even my savings won't last long."

"I'm not asking you for any money."

Her eyes turned cold. "Not now."

"It's the truth! You're my friend, my girlfriend. How much of an asshole would I be if I didn't support you?"

She stood. "I support myself."

The floor vibrated beneath our feet, and we turned to Nikki jumping up and down. "Stop! Stop it right now. You are not allowed to have this conversation until you stop fighting. If you fight, you will hurt each other. If you calm down, all the way down, then you can communicate." She pushed two full shot glasses in our direction.

I shook my head no and pushed them back.

"Why not? It's not worse than the drink she made."

"I'll drink it. She won't."

Nikki popped a hip out. "Controlling much?"

I faced Jas and stepped away from the table. Either way, this was up to her. I wasn't about to police whether she drank or not; it had been instinct to shield her.

She eyed the glass and shook her head. "I don't want to drink in case I have a problem with alcohol."

Nikki nodded. "Fine. Then kiss him. Because you two need to calm down, and those are the only options I have."

"You've never suggested that before."

"You've never fought like this before. You've never really fought, not until now." Nikki rolled her head and glanced at Pete. "This is going to be bad."

He nodded, but by the look on his face, I wasn't sure he was nodding about us.

This was a mess, one big fucking mess. But Nikki was right, we all needed to relax. I circled the table until I reached Jas. She didn't move away, but a hesitance lurked on her face. I wrapped a hand around her neck, not missing the goose bumps popping up on her skin. A knot uncoiled deep inside as I realized I still had this effect on her. I tried to convey with my eyes the love I had for her, but even if she got it, I didn't know if it would help or not.

I brought my mouth down to hers and kissed her. Not sweet, not hard. Us. I kissed her until she relaxed, until a connection sprouted between us again.

When I pulled back, part of her hard shell had cracked. She'd just apply more duct tape, like she always did. My new goal was to get her to give it up. For good.

I pointed to Pete and Nikki and the drinks now in front of them. "Go ahead. Drink." They both glared at me, and I nearly laughed; this was going to be good. "We all have problems today, but I want a nice evening. So drink, talk, or kiss, anything so we can all settle down when the pizza arrives."

Jas patted my back, sliding under my arm. "He's right." I rested my arm across her shoulders. It had been far too long since we'd acted like a team.

Pete studied his hands, shuffled a foot, acting twelve. Nikki stared at him with a longing in her gaze. Anyone with a set of eyes would know where this headed.

Jas stomped on the floor. "Start responding, or I'm making you another shot. And another, until this situation between you is solved."

Pete reached for his drink, but Nikki stopped him, placing her hand over the rim before he could make contact. "You surprised me yesterday, that's all. Not in a bad way."

Pete didn't move. He stood stiff. Nikki shook her head, signed *stubborn*, then rose to her toes and pressed her lips to his.

Jas leaned on my chest, signed *sweet* against my chin. So many words came to mind as I wondered if we were like this or if they were going to have the same issues as us. Instead, I tightened my grip around her waist.

Pete and Nikki pulled apart, both looking embarrassed as all hell. "Feel better?" Jas asked.

Nikki shook her head and tossed back her shot. Pete wore a big-ass smile but did the same. The doorbell flashed, and I untangled myself from Jas to get the pizza. Things were changing all around, but tonight the four of us would hang out, as we always did. And tomorrow, with any luck, we'd still be able to.

THANKS TO JAS's mixology skills, I woke up in the morning with the light filtering in through my eyelids causing splintering pain and the taste of sawdust in my mouth. I rolled over, ready to press my head into my pillow, only to find I had no pillow.

I didn't move, though I wanted to sit up and investigate my surroundings. The hard surface beneath me was the first thing to register. My bed was the floor. With a turn of my head, I tried to let some light in, only to have my hearing aid create a high-pitched feedback in the process.

I hadn't even taken the aids off. What had she given me?

I managed to open my eyelids, letting in no more than a crack of skull-crushing light. My eyes watered, but I blinked in the area. The living room. I'd slept in the living room. And so had Pete, on the floor as well, and Nikki, on the couch.

The only one missing? The sober one.

My back ached from the hardwood floor as I rose to a sitting position. With a tug, I removed my aids—the removal feedback noise only making my head worse—and used my shirt to wipe down the wet wax left behind.

As my senses woke up, the scent of coffee drifted to my nose. I would have guessed the savior to be Blake, but Jas walked in from the hallway. Unlike how I felt, she looked wide awake and happy.

She noticed I was awake and cringed. "You OK?"

I placed one hand on my head. "My head on? It feels like it fell off and rolled into a pile of shit."

"I'm sorry. You all kept asking for more, and I forgot to keep count. I have pain meds."

I pulled myself up from the side of the couch. "That's a start. What time is it?"

"Eight. I had hoped the coffee would wake you all up."

Whatever had woken me, it wasn't the coffee. I tapped Nikki's foot and kicked Pete's on my way to pain meds and coffee, not letting the black coffee cool before it burned the pills down my throat.

"So you slept in my bed all alone while I slept on the floor?"

She didn't react to my joke, biting a corner of her lower lip. "I tried to get you up and into your own bed, but you were dead weight, I couldn't move you. And Blake stayed at Shawn's, so I had no help. I'm sorry."

I pressed my throbbing head against hers. I didn't mean to make her feel bad. "It's OK. Do we wake them or let them sleep?"

"I'll make cheesy eggs. They need food; maybe the smell will wake them." She moved to work, but I held onto her wrist.

"Are we OK?" It could be the hangover, but I swore the divide between us had expanded.

She threw on a fake smile. "Of course." She made to leave, but I didn't let up my grip.

"Don't change us. We are who we are. Dating doesn't change that. Your job doesn't change that."

She pulled her hand back. "Everything changes everything." Then she set about cooking. The smells did wake our friends, who were just as miserable as I was. Coffee, meds, and cheesy eggs didn't make much of a difference, but we did manage to fake normal.

Something we were all too damn good at.

"It will be a long time before I accept another drink from you," Pete signed to Jas.

She scrunched her eyebrows. "I know. I guess it's a good thing I no longer work in a bar."

He shook his head, then placed a hand on top. "A long time means maybe a month. Keep searching."

Jas focused on her food, defeat written in the slouch of her shoulders. I couldn't sit back and watch her self-destruct. I had to do something. But she had to be willing to accept help.

I walked Pete outside when he left. Nothing like fresh air to point out how much stress the apartment held.

"I need to help Jasmine," I signed.

"Good luck with that. She's shutting down hard because of all this."

I glanced up at the apartment. "She shouldn't have to. I want to take care of her."

Pete shook his head. "Have you met her? She won't accept that."

"What other options does she have? If we save together, she can open her bar."

"In what, five years? How much do you think you'll make as a social worker?"

I rubbed my neck. "Her happiness is what matters. If she's not happy, it doesn't matter what job I have."

Pete narrowed his eyes. "Whatever you're thinking, stop."

"It's for the best." I didn't have to tell him my thoughts, he knew.

"You'll be miserable working with your father."

"Jasmine will be miserable working anywhere else. Once she's happy, then I can reconsider."

Pete shook his head and pulled out his keys. "I'd suggest you think this over; you're setting yourself up for a rude awakening."

Maybe so, but it was something I had to do.

Chapter Thirty-Six

Jasmine

NIKKI LEFT SHORTLY after Pete did. I tried to tempt her with a movie, but she spouted some bullshit about homework. I suspected her intent was to give Dev and me time to talk, not realizing we needed the distraction.

Dev closed the door behind her. The place was large and empty with just the two of us. I would have set about cleaning, but I had already done that while the hangover victims nursed their heads.

No other distractions remained. I wrung my hands together, staring at the many feet of hardwood floor between us. Dev's eyes burned my skin, but I kept my gaze down until his foot tapped, forcing me to look up.

"You know that part of being in a relationship is accepting help, right?" Dev asked.

"Jump right into hell, why don't you," I muttered with my hands.

"I'm serious. It's killing me to see you in pain, but you won't let me help. And anything I do makes it worse."

"Maybe I want to be on my own."

"Maybe I thought I had a best friend and girlfriend."

"What does that mean?"

"That means that best friends, couples, they work together. They lean on each other. They support each other."

I laughed, even though it tasted bitter on my lips. "True. That's what's happened for our entire lives. But now I need to stand alone."

Dev stomped. "You have stood alone. You've lived alone with no help from anyone else. Did you really never want more than that?"

I kept my hands at my sides. Some days the answer was yes, other days no; an easy response wasn't possible.

He ran his hands through his overgrown hair. "I'm going to shower."

"We have to finish this fight at some point." As much as I hated it, all the going around in circles might be worse.

He scratched at his scruffy jaw, wariness lurking in his baby blues. "I know. I'm not ready to lose you."

He left, and I crumbled to the couch. We both knew where this headed. But we wouldn't know how bad it would be until the moment arrived. I rubbed at the ache in my chest. Life without Dev, it wasn't something I could envision. No one else understood me like he did. No one else had that connection he had. Add in the feel of his body against mine, and I knew there would never be another like him. Even if I also knew I never got to keep what I wanted.

One thing was clear: I wasn't ready to lose him either.

I followed him down the hall and turned the bathroom handle. Unlocked. I slipped inside. Steam filled the room, and his shampoo or soap already teased my nostrils. His clothes were scattered on the floor. Through the white curtain, I made out the tantalizing outline of his form, but nothing more.

I undressed, tossing my clothes in a pile. My heart beat fast, and anticipation licked through me, as if this was somehow taboo, even for our new sexual relationship. I pulled back the curtain, and there was Dev, eyes closed, head back as he rinsed shampoo out of his hair. The entire front of his body was available to my view, and he had a lovely body, all hard muscle and a light dusting of hair.

He lowered his head and opened his eyes, catching me standing there. I didn't know if I'd let in cool air and alerted him, but I hadn't dared move farther and startle him. His gaze roamed over the little bit of me visible, focusing on my bare breasts. His gaze alone caused my nipples to harden. "What are you doing here?" he asked.

I stepped in and closed the curtain behind me. "I think that's obvious."

"You need to shower?"

I shook my head. "I need you."

He held out his hands, offering all I ever wanted, and I moved to him, pressing my dry body against his water-slicked one. He kissed me with wet lips, his body stirring between us, melting me with heat and promise. I wrapped my arms around him, wiggling against him, all but desperate for a physical closeness while our emotional one remained strained.

Dev spun me. The water cascaded on me as he pressed me against the wall. "I love you," he signed, before kissing my neck and shifting a leg between mine. He didn't give me a chance to respond. I wasn't sure I could, with my own emotional upheaval. I ground against him as his hand found my breast and teased my pebbled nipple.

A sense of exhilaration consumed me. After the last few shitty days, this was exactly what the doctor ordered. I ran my fingers up his thigh, down his abs, and wrapped around his silky length. Dev let out a breath as I began to pump, then retaliated by sucking my breast into his mouth.

All in all, pretty top-notch retaliation.

I let go of him to wrap my legs around his waist, giving him greater access to my chest. The steam of the shower competed with the steam in my veins, a combustible combination. My core throbbed with need. I grabbed his hand and brought it to where I needed him most.

He shot me a sexy-as-hell smile. "You want?" he asked, before putting his hand back where I had requested and slipping a finger inside.

I arched, and my nerve endings did a happy dance and clenched around him. "I love you," I signed, meaning it more than ever before with his hand inside me.

His smile widened, and he sucked on my neck, fingers sliding in and out. My body tightened and climbed. I dug my nails into his back. When his lips met mine again, I burst, my orgasm spinning on and on until the very last notion of reality left.

And then Dev was inside me, and everything built back up. I forced my eyes open, wanting to see the same euphoria I felt on his face. He thrust me into the wall, our bodies moving as one. The moment was so special, so rare and wonderful. Nothing outside of this shower mattered. Here we were—us. We gave and took and came back for more.

He set me off again, then followed. We clutched each other, somehow not breaking our connection. Because once we did, reality would settle in.

Unfortunately, it settled in before we parted, as realization hit us at the same time. We had not been prepared for sex in the shower.

Dev slipped out and stepped back. "That was dumb."

I half laughed, not knowing what else to do. I'd never forgotten a condom before. "Yes. It'll be fine." I hoped. According to sex ed in high school, I was close enough to my period that everything should be okay.

He rubbed his neck, then tossed me the bar of soap. "You promise you won't cut me out of anything that happens because of this."

I soaped up. "Nothing will happen."

His jaw set hard as he glared at me.

"I promise."

"We should pick up the Plan B pill to be sure."

It was for the best, but I couldn't deny that something felt off about the suggestion. Not that I was 100 percent confident, just that the notion felt so final. "Fine."

He brushed his hair off his face, leaned against the far corner. The tension built back up. The fight brewing. I tossed the soap back to him. "We are not fighting in the shower. Not after sex."

"I could grab a condom, and we could end happy." Only his smile faltered. The happy moment shattered.

I rinsed myself off. "How can we know what's coming so well and not have an answer?"

He switched places with me so the water could remove his soap. "Because we're us."

I nodded and stepped out of the shower. I dried myself off before wrapping the towel around me. Dev opened the curtain, unease following. I wiped a spot on the fogged-up mirror and picked up my comb. Better to attempt to tame my unruly curls than deal with the elephant in the room. Dev came up behind me. We looked darn cute together. "Maybe it won't be that bad," I signed.

He leaned into me until his hands came in front of us both. "Until you are willing to accept help, it will be."

I spun around to face him. "What do you mean?"

"Do you really want to have this conversation while naked?"

I had a towel around me. "Yes."

He rubbed his neck. "We both know it may take a while for you to find a job. If we are a true couple, then I'll help support you."

"You shouldn't have to."

"You have any better offers? If you don't lean on me, who helps?"

"I'll figure it out."

"So you're not willing to accept help."

I stared at him, and my eyes drifted to the water droplets on his chest. "You're right. We need to get dressed." I moved to the door, only he stepped in front of me.

"No. Not another delay. We need this out so we can get through it."

I clenched my jaw but didn't move to escape. I didn't want anyone's help. And I suspected that was our breaking point. Devon Walker was biologically wired to help.

"I have an idea," Dev began slowly. "I'm going to drop it out there. You finding a job will be hard. I have two available to me. One will allow us to save money that can go toward your bar fund."

A cold dread settled into my stomach. "My bar is my responsibility."

His eyebrows shot up. "And if, in the future, you got married, you wouldn't share finances?"

I hadn't given marriage that much thought before. He shifted, and I knew he'd read my answer in my expression.

"Well, I have thought about marriage, and that involves sharing things like money."

"But your social work job is the lower-paying option."

"I know."

I backed up. Mom's story. My parents fighting. Her giving up her dream. That's what Dev laid at my feet. "No. You can't do that."

He banged a hand against the door; I felt the vibrations beneath my feet. "Why the hell not? How can you stay alone, without anyone else? What good will that do you?"

I clenched and released my fists. "My mother gave up a dream for my father. She resented him and his bar. The day he died, he thought she was going to divorce him. You want that to be our future?"

He shook his head. "It won't be."

"Really? Are you sure? Because if you start working for your father, do you think that's going to end? And if the bar keeps needing some of your paycheck, when will you ever make it back to social work?"

He pulled at his damp hair. "You're being stubborn."

"I'm not stubborn. I'm practical. The only person I'm responsible for is me."

His shoulders slumped, and a trace of pain crossed his face. "I can't believe I never saw this before. Where are you in ten years? Twenty years? Outside of your bar, what does home look like?"

A studio apartment above my bar. Maybe a cat. I didn't dare sign that.

More pain came to his eyes, which were no longer a vibrant blue, but a dark mess of stormy waters. "Where am I?"

Married to someone else. "I don't know."

"Don't lie. Don't you dare lie to me."

I glanced at the yin on my wrist. What had we been thinking? "We're not meant to be."

"Bullshit. Do I not make you happy?"

"It's not about being happy. In case you've missed this in the past ten years, nice things don't work for me. The less I have, the less I hurt."

"If you keep selling yourself short, you'll never have the things that life is made of. I'm standing here—naked, I might add—ready to give you everything I have. And you're running away."

"You can't give everything to a woman who has nothing."

"Watch me."

I stomped, frustrated beyond hell. "No! I won't let you one day turn around and hate me for always being at a bar. This future you imagine, does it involve nice calm family dinners at home, curling up to watch a movie after the kids go to sleep? Or does it involve you alone, because your wife is at the bar she owns all night? Every night. And you get a few hours a day because you are on different sleep schedules. That's my life if I marry someone."

His hands stayed by his side. Only his chest moved. Because I'd caught him.

"Our futures don't line up."

He shook his head. "I knew all that about your future."

"But I was your friend. The person you visited on your free nights. Not the person you waited for to come home."

He leaned against the counter. "There's nothing wrong with your future."

"Same. But do you want it?"

He looked at me, and I turned my attention to fixing my towel. I couldn't see his face, couldn't bear to be right.

He waved, and I forced myself to look at him. "We need time to figure this out."

I swallowed and reinforced my shell, the one I had somehow managed to take down. In that moment I realized how much I wanted this, a real shot at a relationship with him. "Talk to your father. Take the social work job."

I left the bathroom, went into his bedroom, and pulled on clothes. I couldn't stay here, and I needed an excuse to leave. When Dev joined me, he leaned against the wall, towel around his waist. "I promised my mother I'd visit her. Almost forgot with caring for the hangovers."

He didn't smile, he didn't move. He nodded. We both knew if I had my way, I wasn't coming back.

Chapter Thirty-Seven

Devon

JAS LEFT. I watched the door for an hour for some inane reason. She was gone. Two hours prior, I'd had her in my arms in the shower, nothing between us. Now I had no clue when I'd see her again.

I closed my eyes and faced the ceiling. Future. It all boiled down to future. I wanted her, no matter what package that came with. Why the hell hadn't I signed any of that?

Because I hadn't thought it out, not really. I had this idealistic image in my head, the typical two-parent, two-kid one, probably sexist as all hell. And I had shoved Jas into that image. Not because I truly wanted the image. All I knew was that my future involved her.

I hadn't taken the time to figure out what that meant. Who would at my age? A relationship with her had felt like a distant dream, so far from reality that mapping out details would've been impossible. We'd each been working toward our careers, not thinking about marriage and children.

I stopped now—I had no choice at this point—and really thought of what a future with Jas would be like. The bar was a no-brainer; that's where she'd be, if she could make it work. And a part of me always knew I'd finish up my day job, then spend my nights at whatever bar she worked at.

But that was us young. I tried to age us, to toss a few kids into the mix, and recalled all those times I'd hung out with Jas and Eddie at his bar. If Jas and I had kids, that would be their lives too—growing up in a bar.

I could almost make out two kids with dark curly hair. I was either an idiot to be thinking this now or spot-on, thanks to unprotected shower sex.

So maybe I hadn't thought it all through ahead of time. But Jas was the person I wanted, including the package she came with. Only my wants didn't line up with hers.

Life certainly was a fickle beast. I'd almost given up the career I wanted for a future with a woman that might not happen.

The only thing I was certain of anymore was that I needed my own future. Jas would never let me take the accounting job to help her. And that grated. She wouldn't let me do shit. She locked the door and threw away the key.

I grabbed my keys and left, not able to stay here alone with my thoughts. I needed to help, needed to do something, anything for Jas. Even if it was part of the cause of the fight, changing myself wasn't the answer. Not when there was something she needed, thanks to my mistake.

I fixed my mistakes.

There might have been a little voice inside suggesting it wasn't a mistake. I squashed it. We were too young, and trapping Jas would only make things worse.

I went to the pharmacy and found the Plan B pill, doubly glad I'd done so when I caught the price. Jas would've risked it for that amount. Though the cost of the pill sure beat the cost of raising a child.

Our child.

I turned the box over in my hands, reading the information. This would prevent what we weren't ready for. That was all. Though I couldn't deny it felt like another element killing our connection together.

Didn't matter. Her choice. With all the instability and turmoil in her life, I didn't dare pile anything more on her shoulders.

I bought the damn package.

Jas wasn't there when I got home, but I really didn't expect her to be. I set the package by her charger. I should have sent her a text, let her know I'd gotten it for her. The words were too final. Either she'd get one herself, or she'd come here and make up her own mind.

I couldn't handle any further thoughts on this topic, so I left again, in hopes she'd come here and give me some answers. I drove. With no destination in mind, autopilot led the way. Right to my parents' house.

Fuck it. I already lost Jas, might as well round out the day and piss Dad off as well.

I stalked up the stone pathway, about to enter the house without warning like I always did. But since I had moved out, I never stopped by this unexpected.

I sent them a text. While I waited, I sat on the step, looked out into the little cul-de-sac neighborhood I grew up in. Two-story houses surrounded by trees and manicured lawns, a few bikes strewn on driveways. Odds were I wouldn't be able to afford this for my family.

More importantly, now that I really considered it, I didn't want it. Not at the expense of my job. And who knew? Maybe at some point, in the right area, I would be able to afford a little house.

With Jas. The only constant in my future thoughts. I tried to fit her into a neighborhood like this. She didn't fit. It wasn't what she wanted.

Damn, we really were a mismatch. I rubbed at my yang before catching myself and pulling my thumb off the still-tender flesh. Too bad she had my heart.

My phone vibrated, and I let my parents know I was already here before entering the house. I found them in the kitchen, Dad reading the newspaper, Mom doing schoolwork. They glanced at me and both looked a little surprised.

"You OK?" Mom asked.

I ran a hand through my hair. Hadn't even taken a comb to it. I didn't know if I still looked hungover or like a man whose heart had been trampled on. "I'm fine."

Dad laughed. I tapped the table until he looked up, prepared to wipe the smile off his face. "I'm a social worker. Not an accountant."

Mom placed a hand on my shoulder, then collected her work. Either to give us space or get out of the fire.

Dad leaned back. "You can help people with taxes."

I shook my head. "I can help people as a social worker. There's a position open; they want me to apply. I want to apply."

"You don't want my business?" His face held no emotion, gave nothing away.

I steeled my spine. "No."

Dad stared, a cold, hard glare that would have made a younger me squirm. "We need more Deaf accountants."

I returned his glare and forced my body to remain still. "We need more Deaf social workers."

We stared at each other, and I wondered if this would be another relationship I tarnished today.

Dad rubbed his neck, then dropped his shoulders. "I hope you're not leaving during tax season."

I breathed a little easier. "Not until I graduate."

Dad nodded. "You sure about this?"

"Yes, very."

"Does this have anything to do with Jasmine?"

Quite the opposite. "No, this is me."

"You going to be able to support her?"

I knew it was common knowledge social workers didn't make much, but I'd be able to live. Just not expedite Jas's bar. "She supports herself."

Dad lifted an eyebrow. "I raised you better than that."

"Life raised her to be that way."

Dad really looked at me for the first time in a long time. "You OK?"

No. I contemplated telling him but wasn't ready to share. Not his problem, anyways. "Yes, I'm fine."

He sensed something was up though; they both did. Mom insisted I stay for dinner. I pulled out my phone, ready to let Jas know, but stopped. She wouldn't be there anyways.

Chapter Thirty-Eight

Jasmine

THE MOMENT I walked into Mom's room, she began signing, "What's wrong?"

I paused. Stared. Who was this woman with clean hair and clear eyes? "Nothing. I'm fine."

"I wrote the book on 'I'm fine.' Sit. Talk."

I moved into the room, one tentative foot in front of the other. Afraid I'd trigger whatever alternate-reality detonator had created this encounter. I settled into the chair beside her. Mom wore her own clothes today. She crossed her hands across her stomach and waited me out.

"I fought with Devon."

Mom nodded. "You two used to fight all the time. Play fight, your dad would call it. This isn't play, is it?"

Not even close.

Mom looked at my wrist. "He has the other half."

Emotion choked me. Stupid tattoo.

Mom sighed. "Are you dating your best friend?"

"I was."

Mom shook her head. "Now where are you going to live?"

"I don't know yet."

"I can't believe it's that bad. Nothing can break the two of you."

"Like you and Dad?"

Mom paused, leveled me with a glare. "Couples fight. It's part of love. It's what you do after the fight that's important."

I shook my head. "We want different futures. It's not going to work."

She reached out toward me, held her hand in the air, and waited me out. I leaned forward and took it. She brushed my hair off my face with her other. So strange, holding onto my mother like this. "I'm sorry. I wasn't there to raise you properly." She wanted to say more, I knew it, but I came by my stubborn streak naturally. "Why don't you stay at my place? I'm not going to be there anytime soon."

It was an option. A chance to figure out my next steps on my own, without overbearing people breathing down my neck. We switched the conversation to the soap opera she was watching, something even more complicated than my own life. In the middle of our chat, a guy around my age entered the room carrying a tray of food.

Mom smiled upon seeing him, and her lips moved when she signed. "My daughter, the one I told you about.

She's Deaf." Mom faced me. "His name's Will. He's learning ASL."

Will smiled and placed Mom's tray on the rolling cart. "Nice to meet you," he signed, slow and awkward.

I couldn't help smiling back. "Nice to meet you too." Then, I decided to test him. "Why learn ASL?"

Will moved Mom's tray in front of her. "I thought, cool. Now I want to help." His movements were choppy and ungraceful, his grammar off, but he got his meaning across.

On my way out, I spotted him at the nurses' station. I rounded an empty wheelchair to get to him. "Thank you."

Light eyebrows pulled together. "For your mother?"

"For learning ASL."

A smile lit his face, traveled straight up to his eyes. The type of smile that made knees weak. "I like it. Helps me meet good people." He tapped the folder in front of him. "Maybe, one day, coffee? Help me practice?"

I raised my hands and froze. Was he being friendly or asking me out? Did I want someone to ask me out? Then I remembered what Dev said; I hadn't let anyone new into my life since Dad died. And it wasn't like I had much to do with my time. "OK."

The sun had begun its descent by the time I pulled into a parking space at Mom's building. Weariness had taken over, and I yearned for a quiet moment. I'd trekked through these halls countless times on my own, yet somehow I worried about being caught. I kept my head down, determined to ignore any of her neighbors if our paths crossed, not too difficult due to communications issues. Turned out I didn't need to worry. Everyone was in their rooms, and no one stopped me.

Not that they would, but technically I wasn't allowed to stay here. I unlocked Mom's door and stepped into stale air and a musky smell. I had already taken care of the trash, so at least it was an improvement over my previous trip. I opened the windows and took a moment with my nose sticking into the spring air, wondering how my life had come to this. Those were unpleasant thoughts, so I set about cleaning. The place needed it if I was going to stay here. More importantly, Mom deserved a nice place to come home to, especially if her positive mood continued.

I cleaned. I scrubbed. I changed her sheets. And by the time night blanketed the sky, I was to-the-bone exhausted. I hadn't eaten anything since lunch and didn't care if the grumbling in my stomach was hunger pains or upset. I collapsed onto Mom's bed. I knew I needed to send Dev a text so he wouldn't worry. But my cell was dead and my charger at his place. Mom's charger was at the rehab with her.

Truth, being off the grid felt nice. For the time being, no one except Mom knew where I was. Tomorrow Dev would be at classes and work. I'd collect my stuff then, send him a text once I had power.

Until then, I needed sleep. Mom's bed wasn't bad, the full mattress still had a decent spring to it. I tossed and turned. How quickly I had grown used to Dev. To sleeping beside him, curling up with him. The perfect way to end a day.

No more. Never again. From now on, I would be an island. No dates, no loves. Just me and my dream.

My friends would claim that's who I'd been all along. But so what? Clearly that's who I was. What I was. And if I kept this up, I'd never get any sleep.

I threw the covers off me, studied the way the streetlights lit up parts of the room. Noticed one picture was off-center from the rest. My parents' wedding picture.

Below that? My graduation picture.

How had I not noticed them before? From her bed, Mom could see us. A realization took root, and I didn't know what to do about it. How many nights had she spent staring at us while she waited for sleep to claim her? I struggled to reconcile the woman I knew with this strange sense of warmth and caring the image before me created. For so long, I had learned to be closed off from her. My plans, who I'd become, all because of her depression. A depression that Mom didn't want. The pictures said it all: she wanted us. Death took Dad. Depression took her. And the combination destroyed me.

By morning I had managed a few hours of sleep. I wanted to sleep longer, sleep the day away. I had no plans anyways. My body had different ideas.

I waited until Dev's class started and prayed he wasn't skipping because of me. Then I got ready for the day and headed over to his apartment.

His car wasn't there. I had no idea what to make of the strange twinge in my heart. No time to ponder such sensations. I let myself into his unit. It looked the same. No message for me, no real signs of what his night was like. Until I spotted the box sitting beside my charger.

I had forgotten all about it, my confidence in the timing being off strong enough to bury the need. But Dev hadn't. Not much of a surprise from Mr. Helper. No note, no message, just a box that prevented pregnancy.

An option. I knew his intent; I knew why it waited for me. Dev took care of his own.

I stared at the box, fighting a growing unease in my gut. Then I shoved it into my purse. I grabbed my duffel and collected my items; clothes and toiletries didn't take up much room. It didn't take long. It never did. I only took what I needed for Mom's. The rest stayed.

Including Dad's box.

Two hours later, I sat at Mom's kitchen table, a glass of water in front of me, next to the opened Plan B box. I read the instructions and warnings over and over again but still couldn't bring myself to puncture the package and release the pill.

I turned the package over again, my nails doing nothing to release the dosage. *Take the damn pill, Jasmine*! It was so simple. All I had to do was swallow the pill and go on with my day.

The responsible thing to do was take the pill. Dev wanted me to; he bought it. Or he didn't want me to. I didn't know anymore. But I knew we weren't ready for the ramifications. Knowing each other for fifteen years didn't change the fact that we were too young and our foundation was too shaken. This was one huge commitment neither one of us was ready for.

Which didn't explain why I put the contents back in the package and drank the water. Definitely half empty now.

The timing wasn't right. That's why I wasn't taking the pill. No reason to put chemicals in my body if there was only a slim chance of getting pregnant anyways. I'd be fine.

Or foolish. I wasn't one to take risks. I had my bar to own. And perhaps that single-minded view hadn't done me a ton of favors over the years.

I finished the water. I could always take the pill later. I still had time. It hadn't even been twenty-four hours yet. No use freaking myself out over a tiny little pill.

I closed my eyes. I had no clue if I was doing the right thing or not. *Take the pill.* I got up and collected my phone from its charger instead. Later. I'd worry about it later.

Chapter Thirty-Nine

Devon

Two p.m. That's how long it took to get a text from Jas.

Jas: Staying at Mom's. Cleaning up for her return.

Bullshit. Connie had months before she'd be well enough to return home.

I pushed my cell away and returned to my work, doing my best not to stare at words from…who was she to me anymore? My ex? My former best friend? Just Jasmine?

None of those labels felt right. The whole situation sucked. The only thing good about the damned day was knowing I no longer had to work here after graduation.

My phone vibrated again, and I lunged for it like an addict. Only it wasn't from Jas.

Pete: If you two are done fighting, we can all hang out again tonight, but Jas isn't allowed to mix any alcohol.

I tapped my phone, figuring out the best way to respond.

Me: We're done. Text her if you want to hang.

Pete: What do you mean: done?

Me: What do you think I mean? She's staying at her mom's place.

Pete: Shit. I thought you two were indestructible.

Me too.

Me: Make sure you know what you're getting into with Nikki.

Pete: Wow, she ran you over if you're warning me.

I tossed my phone back on the desk and gave serious contemplation to fucking it all and getting the hell out of there. Blake stopped in before I had a chance to move.

"You need to spend a healthy amount of time with that punching bag."

Best idea of the day.

Blake pulled two sodas from the fridge and handed one to me. "Any update on Jas?"

I showed him the text.

He pressed his lips together. "You two do a lot of damage. You going to fix things?"

"I can't."

Blake leaned over my desk. "Don't turn this into your job, where you push it off until the last possible minute. If you do that with her, you'll lose her for good."

I shook my head and was saved by Dad entering. "You get through to him?" he asked Blake of me.

"Not yet. He needs to grow some balls."

Fucking family.

Dad joined Blake in leaning over me. I should have stood up to show them I was taller. "Women don't wait. They move on, and their anger grows."

I pushed my chair back, needing some space. "What she wants and I want are different. I found out her future doesn't involve me in any role other than friend." Like the label, it didn't feel right. But the answer lay in her hands.

Both men straightened. Blake signed first. "I suspect she's lying to herself."

"This is who she molded herself into. It's up to her if she wants to change."

Dad eyed my wrist. "What are you going to do about the tattoo?"

"Keep it."

A wry smile crossed Dad's face. "When a man loves a woman, he does whatever it takes to keep her."

"If I try, she'll run the other way." And it grated, this powerless feeling. This knowledge that even though I knew her better than anyone else, nothing I could do would fix things.

"So maybe you need a different tactic." Dad patted my shoulder and turned to the door. I gave Blake a meaningful look. He shook his head.

"When a man loves a man, he needs to get over himself and move out."

Blake rubbed his neck, then stomped and called for Dad in a loud voice. Dad and I had similar hearing levels, Mom had none, and Blake had no hearing loss at all.

Dad faced us, eyebrows raised, looking back and forth to figure out which one of us called for him.

"I'm planning on moving in with Shawn," Blake signed.

"The guy we recently met?"

"My boyfriend, yes."

Dad nodded and pointed at me. "You going to be able to afford your own place?"

"I'll figure something out."

Dad studied Blake. "You're serious about him?"

Blake squared his shoulders. "Yes."

Dad looked between the two of us, silence engulfing the room. "Don't mess things up like Devon."

"Thanks," I signed, though neither of them paid me any attention.

Dad left, and Blake collapsed into the chair next to me. "See, that wasn't that bad," I signed.

Blake smiled. "I suspect you softened him up."

"Right, whatever you want to believe."

"Need help figuring out how to win Jasmine back?"

Not yet. I needed to make sure it was right for her. "We'll see."

I ARRIVED HOME to an empty apartment. No chance to see Jas getting ready for her old job. No chance to find her waiting for me. My heavy heart weighed me down, fought against the growing desire to fix this. That's what I did. I fixed things. But this issue between us had no fixing.

I went to my room to change into workout clothes and froze at the sight of my closet: half empty. None of Jas's clothes were hanging up. I checked around, finding her other knickknacks and things gone. She had ripped herself right out of my life.

Then I noticed the box in the bottom of my closet, the one that held her father's belongings. A glimmer of hope ignited. Her box would have been safe at her mother's apartment, but she'd left it here, with me.

She'd be back.

Chapter Forty

Devon

One week had passed. Seven long days. Seven longer nights. No more communication from Jas. I left the ball in her court, waiting on her. I feared I'd be waiting for too damn long.

For now, I nursed a beer with Blake, a rare night with the both of us home alone.

"Why haven't you gone after her?" Blake asked.

I fiddled with the label of my drink. "She needs time." When I looked up, I found Blake staring me down.

"You can't be serious."

My spine straightened. "Of course I'm serious."

He laughed, the sound grating against my ears. "Same story. Different woman."

"What does that mean?"

Blake pushed his beer aside. "You've always dated like you were trying out a bag of chips, and if you didn't like it, you were happy to toss it aside and forget about it."

"You implying I'm forgetting about Jasmine?"

"I'm implying that it looks that way. You still can't keep a girlfriend for longer than two weeks."

"Jas is different."

Blake held out his hands to the empty apartment. "Looks the same."

I rubbed my neck. This wasn't my intention. But if I tried anything else, she'd have my head. And not the good one either.

Blake's signs interrupted my thoughts. "Why don't you commit?"

I clenched my fists before releasing them. "You know why."

"Sign it."

I took in a deep breath and contemplated ramming my fist into my brother's face. "I wasn't going to commit to someone when my heart belonged to Jas."

"And still, you've lost her real quick."

"Because life got in the way."

"I'm going to offer you some advice that you haven't needed until now: relationships take work. I know she's scared, and life's thrown her some tough shit. More than that, she knows you, knows your track record. Prove to her she's not just another bag of chips." He left his beer on the table, patted my shoulder like I was ten, and left me alone.

It wasn't true. I hadn't let Jas go because her time was up. I'd let her go because...because she needed it. And those thoughts barely held water in my head. Was there some truth to Blake's signs? No, of course not. No one mattered to me the way Jas did.

I pulled out my phone, tapped the screen until Jas's dormant text thread popped up. Then I chugged down the rest of my beer. It took several tries to get some words out that weren't pathetic.

Me: I want to know if you're OK. I miss you. The friend. The girlfriend. Us.
Me: Just tell me you're OK.

I set my phone on the table and finished off Blake's beer. I stared at the screen until my vision blurred. She wasn't going to answer me.

Then, when I was about to give up, my phone vibrated and flashed to life.

Jas: I'm OK.

Come home. Meet me. We'll work something out.

Jas: Miss you too.
Me: So come over.
Jas: Not yet.
Me: I wanted you to be the one to break my longevity record.
Jas: Don't you remember? We've been secretly dating each other for years. I think I've got this one in the bag.

I smiled even as another tiny piece tore off my heart.

Me: The record was made for you.
Jas: I have to go. You OK?

I tapped the phone with my thumb, wrestling with needy-ass words.

Me: I'm fine.

I pushed my phone to the center of the table, where it lit up but didn't flash, didn't change. A minute passed, and the screen turned black. The record would always belong to her. I could only hope we'd work things out and make it even longer.

TWO DAYS LATER, my patience wore thin. I'd had a shitty day, starting with a test I was sure I bombed. I followed that up with a trip to Support Services, where I intercepted an altercation before it turned into a fistfight. Then I headed to Dad's office at his request and spent two hours working on another computer problem.

I needed a beer or Jas to whip up one of her drunk-in-one-gulp concoctions. Only there was no bar to go to, no Jas to serve me.

I settled for the beer in my fridge. Things grew hazy around my fourth or fifth beer—I wasn't sure of the exact count, only that I had texted Pete and he banged his way into the apartment.

"You look like shit," he signed while taking in the mess of beer bottles on the table. I had tried to shape them into a word, but I didn't have enough yet.

"Thanks," I answered, only I signed it with my middle finger instead of an open palm.

Pete shook his head and straddled a chair. "You ready to crawl?"

I shook my head and the room spun. "No. Do you know where she is?"

"No. She locks down, you know this."

Defeat surged up, until I remembered that Pete didn't know where Jas was staying, but I did. I fumbled for my phone, my fingers not following commands, and eventually got the thread up where she told me she was at her mom's.

I shoved the phone into Pete's hands and stood to get my coat. The floor vibrated.

"What the fuck do you think you're doing?"

I swayed and used the wall to keep upright. "We need to talk."

"*We're* talking."

"No. Not you-and-me we, Jas-and-me—us—we."

"You are not talking to her drunk. Go to bed. I'm sitting by the door to keep you in." He stood and crossed his arms.

"I need to see her. Need to show her she's not a bag of chips. Need to find out if she took the pill." My thoughts scrambled together; the only clear thing was that I needed to see her. Now.

"You are making no sense. If you go, you're going to crawl."

I threw his jacket at him. "Fine. Let's crawl."

My plan backfired when we got to Connie's building and I realized I had no way in. Jas's car was in the lot, so I knew she was there. But I didn't know if she'd let me see her.

I picked up a rock and walked along the side of the building, trying to remember which window belonged to Connie. Pete grabbed my shoulder and tossed the rock back on the ground.

"No," he signed in the limited streetlight, "you'll break a window and wind up in jail."

I shrugged free and focused on the front door when it opened. I debated if I could run and grab the door before it latched in time, but then I saw who had exited the building. Someone with blond curls and straight posture. Jas. She carried a bag of trash, and I didn't know whether to be grateful that she threw out trash in the middle of the night or angry that she threw out trash in the middle of the night.

I stomped over to the trash receptacle as she threw the bag in. She caught my movement and turned in a blur of curls, one hand over her heart. Her face morphed, eyes narrowing, mouth thinning. It was then I knew I'd been wrong and should've listened to Pete.

"What are you doing here?" she signed one-handed, the other propped on her hip.

"I needed to see you."

She spread out her hands. "Well, now you have." She made as if to turn, and I knew I had to sign something, fast, to keep her here.

"Did you take the pill?"

Her gaze fell to her shoe, which kicked at a few pebbles. "No. I told you, I'll be fine. We don't need it." Her chin jutted up in a challenge. All I saw was the hurt beneath the façade.

"I'm sorry. I didn't mean to hurt you. You aren't a bag of chips. You're Jasmine. The only bag of chips."

Her eyebrows lowered, and she studied me. "You're drunk. Go home." She looked around. "Wait, how did you get here?"

I pointed behind me to where I presumed Pete was. I didn't sign his name, but Jas waved to a spot over my shoulder. "Go home."

"No. Not until you let me take care of you. Please. I have to take care of you."

"No one takes care of me. And you know that. Our futures don't match."

"Fuck the future! I don't care about that. Work at a bar. Don't have kids. It's fine. We'll make it work."

Her eyes watered. "It won't work." She took in a deep breath, and I noticed all she had on was a sweatshirt. Mine. "I need my box."

Hope evaporated. My one remaining tie to her. "What box?" I wasn't giving it up.

"Don't be an asshole. You know what I'm talking about."

"I thought you took it. I haven't seen it."

Her eyes grew wide, and I felt like a prick. I needed to let her know it was safe and she didn't need to worry. I couldn't bring my hands to move.

We stayed that way, staring at each other, the past few weeks of dating fading away. Years of friendship fading along with it, leaving two virtual strangers. I never thought we'd be this way, even if we lost touch somewhere down the line. Our connection had been too strong for too long. She'd always be my yin.

Now, I wasn't so sure. Maybe in five years I'd meet her again and find her tattoo removed. Maybe I'd find her settled down, married, with kids that weren't mine. Maybe I'd find her on her own, happy as could be.

Maybe I wouldn't find her at all.

"I'm going inside." She glanced over my shoulder. "Take him home and get him some water." Then, without a glance, she walked back into the building and out of my life. Jas always ran, but for the first time, I watched. And did nothing.

Chapter Forty-One

Jasmine

Nikki: Hello, new best friend reporting for duty, though I might go after your ex since you continue to ignore the world! Don't make us choose sides.

I CLOSED MY eyes against Nikki's words. Direct sucker punch. And I deserved every bit of it, even if Dev being described as my ex felt plain wrong.

Me: know. I'm sorry. How's Pete?

Nikki: Good, except we're scared. You and Dev were our idols, and you imploded.

Me: You and Pete don't have our baggage.

Nikki: Sweetie, the baggage is all yours.

I took a shaky breath and checked on my surroundings. The little beverage area at the rehab was nice enough to provide even guests with coffee.

Nikki: How are you? Honest.
Me: Honest? Like shit.
Nikki: Then get him back!

I shook my head at my phone, as if we were on a video call and not text.

Me: He wants a future I can't give him.

Drunk Dev be damned, I knew what he really wanted. And I knew better than to take his drunk ramblings as fact.

Nikki: He wants you and whatever future you come with.
Me: It's better this way. Trust me.
Nikki: Come over tonight and prove it.

Not like I had any plans. And if I didn't agree, I'd never make it out of the tiny beverage area.

Me: Fine.
Nikki: I'm worried about you.

Join the club. I'd never felt quite so aimless before, as though there were two different versions of me but I no longer knew which one was real.

I added creamer to my coffee and sugar to Mom's, then made my way back to her room. I'd spent the last few days here with her—sure beat being alone in her apartment.

Will, the nurse who knew some ASL, waved as I walked past. Since my hands were full, I gave him a nod, then slipped into Mom's room. She gave me a look as I set the coffees down.

"He likes you," she signed.

I turned, finding a clear view of the nurses' station and Will bent over some paperwork. He was too short, too lean, and his hair wasn't dark enough. "Not for me."

Mom picked up her cup and took a sip. "It's hard when you give your heart over to one person."

I nearly spit my hot coffee all over her. "I still have my heart, thank you."

Mom shook her head, her eyes sad. "No, you don't. I watched you give it away in elementary school."

I rubbed my temples. "Can we not discuss this?"

"Today? Fine. Tomorrow's a different story."

I rolled my neck, stretched my toes, and thought of the real problem. "I don't want a family."

"Then you should have thought about that back in elementary school, when you made him part of yours."

"As a friend."

Mom laughed. "You two were always closer than friends. You want to fix your life? He's the answer."

"I don't need some guy to take care of me." I flailed my hands wide, nearly knocking over my coffee.

Mom shook her head. "Not to take care of you, to work together as a team. Your father and his bar, he made it his burden, he shut me out. Together we might have been able to save it. I don't know if the reduced stress would have saved his life or not, but in my dreams, it would have made a difference.

"My point is, you have a problem right now. You bring this problem to your family, and together you can come up with a solution."

"Last I checked, you were part of my family."

Mom's face fell, the wrinkles appeared more pronounced. "I burned that bridge a long time ago. It's amazing you're even here. I'm not the person to help you get on your feet, when I haven't been on mine in a long time." She moved one foot. "Even before the hip injury."

I let the conversation shift from there. Because it didn't matter, not one bit of it. My goal remained the same: own a bar. And live alone. But being alone had lost some of its thrill. Instead of relaxing solitude, I feared now it would feel more like empty sorrow.

THAT EVENING, I rang the bell to Nikki's apartment, though I really wanted to turn around and leave. I dug in my feet. I could wallow on my own tomorrow. Tonight was for friends.

The few I had left. I should have brought chocolate as a peace offering.

The door opened, and Nikki sent me a smile, part relief, part mischief. She pulled me into a hug, and I held her, hard. I'd missed her. I'd missed people and comfort and friends.

She pulled back and bit her lip. "Don't be mad."

A cold bead of sweat slithered down my spine. I didn't move. I knew what I'd find. "You can't play matchmaker."

She popped a hand on her hip. "Why not? You did."

Shit, I had. But her first kiss with Pete was about them both acknowledging a new situation, nothing like the drawn-out fight between Dev and me.

Nikki opened the door wide, the perfect face of innocence. I could leave, try to see her again alone. I was stronger than that.

I stepped in, and there Dev sat next to Pete on the couch. One jean-clad leg crossed over the other, a beer dangling from his hand, showing off his yang. He wore a tight tee shirt with some writing on the chest I didn't stop to read and a day's worth of stubble. It physically hurt to see him. The other night darkness had shielded some of his features, giving the sense of some separation between us. Now even that was gone. I had the strongest urge to run to him. Instead, I stepped away, allowing Nikki to close the door.

Dev's blue eyes locked with mine. Neither one of us moved to sign anything. Out of the corner of my eye, I caught Pete signing, "Awkward," and he was right.

"Should you be drinking?" I asked.

A small wry smile crossed his face. "Just one tonight." Silence resumed and threatened to consume us.

Nikki waved, breaking our stare. "The four of us are friends. I meant what I texted to each of you: I am not choosing sides because you two are in a fight."

Dev's eyes were on me, but I looked at my shoes, refusing to confirm or deny Nikki's comment.

No one moved, everyone frozen in place. It occurred to me that everything had probably been fine before I arrived. I messed it up. "This is crazy. I'm going to leave." I faced Nikki and signed before she did. "We'll meet up another day."

"I do have your box," Dev signed from the couch.

Those eyes, I needed to stop getting lost in them. A coil of stress unwound from my shoulders. "I know."

My chest tightened as words passed between us, a whole hidden conversation, like the ones we used to have all the time. He didn't have just my box; he had me. And I hadn't forgotten it; I left it there.

No matter where we were, what we did, there would always be a connection between us. There would always be an *us* in some shape or form. I didn't know how long it would take for us to figure out the final stage of our relationship.

"I'll talk to you later," I signed to Nikki. I waved to Pete but only looked at Dev. Thoughts battled in my head, thoughts I hoped he'd infer: *I'm sorry, I miss you, I don't know how to solve us.* If he understood, he didn't have any answers either.

I LEFT THE lights off in Mom's apartment—it went with the loneliness. After seeing Dev and the drained look on his handsome face, the isolation grew worse, nearly suffocating. I wanted to stomp, I wanted to scream, but I didn't dare disturb any of Mom's neighbors.

Why was it so complicated? This was supposed to be the easy answer: stick to my path. Only I didn't know what I wanted anymore. I didn't know what my future held and what I should be fighting for.

I hadn't eaten and I wasn't hungry. My stomach was a little queasy, but stress would do that to a person. A nice, long, soothing shower sounded good. Maybe a bubble bath if Mom had any on hand.

No bubbles, but I prepped the shower. Before I got in, I discovered my period had arrived. It should have been a nonissue—go to my bags, grab a tampon, done. Instead it reminded me of that last shower at Dev's place, that last sex with him. The pills I really didn't need to take.

I wasn't pregnant.

I got in the shower, trying to wash my thoughts away. Only I couldn't wash these emotions away, they bubbled up inside until they boiled over. My head rested against the wall, and I cried. For the child that never was but could have been. For that connection between Dev and me that spanned much more than our damn tattoos. For the loss that wasn't really a loss at all.

And when the tears dried and I managed to wash myself, another realization hit: I wanted a child, or children. One day, I wanted to be a mother.

With Devon as the father.

It was crazy. I knew how many sacrifices Dad had had to make to keep the bar afloat and not be with me. But I saw myself in a bar that looked a lot like Dad's, passing a wet mug to a little boy or girl with blue eyes and brown curls. That kid would smile and dry the mug while waiting for their father to pick them up after work. And when I got home so very late at night, I'd kiss that sleeping child and re-tuck them in before waking my husband, who had fallen asleep in front of the television. We'd talk, make love, and go to bed, repeating it all again the next day.

The image was so real; the smells, the tastes were all there. I wanted it all.

If Dev could handle raising a child in a bar, insane hours and all, then the main part of our fight would be resolved.

Well, the second part. I still needed to learn to accept his help.

I stepped out of the bathroom into the dark apartment. Help, or lack of it, was the reason Mom never got her life back on track after Dad died. I had no idea how much of it had been offered, but she never reached out for it. If she had, maybe things would have been different. I would be different. Help was good. I just had to find a way to believe.

The images kept coming, this potential future I'd created. Not ten minutes from now, but ten years from now. My fingers itched to make it a reality. While so many details were out of my control, one area wasn't.

I turned on a light, grabbed my notebook, and turned to a blank page. Instead of random ideas and concepts, I started with a simple checklist of all the important particulars I needed in place before I could open my bar.

The place I envisioned wasn't a dive bar like Len's. A college bar was more my style, so I could put my mixology skills to use. Beyond the drinks I'd serve, the bar would offer a greater purpose: a hangout for the Deaf Community. It would be a Deaf-friendly location, with beer on tap, mixed drinks, and a bright, accepting environment.

My checklist would take time to complete, but it was a start. No more distant dreams that slipped through my fingers. One way or another, I'd make this a reality.

Chapter Forty-Two

Devon

"SORRY," NIKKI SIGNED after she closed the door behind Jas. I contemplated getting up and going after her. She looked like she needed a hug, or maybe that was me selfishly wanting her in my arms again.

I let her go. Not that I wasn't willing to fight for her. She needed time, especially after my stupid drunk stunt. Until she had her own answers, I needed to stay clear.

"We'll figure out how to be in the same room together one day."

Pete shook his head. He shared a look with Nikki, and I held up my hands before either could interject.

"Don't sign anything. I've got this under control."

Nikki glanced at the door, then me. "No. You don't."

That was kinda true. "I know she doesn't need me pestering her right now." Nikki raised her hands, but I kept going. "She needs time or for me to figure out the right answer. I haven't yet, but I will."

"It's so strange having you two separated. I can't remember that ever happening before."

"Growing pains," Pete signed.

I rubbed my wrist, an absentminded gesture, my thumb pressing against my yang. The recovering mark ached like it was brand new, and I'd bet my college education it had little do with the actual healing process. To think, we got the tattoos to prove how permanent we were, and before they fully healed we were as divided as our separated symbols.

Not over, never over. But the metamorphosis stage sucked. There was only one outcome I wanted. I had to pray that when Jas shifted through all her baggage, she'd agree.

I STRETCHED AWAY from the computer, eyes on my phone vibrating on the table with an incoming text, and froze with my hands in the air when I saw who sent the message.

Jas: Got my period, told you it would be fine.

My stomach dropped. Funny how that didn't feel like a good thing. But she didn't want a family, so no use wondering what could have been.

Me: You OK?
Jas: Questions not to ask a woman on her period.
Me: Not what I meant.

I waited. It took some time, but she answered.

Jas: I'm OK.

It was something. I wanted more, more talking, more interacting. I'd take what I could get.

She surprised me when, ten minutes later, another text came through.

Jas: Actually, I'm not OK. I'm sad.
Jas: And I have no idea why I sent that.

I stared at her words as shock worked its way through me. Had she just given me an opening?

Me: It's OK to be sad.
Me: I'm sad.
Jas: We're too young.

My heart picked up to a run. I wanted to have this conversation in person but took what she gave me.

Me: We won't always be this age.
Jas: True.

I didn't push her. She'd opened the door, and I'd win her back.

DAD MUST HAVE sensed I needed to be active; he sent me back to Charlie's place to review his documents and get his signature. An hour later, I sat at Charlie's table with the papers open in front of us. His pictures haunted me; the whole scenario felt too damn close to being my future. Would my mantel show my kids and their kids? Or would it have a faded picture of Jas and images of Blake's kids?

I couldn't get Jas's text out of my head. Did that mean she wanted this too?

"What happened with the girl?" I asked, pointing to the black and white photo.

Charlie took in the photograph with sad eyes. "I loved her before I had all this, and I was too stupid to know what was important. I gave her up to become successful. When I got my money, she'd moved on. Married, had a few kids. I lost my chance."

Not what I wanted to see. "I'm sorry."

"She was happy though. That's all that matters."

Couldn't argue with that one. I turned back to the papers. Charlie owned a few properties, part of the reason his taxes were such a mess. I went over them with him, verifying we had the right information this time, and froze at an address I knew very well.

He owned the building where Jas's father had his bar.

I pointed to the address. "You own this building?"

Charlie nodded. "Bought it seven years ago, thought I could fix a struggling building. Now it's mostly empty."

I held out my wrist, pointed to the yang. "The woman who has the other half of this, her father used to own that bar."

A spark came to Charlie's eyes. "Deaf?"

"Her father was hearing, she's Deaf. She wants to follow in his footsteps, own a bar like he did."

Charlie smiled. "A Deaf bar. That would be something."

"One day. Hard to find work as a Deaf bartender. She's been saving to buy her own place, but that will take time." And accepting help, but I didn't need to share that part with him.

"Deaf help Deaf, yes?" Charlie asked, then tapped the paper. "What else do I need to sign?"

I walked him through the rest, amazed at how small the world was. Wouldn't it have been something if Charlie had known Eddie? I had a feeling Charlie held an answer or two to my problems. All I had to do was ask and find out.

Chapter Forty-Three

Jasmine

I TOOK OFF my coat and draped it over the chair in Mom's rehab room. "That job interview." I held my thumb upside down. "Awful."

Mom frowned. "What happened?"

I settled into the chair. "Discrimination. Simple as that. They kept asking me to speak and if I could lip-read. I showed them how well I can communicate with a white-board, but I don't think I'll get the job."

"I'm sorry."

The experience was dreadful. Not unexpected, but dreadful nonetheless. I'd kept a smile plastered to my face as the two interviewers kept trying to talk to me. At times, both their mouths moved. How the fuck was I supposed to follow that? I wrote on my board, even showed them how I attached it to a clip on my hip to keep it with me when my hands were full. But by the looks on their faces, the glances they shared, I knew they'd find a way not to hire me.

"That's life. Maybe I should work at the packaging company with Pete." It wasn't what I wanted to do, but my options ran thinner by the day.

Mom shook her head. "That's not you."

"Who I am and what life requires are two different things." My phone vibrated, and I pulled it out of my back pocket, thumbing to the new text message I had.

Dev: Meet me at your father's bar.

I blinked at his words.

Me: Bossy much?

Dev: If you trust me at all, do it.

I scowled at my phone. I did trust him. I'd always trust him. Even when he did weird things that didn't make any sense. I showed Mom my phone.

"I think he's trying to win you back."

"By bringing me to Dad's bar? When I can't find work and can't afford his place? That's mean." It didn't help that I kept imaging his place with all my plans.

Mom shifted, closing her eyes briefly as she tried to get comfortable. "Not everything in life is fair, you know that well. Remember that when you see him."

"You kicking me out?"

"You're miserable. I want you happy. I want that smile back. He makes you smile. Why are you here? Go see him."

It wasn't that simple. "I'm not ready."

"You're scared. That's all."

I sucked in some air, ready to fight back. She sent me a stern look, and I relented. She was right. "I don't want to mess things up."

"You can't, not with him. Trust your heart and you'll be fine."

Trust my heart. Therein lay part of the fear that kept me from fixing us. If I trusted my heart, I'd take us both off the market for good. Which should have scared me more. It didn't.

Maybe I was ready.

I collected my jacket, kissed Mom on the cheek, and headed to my car. A half hour later, I pulled into the empty parking lot behind Dad's former building. The sun shifted below the tree line, the sky more purple than blue. One business remained, but it was closed for the night. Shame—this area used to be brimming with life when I was a kid.

At least, from my kid-colored glasses, it had been.

I rounded the building and stopped at the edge. In front of Dad's dark bar stood Dev. He leaned against the dirty glass pane, hair a mess, light stubble along his jaw. I missed him so much it hurt. I wanted to run to him, fling my arms around him, and never let go.

He deserved answers from me, proof that I'd make an honest try at a partnership. I had to figure out a way to show him all that.

I moved away from the edge, and he looked me over, hungry eyes taking me in like I took him in. The pull between us sprang to life, a pull so much more than friendship. There was a true bond between us, always more than just friends.

It really did take us far too long to figure it out.

"Why are we here?" I asked, stopping a few feet from him.

"You look good," he signed.

I felt my frizzy hair. "I just had the job interview from hell. I doubt I look that good."

"I'm sorry." Though for the first time, I didn't buy he truly meant it. "You always look good."

I was missing something. "Why here?" I asked again.

Dev rubbed his neck. Whatever his reason, it had him all tangled in knots. "I have something for you. But I also know you don't want to accept anything from anyone else. So I'm not sure how to proceed."

"I can't really afford a puppy right now."

A small smile ghosted across his lips. I wanted to bring a full one out, then lick it. In what reality did I believe I could stay away from him? "You know what I mean."

I nodded. "You're not still joining your father's business, are you?"

His mouth turned a fraction more. "I applied for the social work position. Dad knows and accepts."

Relief uncoiled a knot in my back I hadn't realized was there. "Good."

His eyes narrowed. "If I hadn't?"

"I'd shake you until you gained some notion of sense."

"You planning on keeping me in line?"

"If I can." My hands moved slowly, shyly. Shy and Devon were not a thing I usually did.

"Where's your freak-out level?" He studied my face. "You look ready to run already."

Oh boy. I was, but that was the nerves. "Under control." *For now.*

Dev knew the truth, he'd see through me, but he also accepted my words as fact. "Blake talked with Dad. He's moving in with Shawn. I'm going to need to find a new place and roommate."

There it was, the door opened to put all this behind us and continue forward. Together. More importantly, my chance to prove my readiness and accept what he offered. "I still can't help with the rent, but I could keep you warm at night."

My cheeks flushed. He had opened the door; I pushed us both through. I bit my lip, worrying over his response. But those lips, they broke into a smile, and my knees nearly jellied.

"I think that's a fair deal. Don't forget your cold toes help prevent overheating."

A tiny laugh bubbled up, but I tamped it down when Dev turned serious again.

He shook out his hands, took a deep breath, then leveled me with his gaze. "I have something for you. Hold out your hand." I followed his instruction, and he reached into his pocket, pulling out a gold key and dropping the metal into my palm.

"I already have a copy of your key," I signed with my other hand. Unless he already had a new place?

"I know." He stepped back, looked at the building beside us. "Remember how Dad had me working with a client, Charlie? I found out that he owns this building."

My heartbeat picked up. "Deaf owned?"

"Yes. Deaf owned. He bought the place after your Dad died."

I stared at the key, then Dev. "What did you do?" My hands shook.

He smiled. It wasn't full and bright but laced with nerves. He took the key from my outstretched palm and slid it into the lock. The door opened.

I placed my hands over my heart. I hadn't been inside the bar since before Dad died. Dev opened the door wide, and I stepped over the threshold.

Cobwebs hung in corners and over furniture. The air was stale, the floors in need of a good scrubbing. But it was Dad's bar.

I ran my fingers across the dark wood bar top, leaving trails in the dust. The cushioned barstools needed an update, but I pressed on one, knowing at one point I had sat there. Dad had sat there.

I turned to Dev, who stood by the door. "What does this mean?"

"Charlie hasn't been able to find a renter. He was really excited about the idea of a Deaf bar. The place is yours, rent-free for a year, negotiable after that. Bring the place back to life."

I looked around again. The bar. Dad's bar. *My* bar. My chest was so full I could barely breathe. I lunged for Dev, wrapped my arms around him. He held me tight, our bodies as one. I closed my eyes, buried my nose in his neck, breathed in his familiar scent. No hug in the world matched Dev's.

Then reality sunk in. My list. All those details cost money. Even with my savings intact, it wouldn't be enough unless the bar was stocked. I pulled back. "I still can't afford it. It costs a lot of money to start up a bar. I need alcohol, mugs, and that's just the start—"

Dev placed a hand over mine, stopping me. "I mentioned this to Dad and Blake. Dad wants to cosign a loan, help get you on your feet. You'll be required to give him free beer." His eyes shifted back and forth between mine, and I knew why. He expected this to be the tipping point. "I know, it's a little odd—"

I shook my head. "Family helps family." I felt it, to my toes. But if I wanted this, my dream, a life with Dev, I had to learn to accept help. And right now, the only thing blocking everything I ever wanted was letting down my guard.

Dev nodded, not getting me. "Of course, but he wants to help you too."

"You and me, we're family, and everyone else knows that. That's why he wants to help. That's why you help."

He grinned, full out grinned, and it was the most beautiful sight ever.

"Have you thought of a second job?"

His eyebrows lowered. "You think the bar needs more finances?"

He was precious; he'd give me everything, even when I didn't deserve it. "I need help. You've got this accounting degree coming your way. Math is your thing, not mine; you'll have to take care of my books."

His face lightened. "I can manage that."

"And I can't do this alone. What do you say, be my nighttime and weekend help?"

He stepped into me, a predator's gaze on his face. "To clarify, do you mean here or at home?"

My body tightened, yearning to feel him again. "Both."

He studied my face, one last question left. "Where are you in ten years?"

I took a deep breath and glanced around. No denying that I saw it, felt it. The images sprang to life in full color. "Helping kids with homework at the bar." I placed my hands on my stomach, almost in disbelief at an admission Dev deserved.

Those lips. That smile. "And where am I?"

"Coming here to pick them up." I held up a hand when he tried to step closer to me. "You understand that's your future if you do this."

"I understand. It's what I want. And I think we have a deal."

"Good." I threw myself at him, meshed my lips to his. He wrapped me against him, turning up the heat with his tongue. Him and me. In my bar. I pulled back. "I never got to kiss someone here before."

"If this place was clean, we'd do a lot more than kiss."

I laughed and kissed him again. Because I wanted to, because I could. He truly had given me everything. And I'd give him all of me in response.

Epilogue

Devon

I PARKED MY car in the parking lot and stretched my neck from side to side. A nervous energy took over, replacing the stress of a long day. I pushed it aside. Thanks to a late-day home visit, I was at the bar early, and I planned on taking advantage of some extra time without Jas knowing.

I crossed the lot, replaying my last client visit in my head. I had inherited this guy my first day on the job by default for being male. George had a penchant for making the female social workers uncomfortable. Heck, he made me uncomfortable at times, especially when he tried to inquire about my love life. I never gave him any ammunition, and we got shit done. Only now he had a medical issue and a doctor unwilling to provide interpretation.

I either needed to get through to the doctor or find one who wasn't an asshole.

My hand gripped the handle to the back door of the bar. I finished my planning for George, gave myself a minute to linger in social work mode. The moment I entered, that was it. I left one job for the other.

I opened the door and stepped into the warm bar. The alcohol smells reached even back here, and I breathed it all in as the door shut behind me. I wouldn't give up my day job for the world, but sometimes it was nice to be in a place where my biggest issue was balancing numbers and filling beers.

I checked the monitor. The black and white screen had most of the bar on view. Instead of some of the more cosmetic upgrades Jas wanted, we'd gotten a surveillance system for the bar. So if either of us were in the back room, we knew what happened out front. There was another monitor behind the bar, ensuring Jas had eyes behind her when necessary.

At this hour, she had a few tables filled and a few patrons at the bar. I spotted her kneeling next to a table, her blond curls always easy to spot on the black and white monitor. She wrote on one of her whiteboards—she had them at each table and scattered across the bar for communication. Through word of mouth, news of a Deaf bar had gotten out, and a fair amount of our regulars didn't need to write down a thing.

This customer did. Jas wore a pair of jeans and one of her halter tops. Less flirty, more business owner. I checked the other tables, but everyone appeared happy; she had the place under control.

In the office, I pulled out some clothes to change into. Jeans and a tee shirt versus dress pants and shirt. Not that I'd picked them out. After I got a beer stain on one of my khakis, Jas had taken it upon herself to grab a spare change of clothes for me.

Bossy woman. Good thing I was in love with her and knew better than to point out our apartment was ten minutes away. If I wanted to stop home first, I could.

In my bar clothes, I settled down at the desk, running over the end numbers one more time. They'd been strong, and I wanted to make sure I knew how strong. Jas had taken her time getting everything set up to open her business. She knew her shit. And the crowd out front would be overflowing soon, a testament to her success.

Granted, that was due to the celebration. Today marked one year since she first opened.

Which reminded me—I reached into my work pants and pulled out the small gift I had for her, transferring it over to my jeans. Then I forced my head into the numbers game; otherwise I'd never get through the figures.

It took thirty minutes, but I verified what I already knew: she'd closed her first year in the black. And if she kept this up, she'd never go hungry again, with or without my help.

I couldn't stop the smile, couldn't stifle the pride. Sure, I'd been here every step of the way. She leaned on me, and I supported right back. But the rest was all her.

The door opened, and Jas shrieked, her hand over her chest, breaths coming fast. "What are you doing here?" she signed.

I gestured to the books in front of me. "I thought I worked here too."

She scowled, and it was just about the cutest thing. "You know what I mean."

"I finished early and wanted to get this done."

She leaned over the edge of the desk, scanning the numbers. I got lost in the hint of cleavage and the way her top molded to her breasts.

"You're not wearing a bra with that top, are you?"

She cocked her head to the side, curls flowing over her shoulder. "How often do I wear a bra here?"

I licked my lips. She let out a laugh, but two delicious peaks of excitement let me know I got to her. Always did. She angled the monitor, verifying the bar was still quiet. "I don't have time for you. Keep it in your pants until later."

"If you wore skirts again, I could have you back on the floor very happy in five minutes."

She crossed the desk, coming to stand beside me, those dark eyes settling on my lap. I thanked my lucky stars that my hard-on grew in the same direction as the other bulge in my pocket. "You think five minutes is enough for me?"

I grasped her around the waist and hauled her to me for a hot kiss. "Wear a skirt one day, and we'll find out."

She shook her head but kissed me again, those warm lips all I ever really needed in my day. Then she angled herself to take in the books. "You planning on letting me know what the result is?"

I pointed to the bottom line. Jas's jaw dropped open. I tapped it up. "I suggest tackling one of those projects you had to push off."

"You serious?" She bent over, studying the numbers.

I held my hand out in her line of sight. "Yes."

She squealed and wrapped her arms around me, holding me tight. Happy Jas. Truly, truly happy Jas. I held out hope that my next surprise made her day even better.

Movement caught my attention on the monitor. I tapped Jas's shoulder and pointed. She leaned forward, studying the newcomers, then hopped off my lap. "I'll see you out front soon?"

I nodded, and she left. I cleaned up the books, then checked my pocket. Still there.

A FEW HOURS later, the bar was filled with customers, regulars, and friends there to celebrate the milestone. I manned the bar area, collected orders, and handled the simple things like beers and sodas. Jas did the rest, all but floating around on her sneakers.

I rested for a few minutes near Nikki and Pete. "Tonight, right?" Nikki asked.

I glared at her. Why I shared important plans with my friends I'd never know. "You haven't let Jas know, have you?"

Nikki whacked my shoulder. "What kind of a friend do you take me for?"

"Excitable," Pete signed, only to have her switch her dagger eyes from me to him. He settled her down by kissing her.

I glanced around and found that most of the people invited were here, including Connie sharing a table with my parents and Blake and Shawn with a few of their friends. The room was a mix of talking and signing. Somewhere, music played. Blake had set up the dials so we could control the sound without hearing it. And along one wall was a flat-screen television, muted, with the captions on, which was actually pretty standard as far as bars went.

I collected the yin-yang goblets Jas and I had painted and filled a beer for myself and water for Jas. I kept them by me as I caught Blake's eyes from across the room. I had a little speech planned, and I wanted to make sure even the hearing people understood.

I stood up on a stool behind the bar, waving for attention. Jas shot me a look, clearly wondering what the heck I was up to. She moved nearby, and I forced myself to make sure I had everyone's attention before beginning.

"As most of you know, today is the first anniversary of Jasmine opening her bar." I paused for applause, both clapping and hands waving. "It's been her dream for as long as I've known her, and I couldn't be prouder of her and what she's accomplished." I nudged Jas's drink toward her and picked up my own, catching the momentary surprise on her face. The goblets usually stayed at home, but I wanted them here for this. Once everyone raised their drinks, I settled mine back down to sign. "To Jasmine. To the bar. To many more happy years to come."

I raised my glass with everyone else, eyes on Jas. There was cheering and drinking, but I didn't take my eyes off her. She grinned and raised her goblet to her lips, then paused, sputtered, and spit the rest out in the sink.

I knew everyone watched us, but I didn't dare check—couldn't, really. She poured the rest of the drink over her hand, catching the item I had deposited in there for her. Eyes wide, she faced me, holding up the sparkling diamond ring, water dripping past her tattoo.

My heart rammed against my rib cage, and I took some comfort in the silent conversation coming from Jas, something along the lines of, *You're doing this now?* Which was better than, *You're doing this?*

I slid to one knee before her, landing in something wet, but I didn't give a damn. I looked up at the woman I loved, the woman I would always love. "I've loved you since you fell off the swing in kindergarten and scraped your knee from under your dress. I've loved you through middle school, when your world fell apart. I've loved you through high school, when I wanted you in a very non-friendly way, but it took until our twenties for us to figure it out. And I'll love you when we're old and gray. Because you are my other half, and nothing in this world matters without you in it."

I held out my hand, took the ring from her. "Will you marry me?"

She bit her lip, but her eyes gave her away, even though she tried to hold it all in. Then she let the lip go, a huge smile crossing her face. "Yes. Of course!"

Cheers erupted around us, vibrations from people stomping on the floor, but I only focused on Jasmine. I placed the ring on her finger, a perfect match. She flung her arms around me, pressing her lips to me, giving me the best present ever: her.

Want more from Laura Brown?
Keep reading for an excerpt from her debut novel,

SIGNS OF ATTRACTION

Do you know what hearing loss sounds like? I do.

All my life I've tried to be like you. I've failed.

So I keep it hidden.

But on the day my world crashed down around me,
Reed was there.

He showed me just how loud and vibrant silence can be,
even when I struggled to understand.

He's unlike anyone I've ever known. His soulful eyes
and strong hands pulled me in before
I knew what was happening.

And as I saw those hands sign, felt them sparking on me,
I knew: imperfect could be perfect.

Reed makes me feel things I've never felt.
It's exciting…and terrifying.

Because he sees me like no one else has, and I'm afraid of
what he'll find if he looks too closely.

The only thing that scares me more than being with him?
Letting him go.

Available Now from Avon Impulse!

Chapter One

Carli

THE MINUTE THE professor opened his mouth, I knew it would be a long semester. The muffled sound struck a vein deep inside my skull, vibrating tension destined to trigger one of my frequent headaches. I slid my hand under my long brown hair, scratched my cheek as a decoy, and then ran my finger over the microphone of one hearing aid. Static rang loud and clear, confirming my suspicions. My hearing aids were fine.

The professor was the problem.

His booming voice ricocheted an accent off the walls of the small classroom. An accent I identified as…not from around here. Dr. Ashen's bushy mustache covered his top lip. Students shifted. Pages turned. Pens moved.

I flicked my pen against a random page of my thick book. Words spilled from his bottom lip, and I couldn't understand one fucking sound. Survival skill 101 of having a hearing loss: blend in. I'd grown skilled at blending, almost mastering the task of invisibility. No cloak required. Take that, Harry Potter.

I always, always, *always* heard my teachers. Until now.

Big Fuck-Off Mustache + My Ears = Not Happening.

Dr. Ashen glared my way. He tapped his textbook and went right on speaking.

I couldn't see his book; tapping it didn't help. Moron. I rolled my eyes and landed on my neighbor's book. I scanned the words, hoping something, anything, would match. Nothing did. What a waste of a class. I shoved my book and slouched in my seat. No way could I keep up. No chance in hell.

With a sigh, I focused on two women standing by the dry-erase board, both dressed in black, heads close as they chatted. They looked much too old to be students, but considering this was an undergrad/grad class, anything was possible. Perhaps they were assistants to Dr. Ashen. They looked to be following him about as much as I was, but that didn't mean they weren't his assistants. They could've heard his spiel one too many times before. I wished I'd heard him at least once.

One of the women wore the coolest glasses with tiny gemstones in the corners. If I ever needed glasses, I wanted those. Chic Glasses Lady glanced at the clock and said something to the other, who had long brown hair in perfect ringlets. If my hair had curls...I shouldn't be shopping for fashion styles in my linguistics class. They moved to get their bags as the door opened.

You know those corny movies where the love interest walks in and a halo of light flashes behind them? Yeah, that happened. Not because this guy was hot, which he was, but because the faulty hall light had been flickering since before I walked into the room. His chestnut hair—the kind that flopped over his forehead and covered his strong jaw in two to three weeks' worth of growth—complemented his rich brown eyes and dark olive skin, which was either a tan or damn good genetics.

Not that I paid much attention. I was just bored.

And warm. Was it warm in here? I repositioned my hair, thankful it not only covered my aids but also the sudden burning of my ears.

Dr. Ashen stopped talking as Hot New Guy walked over to the two women, shifted his backpack, and began moving his hands in a flurry of activity I assumed was American Sign Language. Chic Glasses Lady moved her hands in response while Perfect Ringlets addressed our teacher.

"Sorry. My car broke down, and I had to jump on the Green Line," Ringlets said, speaking for Hot New Guy.

Car? In the middle of Boston? Was this guy crazy?

Dr. Ashen spit out an intense reply. Chic Glasses signed to Hot New Guy, who nodded and took a seat in the back of the room.

For the next two hours—the joy of a once-a-week part-grad class—I watched the two interpreters. Every half hour or so they switched, with one standing next to Dr. Ashen. They held eye contact with one spot near the back of the room, where Hot New Deaf Guy sat. I'd never seen ASL up close and personal before. My ears, faulty as they were, had never failed me, at least not to this degree.

From the notes the students around me took—pages of them, according to the girl on my left—this class was a bust. I needed this to graduate. Maybe my advisor could work something out? Maybe—

Beep. Beep. Beep.

Dammit. To add insult to injury, my hearing aid, the right one, traitorous bitch, announced she needed her battery changed. Right. This. Second. And if—

Beep. Beep. Beep.

I reached into my purse, rummaged past lip gloss, tampons, and tissues, and searched for the slim package of batteries. I had no choice. If I ignored the beeping it'd just—

Beep. Beep. Beep.

Silence.

Fuck. My left ear still worked, but now the world was half-silent. And Dr. Ashen was a mere mumble of incomprehension.

I pulled out my battery packet only to find the eight little tabs empty.

Double fuck. No time to be discreet. I tossed the packet onto my desk and stuck my head in my bag, shifted my wallet, and moved my calendar. I always had extra batteries on hand. Where were they?

A hand tapped my shoulder. I nearly shrieked and jumped out of my skin. Hot New Deaf Guy stood over me. It was then I noticed student chatter and my peers moving about. Dr. Ashen sat at his desk, reviewing his notes. All signs I had missed the beginning of a break.

Hot New Deaf Guy moved his fingers in front of his face and pointed to the empty battery packet I had forgotten on my desk.

"What color battery?" asked Perfect Ringlets, who stood next to him.

"I...Uh..." The burning in my ears migrated to my cheeks. I glanced around. No one paid us any attention. Meanwhile I felt like a spotlight landed on my malfunctioning ears. Hot New Deaf Guy waited for my response. I could tell him to get lost, but that would be rude. Why did my invisibility cloak have to fail me today? And why did he have to be so damn sexy standing there, all broad shoulders and a face that said, "Let me help you"?

He oozed confidence in his own skin. Mine itched. Heck, his ears didn't have anything in them, unless he had those fancy-shmancy hearing aids that were next to invisible. The kind of hearing aids I assumed old dudes wore when their days of rock concerts gave them late onset loss. Not the kind of aids someone who had an interpreter at his side would wear.

At a loss on how I was supposed to communicate, or where my jumbled thoughts were headed, I waved the white flag and showed him the empty packet like a moron.

He nodded, twisted his bag around, and found the batteries I needed.

I glanced around the room again. No one looked at us. No one cared that a hot guy holding out a packet of hearing aid batteries threw my world off-kilter.

This class was going on the List of Horrible Classes. Current standing? Worst class ever.

He tapped the packet and signed. A few movements later, much like a speech delay on a bad broadcast, the interpreter beside him spoke.

"Go ahead. Sharon says this guy has a thick accent. Must be hard to hear."

This could not get any more humiliating. I glanced at Perfect Ringlets, who I hoped was Sharon, and she nodded.

"Thank you." I took out one battery, pulled off the orange tab, and popped it into the small door on my hearing aid before shoving it back in my ear. Hot New Deaf Guy still hovered over me, wearing an infectious smile, a smile that made my knees weak. I handed the packet back. "You don't wear hearing aids, why do you have batteries?"

He watched Sharon as she signed my words while putting the batteries away. "I work at a deaf school. Most of my students have hearing aids and someone always needs a battery. I keep a stash on hand," he said via the interpreter.

"That's nice of you."

He smiled again. I wished he would stop. The smiling thing, I mean. Every time he did, I lost a brain cell. "My name's Reed." He stuck out a hand when he finished signing.

I looked at his hand, a bit amazed at how well he could communicate with it.

Not an excuse to be rude. I reached for his outstretched hand. "Carli."

Sharon asked me how I spelled my name. Reed looked at her instead of me. When I touched him, a spark of some kind ignited and dashed straight up my arm. A tingling that had nothing to do with my ears, or his ears. His eyes shot to mine and I froze. Unable to move or do anything human, like pull my hand back. All I could think of was the fact that I'd never kissed a guy with a beard before.

I broke contact before I turned into a tomato. "C-A-R-L-I," I said to the interpreter.

He signed something to her that she didn't speak to me. Then she walked away and he squatted next to me. Soft jeans flexed over his knees, molded to his sturdy frame. He reached for my notebook—still blank—and pen. Even with the beard, he had a soul patch beneath his full bottom lip. My own bottom lip found its way into my mouth and my teeth clamped down. I tried to stop but couldn't. A hot guy was taking an interest in me. It wasn't a common occurrence.

Why don't you have any communication accommodations?

He wrote in scrawly, messy words across an angle on my notebook. Close to me, so close if I leaned a little our shoulders would brush.

I shrugged, careful not to brush him, and seized the pen.

What would I have? I don't sign.

He laughed, the sound low, guttural, and without restraint. A bit jarring since not a single other noise had come from him. As he wrote, I glanced around again. Still, no one watched us. I swore eyes bored into the back of my head but couldn't find any proof.

You could have a CART provider.

I wanted to write *what the fuck is that*? but figured it might be boorish. Instead, I stared at him, slightly less boorishly.

He laughed again, the sound no longer low, but free, without any societal restrictions. It hummed in a quiet manner across my veins. He started scribbling again.

CART, I forget what it stands for. You know those court stenographers who type everything in court?

He looked up at me while I read. I nodded. I'd seen some frumpy librarian-type woman positioned near a judge in images before.

The university provides that to Deaf and Hard of Hearing students. You should take advantage of them, especially in a class like this.

He capitalized *deaf* and *hard of hearing*. I had no idea why. Everything about this conversation contradicted with my upbringing. I wanted to squirm, allowing only my foot to tap a jittered dance. I'd never spoken to a deaf person before. I'd never had one sitting in front of me, full of a normalness I never possessed. I picked up the pen.

I can handle things on my own.

Motto of my life. My father all but had it engraved over the front door: handle it yourselves. Next to that? Perfection is never overrated.

Reed studied me with intense eyes. My breath caught as I resisted the urge to lean in closer. I tried to look away, really I did, but found I couldn't.

I'm sure you can. But getting help to hear is being independent. Without Sharon and Katherine, I wouldn't be able to take this class. And without CART, neither will you. I can get it set up for you. Give it a try. What do you have to lose?

He reverted to studying me intently as I read his words. I looked at him and wondered how to respond. This was so completely out of my comfort zone, yet he had a point. Without help, I was dropping this class.

Dr. Ashen made a loud noise. Startled, I looked up, creating a chain reaction when Reed glanced over to the interpreters. He quickly scribbled something on my paper before heading back to his desk.

I took a deep breath, ready for the last hour of the class. If a God existed, my inability to hear the professor was only due to my hearing aid battery dying.

Nope. Was it too late to convert to atheism? I understood the spittle from Dr. Ashen more than any of his words. I turned my attention to the interpreter. Chic Glasses Lady, Katherine, stood nearby, out of spittle range. They must have learned fast. Her hands moved smooth and easy, her face full of expression.

I knew I wasn't going to hear anything for the rest of the class. My head ached, and I was done pretending for the day. Instead, I focused on Katherine's hands, fluid movement from one sign to the next. The beautiful motion transfixed me.

Something deep inside me shifted. I had no clue what she said. But I felt it. Her words made sense on some level.

I knew exactly one sign, *I love you*, and that wasn't about to help me. I spent the rest of the class watching her, no longer hearing Dr. Ashen.

When I finally looked at my paper, Reed had written a phone number down, plus *text me if you want to talk.*

Students around me wrote notes. The interpreter signed. Dr. Ashen continued saying nothing I could infer. And I really didn't want to delay my graduation. I didn't come this far in my quest to be a teacher to fail now.

I pulled my phone out of my back pocket and plugged Reed's information into a new text message.

Me: How do I get this CART thing?

About the Author

LAURA BROWN lives in Massachusetts with her quirky, abnormal family. Her husband's put up with her since high school, her young son keeps her on her toes, and her three cats think they deserve more scratches. Hearing loss is a big part of who she is, from her own Hard of Hearing ears, to the characters she creates.

A Letter from the Editor

Dear Reader,

I hope you liked the latest romance from Avon Impulse! If you're looking for another steamy, fun, emotional read, be sure to check out some of our upcoming titles.

If you're a fan of historical romance, get excited! We have two new novellas from beloved Avon authors coming in August. JUST ANOTHER VISCOUNT IN LOVE by Vivienne Lorret is a charming story about an unlucky-in-love viscount who just wants to find a wife. But every lady he pursues ends up married to another…until he meets Miss Gemma Desmond and he vows not to let *this* woman slip through his fingers! This is a delightful, witty story that will appeal to any/all historical romance fans—even if you've never read Viv before!

We also have a fabulous new story from Lorraine Heath! GENTLEMEN PREFER HEIRESSES is a new story in her Scandalous Gentlemen of St. James series. The second son of a duke has no reason to give up his wild ways and marry, but when an American heiress catches his eye, the prospect of marriage seems *much* more appealing. As any true #Heathen (a Lorraine Heath superfan!) knows, her books are deeply emotional and always end with a glorious HEA. This novella is no different!

Never fear, contemporary romance fans…we didn't forget about you! Tracey Livesay is back at the end of August with LOVE WILL ALWAYS REMEMBER, a fun and sexy new novel with a *While You Were Sleeping* spin! When a woman awakens from a coma with no memories from the past six years, she's delighted to learn a handsome celebrity chef is her fiancée…or is he? Don't miss this wonderful, diverse romance that will have you sighing with happiness!

You can purchase any of these titles by clicking the links above or by visiting our website, www.AvonRomance.com. Thank you for loving romance as much as we do…enjoy!

Sincerely,

Nicole Fischer
Editorial Director
Avon Impulse